Maud & Addie

Maureen Buchanan Jones

Fitzroy Books

Published by Fitzroy Books
An imprint of
Regal House Publishing, LLC
Raleigh, NC 27612
All rights reserved

https://fitzroybooks.com

Printed in the United States of America

ISBN -13 (paperback): 9781646030606
ISBN -13 (epub): 9781646030859
Library of Congress Control Number: 2020940183

Interior and cover design by Lafayette & Greene
lafayetteandgreene.com
Cover images © by C.B. Royal

Regal House Publishing, LLC
https://regalhousepublishing.com

Printed in the United States of America

For Caroline, Melanie, Colleen, Roberta, and Charles
who taught me how to be a sister

Contents

1

I'm Not Trying to Be Anything

Maud leaned over the map drawn on rough school paper, with thick pencil markings showing the edges of Mahone Bay, Nova Scotia, and arrows pointing to Whynachts Cove. An *X* marked where pirates had hidden longboats and unloaded chests of doubloons, jewels, and gold trinkets. At least, that's what Tavis Crandle said. "My great-great uncle was a pirate," he'd added. He licked the end of the pencil to make the lines dark and went over the *X* twice.

Maybe there would be a coin, a pearl, maybe a skull. Pirates often left skulls. Maud believed Tavis, because she had been to the caves, The Ovens, on the south side of Lunenburg Bay, where the high tide ocean thrashed. Sweeping low tides left ghostly, echoing caverns that only the bravest entered. Everyone knew that pirate spirits haunted The Ovens. If she could get to Andrews Point, she could explore and show Tavis that she had pirate blood in her too.

"Maud! We're late!" Maud's sister, Addie, yelled from the bottom stair. It was June 11, 1910, the day of the annual Mahone Bay Social. Maud folded the map and stuck it in her pocket, along with her father's old jackknife, a ball of string, and three favorite marbles. She grabbed her straw hat and ran down the stairs.

"It's your fault if we miss the carriage." Adelaide Campbell was almost twelve, nearly one year older and no one would guess she was Maud's sister. Because their birthdays were both in June, Maud's before Addie's, they were both eleven for seventeen days. Addie hated this fact, even though it was clear she was the older sister. She was tall, blue-eyed, and blonde with thick curling hair. Maud was stockier, freckled, and brown-eyed, with auburn braids.

The Campbell girls lived in Halifax but spent summers in Mahone Bay. This summer, like so many summers, their parents were away on a two-month business trip to India, exploring new contacts for tea blends and shipping routes. Usually they were left in the care of Cook, which is what the girls called her. She was certainly the cook and housekeeper, but she was Winifred Cook by name and had been with the Campbell family since their mother was little.

But Minerva Cosgrove had arrived two days ago, one day after Mr. and Mrs. Campbell had sailed. Maud and Addie were used to being left for long periods of time, but Min was new and strange. She was tall and quiet with the largest dog Maud and Addie had ever seen. Their cat, Overly, circled the massive Newfoundland, tail up and sniffing. Min scooped up the cat, asking who had named him Overly.

"I did," said Maud. "He's overly large."

Min's mouth twitched and her eyes sparked, showing a part of her the girls hadn't expected. When Min first arrived, Cook said, "Some folks take hard roads, they do too."

To figure Min out, Addie started a charcoal sketch while Min slept on the chaise longue in the backyard, drawing a profile and coaxing a story from the spare lines. She thickened a line and thought about hard roads. She was surprised to see a beautiful woman on the page. Addie looked at Min's face. When awake, Min seemed behind a kind of screen.

Overly brushed his tail across the charcoal. "Bossy boy," Addie said and hugged him up.

"He's telling you not to be so serious." Min's voice drifted toward her. A feeling came over Addie that Min had been following her thoughts.

"Do you girls play cards?" Min asked them. She pulled a deck from her pocket and shuffled. She taught them to play cribbage, while Chester put his head on Addie's lap. "He knows good people," Min told her, then wagged a finger at Maud. "You counted your points twice, lady. Don't be so tricky!" They laughed, and something, especially in Addie, leaned toward the equality in Min's voice.

That morning after breakfast, Min went upstairs, leaving Maud and Addie at the kitchen table looking at each other. Maud raised her eyebrows and shrugged. Addie leaned in.

"You shouldn't have asked her why she needed so much milk in her tea."

"She spilled it. You saw her hand shaking," Maud defended herself.

"You embarrassed her."

Maud slapped the table. "I want to know what's wrong with her."

"Maud!" Addie exclaimed. "You can't say things like that—"

Maud cut her off. "Cook knows something. I can tell. I'm going to find her." But there was no need. Cook came into the kitchen and looked from one to the other. "What's wrong with Min?" blurted Maud.

Addie studied her tea.

Cook set herself at the table. "There's nothing wrong with her," Cook said. The sharpness in her words startled them. "Min's as true a friend as you'll find, and her mind's as quick as they come. I thought..." Cook looked out the window and brought her hands into her lap. "I thought you'd like her, for all love."

"But—" said Addie and stopped.

Cook waited. When Addie didn't continue, Cook said, "Min needs a bit of company. Now finish your breakfast, so."

When Cook had gone upstairs, Maud burst out, "I told you something is wrong."

Addie turned to her. "I like Min. I think she's sad."

Maud tapped her spoon, then hit her cup once, hard. "Something isn't right." She banged out the kitchen door.

Addie fidgeted around the kitchen, trying to make sense of what they couldn't know because neither Cook nor Min would say it plain. Under the table a bit of envelope caught her eye, a scrap of paper with slantwise writing:

Inside every bird is another bird
identical like a keyhole
that makes it possible to fly.
Inside every cat is another cat
simultaneous like an echo
that makes it possible to purr.

It wasn't Cook's handwriting and Maud certainly hadn't written it. Addie looked out the window toward the chaise lounge, but it was empty. She read the lines again, then put the paper in her pocket. She didn't think it would be missed.

Min was one mystery after another, and Addie wanted to read her slowly, the way she read novels.

"Does Min write poetry?" she asked when she found Cook upstairs folding sheets.

"Now what will you be asking that for?" Cook countered.

Maud knew this trick of Cook's and easily lost patience. But Addie accepted it as a way to understand things from the side. Sometimes she got better information this way.

"She seems sensitive and full of feelings," she answered.

Cook laughed and handed her a pillowcase to fold. "We're all full of feelings. Doesn't mean we write poetry."

"But she doesn't say her feelings, so she must put them somewhere."

Cook fitted together the edges of a double sheet and shook it straight. She didn't answer right off.

"You could be right. I'm thinking you want to know about Min. Ask. If I can say, I'll answer."

Addie pulled the bit of paper from her pocket and held it out. "Is Min very sad?"

Cook read the lines and looked up into the middle distance. "She has her right share. But you're not to worry, she's tough."

"Tough people don't write poetry," Addie stated.

Cook snorted and looked at her directly. "I don't know about that. I'm not much for reading."

"Have you been friends long?" Addie asked.

Cook nodded. "Since she was small, and I was learning to roll pies."

Something in this satisfied Addie. "Even if she's not tough, she has you."

"She does," said Cook. "And I have her."

They folded together for a while and then Addie said, "I think there's a Min inside Min who needs to cry."

Cook put her arms around Addie and squeezed her hard. "Just don't be telling her that," she said.

That afternoon, with her map in her pocket and ready for the Social, Maud landed at the bottom of the stairs and headed for the kitchen. Cook was bent over a large picnic hamper, packing it with containers.

"Eat the salad first, otherwise it will go sour," she told Maud without looking at her.

"I don't like salad," Maud answered, then added, "Why did Mama ask Min here to watch us? Why not just you?"

Cook's hand hesitated, then went on putting containers into the basket. "Don't you like her?" she asked.

"She doesn't do much. She's odd."

"Minerva Cosgrove is family. She needs a bit of rest is all," said Cook, looking sideways at Maud.

"Rest from what? She's not minding us."

Cook brushed the front of her dress and stood straight. "Min is my friend. I invited her."

"Do Papa and Mama know she's here?" Cook didn't answer but went back to wrapping gingerbread and putting it in the basket. "They don't, do they? What's wrong with her?"

"She's getting rid of a bad habit, and that's hard work. It makes her tired and she needs help."

"What habit?" Cook shook her head. "I hate secrets!" Maud said.

Cook put her hand on Maud's head. "You're a right one for knowing." She let out a breath and sat. "Years ago Min was given laudanum after she fell off a horse and hurt her back. She's had other hurts and couldn't let go of the drug. Now she's doing her best to come out of its fog. You can see it in her eyes. Not having the stuff knocks them wide and drifty, but she's doing her best."

"She shouldn't be here," Maud stated. She took the basket handle in both hands and said over her shoulder as she went through the door, "And I say she's odd!"

When she arrived on the front steps, Addie confronted her.

"You look like you've been helping Cook sort the pantry. It's the June Social! Everyone will be there." Addie spun and her blue-striped dress bloomed. She squinted at Maud's face. "You have a smudge."

"I don't care." Maud rubbed her cheek with the back of her hand and walked past Addie to the front door. She stepped onto the gravel drive and looked up and down the tree-lined street. The town was quiet for mid-morning. Addie was right. A carriage was supposed to pick the girls up, but there was no sign of one. No wagons rumbled down the street, not even Reverend Beal's 1908 REO motorized Runabout.

Addie paced, watching the hem of her skirt sway around her white leather boots. Although a bit old fashioned by Paris standards, her petticoats held yards and yards of fabric. The day was going to be perfect, fair and humid, with every prom-ise of romance. Maybe Philip Tierney would sit next to her in the carriage. Addie was ready, from her lace gloves to the sea-blue pleats at her bodice and the organdy inserts in her elbow-length sleeves. A satin ribbon circled her waist and held a crocheted bag containing a handkerchief, wire-rimmed spectacles, and a novel. The final item, the one that made Addie most happy, was a straw bonnet with a wide brim, matching ribbons, and silk forget-me-nots.

Maud shoved her hands in the pocket of her maroon cotton skirt. The tie on her matching middy blouse was slightly askew, but Maud's sturdy black boots were laced and ready for the walk to Andrews Point should the opportunity arise. If that idea failed, she planned on winning the Social's hundred-meter dash.

After ten minutes of Addie pacing, Maud lost patience. "Stop swishing. No one's coming because Min didn't send for them."

Addie faced her sister. "What do you mean?"

"Min doesn't care. She takes loads of laudanum."

"She does care!" Addie shot back and darted into the house. "Min! Min!"

When no answer came, Addie went through the house and onto the back porch. Min was sleeping on a chaise longue under the big elm tree. Addie stepped off the porch and walked to the chaise, thinking about Maud's statement and the last two days with Min.

In the backyard by the lounge chair, Addie touched Min's arm. Min was half asleep and when she opened her eyes her pupils were soft and wide. Addie thought Min was beautiful and dreamy. She wanted her eyes to look like that.

"Min?" prompted Addie. "Are you awake?"

"I am, dear," Min replied. "What do you need?"

"Did you send for the carriage?"

Min half sat up, winced, and let her head rest again. "Carriage?"

"The one for the Social. It should have been here by now."

"I think Cook did. I'm sure she did."

Chester was asleep at Min's feet. He put his head up and licked Addie's hand as if to reassure her. Addie crouched and cupped his face. "You're a beautiful boy," she whispered.

Min smiled. "He is. And smart. He keeps the chickens safe when Gillhooly goes for a strut."

"Chickens! Who's Gillhooly?"

Min laughed and shaded her eyes to see Addie more clearly. "I have chickens at home and a very large goose. The neighbor boy is caring for them. They're good company in their own silly way, but Chester never leaves me, nor I him." Min's hand dropped and found Chester's ear, curling around the velvet.

"Mama told us you're her cousin," Addie said, concentrating on the dog.

Min pulled her hand back. "If that's what she said, I'm sure she's right." Addie tried to read Min's face, but it as was if a veil had come between them. "My head hurts," Min said. "Would you find me some headache powder?"

"I'm sorry," Addie said. She went into the house and to Mama's room. The mahogany dressing table, with glass top and curved front, supported a beveled mirror. The glass, the bottles, and the dishes were like lights on water, shimmers and multiplications of sparkles: Eau de Paris, lilac toilet water, dusting powder in cut glass, lipstick tubes, eye pencils, a porcelain dish of hair pins, pomade, a crimping iron, a silver-backed comb and brush, a Wedgwood dish of rose cream. Nearly hidden in the miniature circus were two small bottles. One was marked headache powder. The second was corked with no label. Beside it rested a tiny crystal cup meant to measure alcohol like Papa's brandy. Mama took laudanum three drops at a time for aches. Addie put her hand out to lift the bottle of Eau de Paris to perfume herself for the Social but found her hand on the bottle of laudanum. Would it make her eyes look dreamy like Min's? She pulled the cork and put the bottle to her lips. One large swallow. She coughed, put down the bottle as if it had stung her, and looked in the mirror to see if the liquid had worked. Addie saw her own surprise. She corked the bottle and headed outside.

Min had drifted off again. Addie set the headache powder on the table next to the chair and joined Maud at the front of the house.

Maud sat on the steps practicing mumblety-peg with her jackknife. "It's gone," announced Maud.

"What's gone? What do you mean?" Addie looked into Maud's face.

"The carriage went past minutes ago."

"But they can't leave without us. They can't!"

"You took too long." Maud pulled one side of her mouth crooked. "Your hair doesn't look any better."

"I wasn't fixing my hair, I was…" Addie turned a slight pink and changed her answer. "Min needed me." Maud picked her knife out of the dirt, snapped it shut, and put it in her pocket. "They were supposed to wait," Addie fumed. "We're on the list for the last carriage."

The town stables had organized rides to the seaside grounds where the Social was taking place. The shared rides saved everyone from bringing buggies to the headland and would have let Addie practice flirtations.

"We'll never make it, even if we could ride the horses directly. There's no time!" Addie fretted. She searched the road, as though a ride would appear if she looked hard enough.

Maud, on the other hand, was quite focused. "We could take one of Perry's dinghies and row across," she offered. Addie gave a dismissive wave and continued pacing. "We could, you know," Maud continued. "If we take a boat, we'll arrive the same time as the carriages. It's a shortcut."

Addie stared across the yard.

"I'll row," Maud added, knowing Addie would never touch oars with her crocheted gloves.

"It would be so undignified!" Addie wailed.

Maud shrugged. "Everyone would notice you."

That got Addie's attention. "All right. Only because we're late." She wanted to be seen and be part of conversations. Maud swung the heavy hamper, whistling loudly. "Stop that," scolded Addie.

Maud ignored her and blew harder as she whistled.

Addie tilted her parasol to block her view of Maud, as if not seeing her meant not hearing her. Maud whistled louder. "Honestly, Maud. You sound like a ship's whistle blasted for calamity!"

The whistling cut off as Maud laughed. "That makes no sense. You just like the sounds of the words."

"At least I know a few words beyond blacksmith words."

Maud whistled "Camp Town Races."

Addie looked disgusted.

Quiet streets led to the dock, and the dock itself was deserted when the girls arrived, with Mr. Perry's six sailing dinghies tied along one side. The three church steeples stood silent on this side of the bay. Maud ran the length of the wharf to find someone, while Addie called, "Hello?" The boats, moored to the wharf with masts dismantled and rigging secured, had a pair of oars shipped along their gunwales. Maud grabbed up the picnic hamper.

"There's nothing for it but to row across in one of these," Maud said, pointing to the small boats.

Addie crinkled her nose at arriving in a dinghy meant for squalling children and sunburned out-of-towners. "There must be someone we can ask." She played with her hat ribbons.

"There's no one, Addie. Look for yourself." Maud spread her arms to show the emptiness of the docks. "Everyone's gone. You can row across with me or stand here looking fetching."

"I'm not trying to be anything!" Addie shot back.

"It's working." Maud heaved the basket and turned toward the dinghies.

"Fine." Addie followed Maud to the dinghy that looked cleanest. Maud lowered herself and the picnic hamper down the ladder and into the waiting craft, then steadied it against the wharf while Addie came cautiously down. With her skirts and parasol in one hand, Addie was slow. The brim of her hat made it hard to see where to place her feet.

"The carriage rug, Addie." Maud pointed.

The thick plaid blanket peeked over the dock's edge.

"We don't need it. We'll get it when we come back." Addie arranged her skirts.

Maud twisted her mouth, climbed the ladder, and grabbed the rug. "My Lady Morning Glory will be happy to sit on it at the Social." Their father called Addie this when she was most concerned with her looks. He said it sweetly to make Addie smile. Maud's delivery made Addie feel pinched.

Maud sat on the front thwart with her back to the bow and undid the painter from the wharf. She adjusted the oars in their oarlocks. The boat wiggled, then slid from the wharf with Maud's strokes. Addie, on the rear thwart, removed her glasses from her bag and perched them on her nose. She pulled out her book and separated herself from Maud as effectively as if she had stepped into another room. Maud was happy to let Addie read, whistling as she plied the oars, imagining the caves' mysteries.

Cutting across the bay meant a twenty-minute boat ride. Maud rowed, keeping an eye on where she would have to curve around the point to explore the caves later.

The dinghy, not even twelve feet long, was made of sturdy fir and braced with oak knees at the bow and along the chine where the ribs met to form a point. The wooden centerboard, when released, would knife straight into the water and help steady the boat against the force of the wind. Because she wasn't using the sail, Maud made sure the centerboard was up and secure within its box at the center of the boat. She checked the rudder, raised and latched to the boat's transom, and began to pull the oars in rhythm, her whistling fading as she worked.

Halfway across the bay Addie yawned and put down her book. "The sun is making me sleepy, Maud."

Addie, not realizing that it was the laudanum that made her head groggy, curled up in the bottom of the boat, kicking a tin beach pail as she did so. She fell into a lazy slumber as Maud rowed steadily, eyeing the shoreline. The offshore breeze pushed the ocean into small peaks. Seagulls hung on the air, calling raucously. Striped cabanas for the picnic rippled with the wind. From a distance they looked like birdhouses punctuating the beach.

Maud maneuvered the dinghy across the bay and soon its bottom bumped and scraped the sand. She shipped the oars, pulled off her boots and stockings, and stood. She was about to step out of the boat when she stared at Addie, still dozing with her head on the rear thwart. "Addie!" Maud yelled.

Addie sat up like a gun had gone off by her head. Her eyes were filmy and unfocused. She stared about, squinted, and rubbed a hand over her mouth. She felt slow and stuck and slightly sick.

"Addie, get out and help me push." Maud was over the side and hauling the boat onto dry sand. Addie made no move to take off her boots or stockings, much less get into the water and push. "Get out!" Maud gritted through her teeth.

"I'm not dragging my dress through saltwater," Addie replied, her hat tied a little crooked. She adjusted her gloves and opened the parasol.

Maud raised herself on the gunwale, tipping the boat. Addie pitched sideways and seawater slurped over her lap.

"Aghhh!" Addie gasped. "You beast!" She grabbed both gunwales to keep from toppling over the side.

"I'm not pushing you up on the beach. Get out." Maud set her mouth.

Addie crawled forward around the centerboard, over the front thwart and onto the bow. She tossed her parasol and hat onto the beach, flinging her boots and stockings beyond the water's reach. She backed herself off the bow, reaching with her toes for the shallowest water. She pushed off and ran tiptoeing onto dry ground. Maud shoved the boat, nearly ramming Addie, and then grabbed the bowline and pulled the boat from the water's edge. By the time she grabbed the carriage rug and hamper, Addie had her boots back on and was smoothing her hair and skirt. Maud thought about leaving her own boots behind but remembered the race. She needed them for speed.

They climbed above the beach and arrived at a festival of cabana tents, arenas for games, families unpacking picnics, and blankets spread for relaxing.

2

You Won't Say a Word, Will You?

Maud plunked the blanket and hamper onto the first open spot of grass.

"No one will see us here," Addie protested.

"Then you carry the blanket." Maud thrust the blanket at Addie, which smothered her face until she snatched it down.

"You little toad!" Addie threw the blanket back.

It caught Maud sideways and draped over her head. Maud didn't bother to pull it off. She swung the hamper and caught Addie in the back with a thwack. Addie lifted off her heels and stuttered forward. Her hat slid over her forehead and she tripped over a tent peg. Stumbling a few steps, she nearly collided with Mrs. Beal, the reverend's wife. Addie caught herself, pushed her hat out of her eyes, and lunged back at Maud.

"You girls are hoodlums! Where's your mother?" Mrs. Beal demanded. She pointed a finger at Addie. "You're not fit to be out by yourselves."

Maud, with the wadded blanket under her arm, trotted behind the cabanas to the lanes for three-legged races, the egg balancing race, and the fifty- and hundred-meter dashes. She dipped behind a picnic table where Mrs. Clausson was setting out pies. She spread the carriage rug, put the hamper at one corner, and set off to find Tavis and the marble match. She also wanted distance from Addie.

Addie regained her balance, patted herself into order, and gazed over the crowd. Evelyn Brighty, standing beside her mother, waved to her. It was the kind of wave that said, *I see you, and I'm supposed to be polite, and I want you to know that I'm here first.* Addie waved back with a wave that said, *You may be here first, but I'm not with my mother.*

Addie dismissed Evelyn and strolled along the tents and picnic tables. The Mahone Bay Community Band played "The Daring Young Man on the Flying Trapeze." Father Cavanaugh, with cassock sleeves rolled up, shaved ice from an enormous block. A man from Lunenburg had a feather candy machine where the youngest children gathered, watching white fluff spin white onto sticks. Addie almost stepped up to buy one, then remembered Evelyn Brighty's eyes. She put her head to one side at the children clamoring for sugar. Then she saw Philip Tierney setting up a penny pitch next to a booth with milk bottles stacked for knocking down. Everything was fuzzy to Addie, soft around the edges. Her head was like one of the balloons Mr. Iverson was filling and tying off with string. "My head doesn't have a string," she thought and giggled at the image of her head floating over the Social. She giggled again and her stomach floated and swayed. She put her hand out to steady herself, noticing how everyone belonged.

Mr. Crandle pounded horseshoe stakes into the ground for the pitch. A clump of girls, Estelle Ramorgen, Lydia Murchey, Anne Sheehan, and Hope Barstow crowded the edge of the bandstand. Their shoulders bent inwards, nearly touching. They watched each other as much as they watched the crowd. Lydia saw Addie and threw her arm up in a wave. Addie beamed back and picked up her pace, but before she reached the group, Evelyn Brighty wormed herself into the huddle. Addie's stomach tightened, but she kept going.

"Hi, everyone." Addie smiled around the circle and spun her parasol.

"Your dress is beautiful!" exclaimed Lydia. "Is your hat from Halifax?"

"Montréal," answered Addie. "You all look pretty too. I wish I looked as good in green as you do, Lydia."

"I saw that dress in the Sears book," said Evelyn. "It was last year's."

Addie's neck and cheeks heated to pink. There was nothing true about what Evelyn said. But everyone believed her or didn't cross her, because no one knew who would be her next target.

"Mama won't have a Sears book in the house," Addie answered.

Evelyn pointed to Addie's shoes and the hem of her dress. "Ew, what's that? Did you swim here?"

The girls giggled. Addie's cheeks went from pink to pale. Sand encrusted the edge of her dress and a strand of seaweed curled at the hem. Her balloon head leaked air. She drifted out of the circle, past the racing lanes and over the field where blankets and hampers dotted the grass. She found their hamper and sat on the plaid rug without unfolding it. The band bleated "Bicycle Built for Two." The hot sun and noise confused her. She took off her hat and pulled her hair off her neck. The girls hunched together with Evelyn tossing her head. Addie closed her eyes to let the rocking inside her slow down.

"Here, I thought you'd like this."

She squinted and saw a hand with a piece of paper. The hand was attached to Philip Tierney's arm. He partially blocked the sun, but its rays poked around him. Her eyes watered as she tried to smile. She took the paper, but before she could stand up or answer, Philip walked away. On the paper was a poem: "The Wild Swans at Coole" by William Butler Yeats. Addie read it twice. She was giddy. The poem was about swans and sunsets and beating wings and it had the word *love*. Philip had given her swans and love. She closed her eyes and pressed the paper to her chest.

"Are you all right?" Lydia crouched next to Addie. "Don't mind Evelyn. She's mean to everyone just the same."

Addie folded the paper and put it into her pouch with her glasses.

Maud had found the marble pitch beyond the penny toss. Tavis, Rufus Handy, Nathaniel McCallock, Alex Curren, John Enslow, and Lydia Murchey's younger brother, Hugh, were on their knees for a game of Taw. Alex knuckled his first marble into the circle. "I'm in," announced Maud.

The boys groaned and Rufus waved her away.

"You're only scared," she said. They hooted, and Nathaniel blew a raspberry at her. "It's true. You know I can beat you." She stepped closer.

"Let her play," said Tavis.

That earned him louder hoots.

"You're sweet!" shouted Rufus.

Tavis twitched a shoulder. "Sweet's got nothing to do with it. She's got the best marbles. Win those and you'll have something to crow about."

The boys looked from Tavis to Maud. "We can't let a girl in. We just can't," said Rufus.

The boys nodded. Tavis nodded too.

"Now I know I'm better than the lot of you," Maud said and turned. She tasted anger and wanted to kick their pitch to a pocky mess.

"One game," said Rufus. "Then go waltz with the girls."

The boys snickered.

Maud's best marble was mossy green, a real masher. Nudging her way in, she kept her mouth still as each of the boys shot their marbles into the circle, either knocking another fellow's out or careening straight through the circle and out. It was Maud's turn with two marbles left on the pitch—Nathaniel's huge cat's eye and Rufus's clear and speckled galaxy. She knuckled her marble and sent Rufus's galaxy zinging out of the ring. A clear win. The boys laughed, and Tavis slapped Rufus on the back.

Nathaniel grabbed his marble, yelling, "It's a draw. Rufus and I are even!"

The boys swarmed and pounded toward the racing lanes. Maud pulled her marble from the dust. They would never say she'd won, and she was lucky they hadn't taken her masher. Someone shouted that the hundred-meter race was next. The band played and people sang along: "Casey Would Waltz with The Strawberry Blonde."

Maud placed herself on the starting line.

Mrs. Beal talked to Mr. Kenney, who officiated the races. "It's not right," she said. "The girls have their own race."

As the gun went off, Mrs. Beal grabbed a handful of Maud's middy blouse. Off balance, Maud took two steps sideways while boys streamed down the field. She pumped her legs and kept her head down, but it was no good. Her shoes could have had wings and she wouldn't have overcome Mrs. Beal's hold on her. It was a horrible race, a horrible Social. Maud had had enough. She wanted to leave. She didn't want to smile and eat pie or share anything from the hamper. She hated the smaller children with sticky faces and grabbing hands. Mostly she hated the boys. Addie was across the field with Lydia. No help at all.

"Come on," Lydia said to Addie. "The three-legged race! Be my partner." She pulled Addie to her feet and they set off toward the racing field, Lydia hauling Addie by the arm like a too-heavy kite.

They wedged their way onto the starting line after Lydia grabbed a gunnysack. "Tie up your skirts!" yelled Lydia over the laughing and jostling crowd. Lydia stuck her right foot into the sack. The gun went off, and couples hobbled and lurched down the field. Addie's left foot was on the sack, but her skirts wouldn't stay tied. Her dress was scrambled fabric and her foot lost the sack's opening. Her foot stabbed, missed, stabbed again, and found something like a hole only to find it was part of her skirt. She and Lydia tumbled, skirts, petticoats, shoes, legs, sack, and bloomers flashing as they crumpled. The crowd divided between watching the winner and the commotion mid-field. When Lydia and Addie twisted themselves upright and then collapsed again, everyone cheered. Lydia freed herself, her face scarlet. She backed into the crowd to disappear. Addie crawled until Old Mr. Dunmore set her upright.

"You're a bit wobbly," he said, holding her elbow.

"Thank you," she murmured and slunk behind the cabanas. Her stomach lurched, her head ached, and her eyes glazed.

Maud watched, hoping to laugh, but she didn't. Addie's humiliation was too much like her own. A woman said, "Someone should teach that girl comportment." Maud thought someone should teach that woman to mind her own business.

"You almost won." Tavis was next to her.

"I did win. Nathaniel is a ninny."

"Never mind. Have you got the map?" Tavis moved to a picnic table. Maud spread the paper out, and they bent over it.

"How do you know for sure?" she asked.

Tavis tapped the map with his finger. "People talk in my father's shop. A man from Boston said Pirate Black Bart stowed his loot one stormy night. It wasn't a huge treasure, so no one's looked for it. This man said it was here in Mahone Bay." Tavis let the words sink in. "It's around the point and I'm going for it tomorrow." He pointed across the bay.

Maud followed his finger, then looked at him. She knew he'd told her about the cave and let her see the map so she'd help keep the other boys away. He wasn't asking her to share the adventure.

"You won't say a word, will you?"

"No," she said. "I won't say anything."

Tavis grinned and put the map in his pocket. "You're all right, Maud, you are."

He sauntered off, leaving Maud to wish harder that she'd never come. Maud was sick of the Social; she wanted to find the caves and stay forever. She wanted to leave Addie. Her face was red and her hair frizzed when she threw herself on the blanket. Before she could open the basket, Addie's voice and shadow came over her.

"Don't root around in there. I'll serve it."

Addie didn't look much better than Maud. Her ribbons were loose, her dress was rumpled, and a greenish tinge bordered her eyes. She sat on the opposite corner and set out the food tins that Cook had packed. Seeing the the potato salad, the green in Addie's skin deepened. Her eyes were pinwheels. The laudanum giddiness had worn off, leaving nausea and vertigo in its place.

"What's wrong with you?" Maud demanded.

Addie ran behind the cabanas. When she didn't return, Maud shrugged and pulled a piece of chicken from the basket. She took a few bites, then decided she'd better see about her sister.

Families were leaving, and the band played "God Save The King," a sign that the Social was ending. The races were done, and Mrs. Curran's pie had won the blue ribbon. Children either slept in their parents' arms or cried because they wanted to stay. Mrs. Beal packed her basket, and the boys at the far end of the field had a rough skirmish. Maud wanted to spit at them all.

The cabanas, no longer needed for changing into bathing costumes, were empty. Addie, behind a yellow-striped cabana, looked like she was going to heave her insides onto the grass.

"Too much spun sugar?" Maud asked.

The words, the image, the taste, gave Addie the momentum

to vomit up everything she had eaten, even breakfast. She tried
to keep it off her shoes, the hem of her dress, but it spattered
and stuck.

"Eew! Don't let Evelyn Brighty see you doing that!" This
almost made up for Tavis and the map.

"Shut up, Maud," Addie gasped. Her head shrank and everything was far away.

"The carriages are leaving. You can get a ride if you go
now," said Maud.

Addie gulped in air. "I'm not getting into a carriage like this!
Besides, what are you going to do?"

"Someone has to bring the dinghy back."

"I'll go with you. No one will see us if we wait."

"You can't!" Maud blurted. She wanted the dinghy, the
caves, the discovery for herself.

"Can't what? You rowed us over, you can row us back."
Addie slumped onto the grass and put her head in her hands.
"Go get the rug and hamper."

Maud wanted to kick Addie. Everything was just getting
worse and worse. Addie moaned. Maud marched across the
field. There were no more blankets spread on the ground. The
ropes to mark the races were down, and the booth for the spun
sugar was boxed up and being pulled away. Maud snatched up
the hamper and the rug and trudged back to Addie. It was no
use. She was never going to beat Tavis at anything.

Addie hadn't moved.

"Sit down and wait," Addie said. She closed her eyes and
rocked, setting off the heaves. Maud listened to Addie retch.
This was not the Social either had imagined.

Finally, Addie's insides quieted and the girls were alone.

Maud stepped from behind the cabana. "It's safe," she said.

Addie got to her feet and walked unsteadily behind the
tents toward the beach with Maud following. Addie climbed
into the dinghy and collapsed by the rear thwart.

Maud shoved the boat with all her rage, sending it in a spray of sand into the shallows. She splashed into the water, gave the boat another angry push, and flung herself up and into the bow. Addie no longer cared about the spray. As the boat rocked, she groaned and leaned over the side.

"Serves you right!" Maud yelled. Startled, Addie looked up, but Maud wasn't yelling at anybody in particular. She grabbed the oars and hauled on them as if she could beat the ocean. The oars thrashed as she rowed with fury, the dinghy jerking with each thrust.

"Maud, stop!" Addie gripped the gunwales, her face pasty. "Just row us back!"

"Would you like to try?" Maud barked.

Addie slumped with her head on the rear thwart. She closed her eyes and breathed through her nose. Within minutes she was asleep, giving in to the weariness that the laudanum had left in its wake.

Without Addie to fight, Maud relaxed her hold on the oars and swung them through the water. The boat steadied and moved forward with an even rhythm. She had her plan and she was going to see it through by angling the boat toward the tip of the peninsula. By her reckoning she could row around the point, examine the entrance to the caves, and row home. With luck, Addie would sleep through it all.

Maud daydreamed, whistling softly and noticing the beach sliding past. The ocean chop increased as the boat hit the wider mouth of the small bay. They were past Strum Island and nearly around Andrew's Island, heading for Whynachts Cove. She grinned at her scheme, the grosgrain ribbon of her middy blouse fluttering. Her body pulled on the oars while she imagined pirate skulls and Spanish gold. She was deep in her daydream when the first rolling swell rocked the boat and turned it purposefully out to sea. Maud dug in her starboard oar and pointed the dinghy in her intended direction, but the

next swell was larger and hauled the boat again for the open
sea. Maud pulled on the oars with all her muscles. Between
each rising swell, she had less and less time to maneuver the
boat. Very quickly the boat, with the help of an offshore
breeze, was pushed directly into the open ocean. The cabana
tents were dots. The church steeples were small spears.

"Addie! Adelaide!" Maud cried. "Help me!"

Maud poked Addie with her boot. Addie, smothered in the
laudanum, couldn't hear Maud's cries. Addie, too, was adrift
and untethered. Her head lolled on the wooden seat and she
moaned. Maud screamed, directing her voice toward shore.
Balancing upright, she opened and closed Addie's parasol rapidly, hoping someone would see the blinking spot of white.
Maud tried to remember Morse Code and did her best to
flash an SOS: three short flashes followed by three long and
again three short. Maud bellowed and repeated her parasol
code. Maybe a lobster boat or a fishing trawler was nearby.
Gulls screamed back at her. She took the oars again and rowed
against the current, trying to force the dinghy to safety. She
pulled with all her strength and strained against the weight of
the rolling sea until her back and arms burned and her hands
were rubbed raw. Her efforts had no effect. She pushed and
yanked at the oars, doing her best to keep a steady rhythm until
her muscles felt ripped to shreds.

Maud pulled frantically, her eyes locked on the shoreline
dipping beneath the peaks of waves, the cabana tents like
blown specks of sand. The afternoon sun rode above them
in a haze.

Shipping the oars, Maud propped the open parasol over her
sleeping sister and slumped on her own cross brace, exhausted
and numb. Large tears rolled down her cheeks, and she wondered how she would explain herself when Addie finally woke
up. Maud knew that eventually the tide would turn, the wind
would shift, and they would be pushed back to shore. They

might end up far from the picnic or from home and have to walk or ask for help, but they would end up on shore. Maud's fear and sorrow focused on the trouble she would be in once they landed and she had to confess her scheme. The worst, she knew, would be facing Addie when she realized what Maud had done.

Maud let her tears dry and gazed over the gunwale at the shimmering swells with their lace foam and occasional darker green cold. She thought about the swimming races the boys had held off the point on the last day of school. She saw herself, hair bobbed short, beating each boy as they rounded the rocks. The image floated, the sun warmed her, until she too slept.

From above, the girls looked like fairy tale maidens under a spell drifting and asleep until released by love's true kiss. Adelaide, with golden hair and blue-striped skirts filling her end of the boat like froth, looked a prize for any knight. Maud, a stranger damsel, with fierce freckles and a jackknife hand, could also set hearts ablaze. No incantation was at work; no charm was to be undone. Maud and Adelaide were beyond reach. Because of their own desires, the sea and winds had made it so.

3

Say the One About the Stars

The June sun worked its way west and the little boat moved steadily east from shore, toward a fog bank held by the off-shore wind. They passed between Coveys Island and Rous Island. Soon a grayish yellow vapor obscured everything but the boat itself. In curling fingers, the fog stole over the boat and twined itself around the sleeping girls, its touch clammy and cold. The smothered sun couldn't reach through, and the chill roused Adelaide. She blinked. Thinking the fog was from her drug-glued eyes, she rubbed them to clear her vision. She saw they were still in the dinghy and had no way to get her bearings.

"Maud, wake up!" Adelaide shook her sister by the shoulder. "Maud, where are we? What's happening?"

Maud sat up sharply and stared wide-eyed at the fog. "I don't know, Addie. I didn't mean this to happen."

"Didn't mean for what to happen? Where's the beach? Where are we going? Why aren't you rowing?" Addie threw questions like darts.

"The current was too strong. I tried to wake you."

Addie stared at her sister. "How long have we been out here?"

"I don't know. I tried ever so hard to row us back. I screamed and signaled with your parasol. I rowed until my arms couldn't hold the oars and my hands blistered." She held out her bubbled hands. Tears splashed on them and stung where the blisters had broken.

Addie looked at Maud's hands, then looked down at herself. "Look at me! My dress is flattened, and my hair is matted. Why didn't you wake me?"

"I told you, I tried. You were like Tavis's dog after it got into the ale."

Addie avoided looking at Maud. "Someone must have seen us coming across the bay." Even as she said it, Addie knew no one had been on the headland when they first set out across the harbor. Most of the picnickers had traveled in buggies. She shivered. Their clothes were fog damp and they were covered in goose bumps. Maud rubbed her arms for warmth.

They sat in miserable, guilty silence, the ocean swaying beneath them. They peered into the fog, straining for the beach they believed was in shouting distance.

"Maybe if we both yell."

They screamed and hallooed until the fog was full of their voices, but their words didn't reach any ears. Addie felt like she was yelling into her pillow, which she did when her temper got the better of her.

"Maybe the fog will break and someone will see us," Addie said. But the fog was so thick that neither believed it. Addie shivered and pulled the rug around her shoulders. Seeing Maud with her fists in her lap, Addie loosened the blanket and held out an end. Maud pulled the offered end around her. They sat on separate thwarts, the rug stretched between them, each draping an end over her back.

"Let's eat something. There's hot tea in the thermos," said Addie.

Cook had packed plenty of food for the afternoon—boneless slices of chicken, cucumber and cress sandwiches, four hard boiled eggs, potato salad, pickles, strawberries, carrot and bean salad, six slices of smoked cheese, half a loaf of gingerbread, and four date squares. One thermos held hot tea, the other lemonade. In a third bottle was plain water. Napkins, forks, spoons, knives, cups, and plates were stowed in the bottom of the hamper. The food cheered both girls despite the drifting boat and the enveloping fog.

"Let's start with the sandwiches," suggested Addie. "The cress is already wilting."

"I hate cucumber and cress sandwiches," said Maud.

"But they're the right thing for a Social."

Maud primmed her mouth and wagged her head. "They're the right thing for a Social," she mimicked.

"What do you know, you little barbarian. You eat plain brown sugar."

"You don't like those sandwiches either. I know you don't, because I've seen you nibble a little, tear off bits, and say, 'I couldn't eat another bite!' Phony!"

"You have no idea how to behave. Social situations demand sacrifice. You're a baby."

"Baby! Give me one of those." Maud grabbed at the sandwiches.

"No. They're too good for you."

"Give it to me!" Maud snatched the sandwich out of Addie's hand.

"Hey! Give that back!"

"This one's mine. Eat your own."

Addie swiped at Maud, and the boat tipped.

"Watch out!" Maud yelled, laughing.

Addie pulled the other sandwich from the hamper and took a bite. She chewed it with her chin up. Maud tore off a corner along with a cucumber and a swag of cress. She rolled the collection in her fingers and shot it at Addie, hitting her on the cheek. Maud burst out laughing.

"You little pig!" Addie pulled a cress leaf from her sandwich and tossed it at Maud. It fluttered and flopped between them.

Maud laughed at her. "Like this," she said and rolled another wad in her fingers. She flicked it across the boat and it landed on Addie's lap.

Addie flung her whole sandwich at Maud. "You're the most hateful girl in the world, Maud. I wish you'd drown!"

Maud's laughing stopped. "I want a boiled egg. You can have this." She held out the sandwich.

Addie shook her head. Maud pulled her hand back and they sat silently. Finally, Maud flipped the sandwich over the side.

Addie was angry, but also sorry for what she'd said. She picked up the pieces of her own sandwich and tossed them over the side too. She reached into the hamper and pulled out the chicken and hard-boiled eggs.

"Lemonade, too. I'm thirsty," said Maud.

Addie poured two small mugs of lemonade after spreading napkins on their laps and handing out eggs and pieces of chicken. They munched, letting the food replace their thoughts. Soon Addie's chewing slowed, and she peered around, trying to penetrate the gray mist.

"I can't hear anything," she said, looking ahead and sitting motionless. "It's as if we're the only things in the world, Maud. It's eerie."

Maud stopped eating, straining to hear any sounds. But there was nothing, no birds, no wind, not even waves slapping the sides of the dinghy. She twisted, as if turning would make her hearing more acute. Nothing. It was silence beyond the dull drawing room on winter afternoons or the church quiet after the sermon. The silence had a presence of its own.

Addie shivered. "I keep thinking we're in a room with curtains, and when the curtains are drawn back, we'll see that we're about to slide off the edge of the world. It's so lonely."

Maud observed her sister, taking in her fear and helplessness. "When the fog clears, we'll see more ocean. Neither of us is alone."

Addie took a deep breath and gave Maud a thin smile to keep her terror from showing. "No, we're not alone, and I'm glad for that," she answered, swallowing hard. "Let's finish our lunch and have tea and a date square, all right?" Tea, as their mother said, could make anything right. Addie busied herself with tea and Maud hummed a sailing tune rather than let the silence overwhelm them again.

"Do you miss Halifax?" Maud asked, to keep Addie's mind off their predicament, but also because, as she watched her older sister, it struck her that Addie had not complained recently of being in Mahone Bay.

"I miss the bigger parties and the fashions. It's hard to see the lady's books with gorgeous gowns and know they're out of reach in this pokey place. But I like the sea and some of the people are friendly, much nicer than the snobby Perlings or boring Dobsons. Do you miss Halifax, Maud?"

"I miss the docks." She thought this didn't sound right, so she added, "I miss Mama and Papa too. Although staying at the summer house means I can go about the village more. Sometimes I miss our city house and the Spring Garden Road sounds that come up to my window. But here there are so many birds and the wind is fantastic for kites. If I tell you a secret, will you promise not to blab?"

Addie considered while Maud finished a date square. "All right, I promise."

"I've been going to the blacksmiths. Tavis and his father showed me how to shoe horses, how to shape metal, and how to tie knots. It's wonderful fun!"

"Why do you want to know those things?" Addie burst out. "Did you just wander in and say, 'Mr. Crandle, will you teach me to shoe a horse?'" Addie was more bewildered than appalled. She would never ask an adult how or why they did anything. But Maud watched everyone and always asked questions. Addie was surprised that Mr. Crandle had allowed Maud to stay and learn some of his trade.

"Tavis asked if I wanted to see how a horse was shod," answered Maud. She wanted to get back to telling Addie what she knew about blacksmithing.

"Oh, I see," responded Addie.

"What does that mean? Oh, I see!" asked Maud.

"It means, I understand why you spent time at Crandle's Smithy."

"I like to know how things work and how to do things," Maud said, her temper rising.

"Tavis is sweet on you, Maud, and I think you're sweet on him."

"Adelaide, you are the most perverse sister ever! I don't care for Tavis or any boy and never will. He's a friend, someone who likes the same things I do. He likes to show me tricks with knots and do small carpentry jobs." Maud's cheeks flamed and her eyes grew dark.

"It makes perfect sense that he would like you, Maud," interrupted Addie. "Why wouldn't he want to show off and talk to you?"

"What do you mean?" demanded Maud.

"I mean, Maud, that you're pretty in a wild way. A boy like Tavis would find you fun because you ask questions that he can answer. Most girls don't know anything about what boys like to do and only pretend to be interested. You want to find out how the world is put together and listen carefully when someone explains. I wish I could do it, but I can't. I'd like to find someone who recites poetry or talks about novels."

Maud was speechless. It was the first time in a very long time that Addie had paid her a compliment, never mind express an understanding of what made Maud happy or how her mind worked. It was also the first time in ages that Addie had confided her feelings to Maud. Maud didn't want the moment to evaporate.

"Have you met a boy interested in poetry or novels, Addie?"

"Not in Halifax, no. Well, Oliver Harkness used to read all the time, but he didn't want to hear what I had to say about books and made fun of what I read. I mostly know boys who read what they have to but talk mostly about who can wrestle best or who can pitch a horseshoe farthest. If they do express an opinion, it's borrowed from their fathers." Addie looked sideways at Maud. "Can I tell you a secret?"

Maud's interest sharpened. "Of course. I won't breathe a word."

"Philip Tierney talked to me about a Keats poem. He told me it made him understand his own feelings. He got embarrassed, but it was the most romantic conversation I've ever had."

"Was Philip at the Social?"

"Yes, but he's very shy. I told him that I hoped he'd be there. Was that bold?"

"It's silly the way girls pretend to ignore boys they like and boys pretend that girls are a nuisance. What did Philip say?"

"Nothing. He turned red. I found a handwritten copy of the poem in my coat sleeve the next day."

"Well, that tells you everything. I'd say you'd found a match as long as he can get over his shyness."

Addie squinted around her. "Is the fog thickening or is it getting darker, Maud?"

Maud peered into the impenetrable fog. It was like having her eyes bandaged with thick gauze. Her eyes and ears strained to see or hear something, anything, but the world was muffled, and as daylight drained away, the luminous fog dimmed like a candle going out. If the girls could have seen beyond the fog, they would have seen the sun dipping below the horizon

amid reddened streaks of clouds. But the world had shrunk
for Maud and Adelaide. Their world was the bobbing dinghy.
Dark overtook them and left the wet fog hanging. What little
warmth the sun had offered vanished, and the girls felt cold
right through to their bones. Addie shivered steadily and Maud
hugged herself.

"Here, Maud," suggested Addie. "Let's huddle in the bottom of the boat and wrap ourselves in the rug."

Maud slid off the front thwart and pulled the wool rug
with her. Addie slid from her back perch and crawled past the
centerboard into the full warmth of the rug and the comfort
of Maud's closeness. "Oh, that's much better," said Maud with
a deep shiver.

They settled into as comfortable a position as possible and
discovered that by leaning on each other they had warmth,
a bit of cushion, and more firm support than the edge of a
cross brace. Neither could remember the last time they had
sat so closely. "Remember when we used to play Rock, Paper,
Scissors?" asked Addie. "You used to cheat terribly."

"I did not. You were never very fast, that's all," said Maud,
laughing.

"All right. Let's see how well you do now," replied Addie,
laughing too.

"On three then," said Maud and counted out one, two,
three, shooting her hand forward with her index and middle
finger making scissors.

Addie was equally quick and threw her fist into the air between them. "Rock! I win!" she cried.

"Best three out of five," demanded Maud. For the next
hour the girls gestured over and over, raising the limits until
they reached the best fifty-one out of a hundred. Their laughter echoed through the fog, and their banter filled the boat
with company.

"Paper! That's it! I've beaten you fifty-one times out of a hundred!" squealed Maud. "And I didn't cheat."

"No, you didn't cheat. But I gave you a good chase," Addie replied. She stretched her arms and neck and looked up. "Maud, look! A star! The fog is thinning. I know a poem about stars shining bright."

"Can it be sung in front of company?" Maud asked.

"What do you mean, 'Can it be sung in front of company?'" Addie was startled and fascinated. "Do you know poems that can't?"

"Not poems, just one or two songs, and I can't remember the words." Maud wished she hadn't spoken. "Say the one about the stars."

Addie cleared her throat. Her clear voice circled them and stayed within the boat, but as her voice gained strength, the words penetrated the fog wisps that clung to the ocean's surface:

In the deep of the evening stars sparkle and burn
They fill the great night with stories once told
And they point to my home when I've lost the right turn.

There were six stanzas before Addie finished.

"That's very pretty," said Maud. "I like the words 'great night' and 'point the way home.'" The thought of finding their way home stopped their voices. They shivered despite the thick blanket, a net of moisture covering their hair. "There's a song about a sailor's lunch," Maud said before their thoughts overwhelmed them. "It's about a sailor who eats too many clams and drinks too much ale. He can't find a place to relieve himself."

"Oh, Maud, that's awful!" complained Addie, laughing. "Where did you hear it?"

"On the beach. The men were repairing nets and singing. I didn't learn all the words."

"I need to follow the sailor's example."

Maud nodded, not understanding, then she laughed harder as she realized Addie needed to pee. "Well, Addie, how should we take care of the necessities, as the song says?" Maud tilted her head at her sister.

"I don't know!" wailed Addie. She twisted her hands and waited.

"Use this bucket," Maud offered and kicked the sand pail with her toe. Addie looked in disbelief. Maud nodded. "Go ahead."

"Turn around."

It was Maud's turn to look disbelieving. "Take your petticoats off first."

Addie stared at Maud. "Close your eyes."

Maud did, but as soon as Addie finished, Maud pulled off her own petticoat. "Oh, that's much better!" she declared. "Pass me the pail and now you close your eyes."

With the necessities over, and released from yards of petticoats, both girls relaxed.

Addie rinsed the pail over the side of the boat and asked, "Should we have hot tea, potato salad, pickles, and strawberries?"

Maud nodded and they repositioned themselves in the bottom of the boat, wrapped themselves in the blanket, and dipped into the hamper. Nestled together, Maud munched potato salad while Addie sipped tea.

"Don't drink too much or you'll have to pee again, and I don't want to capsize," Maud warned.

Addie giggled, then thought about the truth of it. Maud's body settled more firmly against hers. Addie glanced at her sister and saw that her eyes were half closed, her head drooping.

"Do you remember the song Mama used to sing when we were little?" Maud asked sleepily.

Addie hummed the favorite tune until the words came back

to her in the right order. She sang gently, verse after verse, until she knew Maud was asleep. Addie hummed the melody to herself as she watched veils of mist separate and thin and more and more stars blink their colors far above their vessel. Soon she, too, nodded into dreams.

4

Wouldn't it Be Grand if it Rained

Both girls woke with a jolt. Something large bumped the bottom of their boat. The sky was a stretch of brilliant blue and the sun bore down after the imprisoning fog of the night before.

"What was that?" demanded Maud as she struggled to sit up. Her muscles ached from the cramped sleeping position. She dropped the blanket off her shoulders and eased herself up onto the rear seat.

Addie sat motionless, holding her breath. She gestured for Maud to keep still. They sat frozen like a game of freeze tag. Again a bump from beneath, and they knew it was deliberate, a test to see what kind of creature this boat could be.

"Don't move," Addie whispered.

Nothing happened for a long moment as they watched the ocean surface. Maud was about to move when another thump raised the boat several inches.

"Oh! Oh!" exclaimed Addie.

Before Maud could answer, a dark shape rose alongside, black with streaks of grayish blue and dotted with barnacles.

"A whale!" whispered Maud. "A whale next to our boat!" She pointed and stared.

Addie, wide-eyed, croaked, "It's going to eat us!"

Maud pictured the dinghy capsized and crushed by the enormous creature. Three times the length of the dinghy, the whale swam alongside. The girls gaped when an eye appeared, surveying them. They saw scars where nicks and scrapes had healed. Maud pointed to a long gash that had left a raised gray line. She made the motion of a harpoon.

The whale sank beneath the depths and left the girls with hearts pounding until it rose again on the other side, rolled over, and once more disappeared. Seconds later, well away from the dinghy, the whale exploded out of the sea in a magnificent leap, arced its body, curled its flukes, and dove with a tremendous splash back into the water.

Maud and Addie stayed still for many minutes, but the whale didn't resurface.

"It was a whale!" Addie said reverently.

"It was a whale," Maud repeated. "It leapt so high!"

"I didn't know," said Addie

"What didn't you know?"

"That whales could be so happy."

Maud nodded. "I was afraid it was sharks."

"Don't say that," admonished Addie. "It must be very deep here."

Maud laughed. "Of course it's very deep."

"When you're out sailing for the day, you don't think about what's underneath. This must be a tremendous amount of water for a whale to swim about."

"What did you think was under us?"

"Water, of course. But think about all the space!"

"It's not space, it's water."

"Can you picture it? How deep and wide it is?"

"Well, look around you."

They did. There was no shore, no islands, not a hint of another boat. The sun sparked off the ocean's surface like a million mirrors winking.

Maud folded the carriage rug. "I'm starving. Shall we eat?"

Addie opened the hamper and laid out a breakfast of boiled eggs, strawberries, and gingerbread. When these were shared on their plates, she paused. "Perhaps we should be careful how much we eat." She didn't want to say the words, but the thought was in both their minds. "We don't know whether we'll be home for supper or not."

Maud looked at the food critically. "Let's put the ginger-bread away for another time."

Addie nodded, rewrapped the bread, and stowed it in the basket. "What time do you think it is, Maud?"

Maud squinted at the sun, then looked at the horizon. "Maybe six or seven. The fishing boats should be out soon."

They ate their breakfast, letting the meal occupy their thoughts for as long as possible, neither wanting to face the question that was as stark as if it had been written across the sky. The sun beat down as it rose above the sea, and the sea reflected the blue of the sky, stretching on all sides in a smooth surface of large, rolling swells. Maud finished her egg and strawberries, drank the rest of her lemonade, and put her hands into the water to rinse them. The blisters stung in the salt, but the cool water felt good in the increasing heat of the sun.

"That feels better," Maud said.

They scrunched down again into the bottom of the boat, facing each other and resting their heads along the gunwales. For a long while, the girls lay and watched the deep green of the sea mix with brilliant blues reflected from the sky. They dozed a bit to rest their eyes in the bright light.

A tern drifted overhead, curious about the boat. Maud watched its ash-gray underside rise and fall with air currents. She knew it was studying her, and with that thought the bird glided down and landed on the transom.

"Oh, you are a beauty," Maud breathed. She jiggled her foot to wake Addie, but Addie didn't budge. The bird had very long tail streamers, its cap like jet in the sun. Its bill was blood-red, and just behind its head the feathers were pearl gray.

"Addie!" Maud hissed.

Addie sat up with a start. The tern lifted off, let out a kee-aarm of a scream, circled the boat twice, and flew off.

"You frightened it away!"

"And you scared me half to death!"

They glared at each other for a moment, and then Addie pulled out her glasses and her book.

"Didn't you already read that book?"

Addie didn't answer. Maud pulled a length of string from her pocket, tied the ends together, and looped it around her fingers. Tavis had claimed she played girls' games with string. "Knots," he said. "Men make knots." Maud pulled hard on a loop and the knot unraveled. "Rats!" she spat.

Addie glanced up but went back to her book.

Maud retied the string and began again, but it didn't hold. "Rats!" she yelled and wound the string around the oar. She crossed the ends and made the same knot, pulling on it hard. It didn't stay. "Huh?" she grunted.

"You need a different knot," Addie said without looking up.

Maud paid no attention. She undid the string, retied the ends to themselves, and tried her looping game, only to have the knot come undone once more. "Damn!" she yelled.

"Maud Agnes Campbell!" Addie barked. "That word's not allowed."

"I don't care. No one can hear me."

"I can hear you."

"You have your nose and ears in that book. You wouldn't notice or care if I fell overboard."

Addie pressed her lips, adjusted her glasses, and went back to reading.

"Why are you reading that book again?"

Addie blew air out her nose. "It's a good story. You should use a splice knot for what you're trying to do. Papa told you that before he left."

"I don't remember." Maud balled up the string.

"Give it here." Addie closed her book. She took the string and wound the ends into double, interlocking loops. "Try that."

Maud draped the string on her spiked fingers and wove a design. The knot held.

Addie watched Maud's expert hands. First, Maud looped the string around her fingers, pulling it tight between some and letting it droop between others until she had made a bolt of lightning. She shook the string off her hands and began again. This time she made two stars. Maud hadn't forgotten anything, and Addie knew it. This was Maud's way of getting Addie's attention.

"Do you want to try?" Maud asked, holding her hands toward her sister.

Addie shook her head and went back to her book. Maud picked apart the knot and hung one end of the string in the water, watching the end dip below the surface and trail. She flicked the string in little circles, making a tiny whirlpool beside the boat. Like a fisherman casting a line, she flung the end out and smiled at the small smacking sound the string made when it hit the water. She did this again and again. Addie raised her eyes from the page and arched an eyebrow, but she said nothing and kept reading.

Maud flung the string faster, over and over, then changed to a sideways motion, twirling the string alongside so that it smacked the water harder and whipped through the water with a jet of spray. Maud was aware of nothing but the string. She twirled the string with her whole arm now so that it slapped the water and sent a steady spray of water into the air and into the boat.

"Stop it!" yelled Addie. "Maud, stop!" Wet dots speckled her book.

Maud, startled, laughed, and let the string hang from her hand. "It'll dry."

"I can't turn the page now. I have to leave it open until it dries." Maud shrugged her shoulders. "You're impossible!" Addie twisted until she faced away from Maud.

"You're a bore," Maud retorted and pulled the corners of her mouth to make a face at Addie's back.

Addie reread the damp pages. Maud sat in the stern, her string stretched across her lap. The corners of her mouth still tugged down, she took one end of the string and flicked the other at the centerboard box. She flicked it harder. She thought about knots and about Papa and Mama being gone. They were always gone. The string slapped the water harder. It made a pinging sound. It snapped harder and harder. It zipped in the air before it hit the centerboard. *Whiz! Ping! Whiz! Ping!* She liked the sound, but the motion of her arm made her angrier instead of calming her down. *Whiz! Ping! Whiz! Ping!*

"Ow!" Addie spun around and the boat wobbled.

"Stay still!" Maud yelled.

"You hurt me!"

"It's just string!"

"You whipped me!"

"It was an accident. It didn't hurt."

"It did too. You whipped me across my back."

"You're a sissy."

"You're a ruffian."

"You're noodle-headed!"

"You're a smudge face!"

"Brainless!"

"Hooligan!"

"Priss!"

"Troll!"

"Odd Maud!"

That was the name Rufus Handy called her at school. She hated it. Maud scooped a handful of water and flung it at Addie. "Addle Addie!"

"Ohhh!" screamed Addie.

Evelyn Brighty would whisper the name to other girls when she thought Addie couldn't hear. But Addie had heard, and the name made her face go bright red. Her hair dripped.

"You…you!" She flung a handful of water at Maud.

"Go on!" shouted Maud. "Go on!" She gave Addie another one.

They splashed and flung water at each other. *Whoosh! Splash!* The boat teetered and Addie screamed. Maud laughed. Addie took her parasol and smacked it hard on the water. The spray came back in her own face, making her splutter and cough. Furious, hair dripping, she flung her parasol into the bottom of the boat, turned her back on Maud, and picked up her novel. But she couldn't read. The pages were damp, and her back hurt. But she had no right to be angry with Maud. It wasn't Maud's fault they were out here.

Addie closed her book and turned around. "There are cards in the hamper. Would you like to play?"

Maud rolled the string into a ball and put it back in her pocket. "What do you want to play? Not Old Maid. I hate that game."

"Two can't play Hearts." It was Maud's favorite game.

"Cribbage?"

"All right." Addie shuffled and cut the deck, showing a five of clubs. Maud cut and showed a jack of spades.

"Ha-ha! I deal first."

Hours went by as they dealt, organized their hands, discarded and counted points. Addie won most hands, but they decided not to keep score. Maud pulled herself onto the rear thwart and stretched her arms and legs as far as she could.

Addie did too. "I'm hungry again," she said.

Maud looked at the sun and saw that it was nearly overhead. "I guess we could eat, it's close to noon."

Addie dug in the depths of the hamper and pulled out pieces of chicken and the rest of the potato salad. "I think this might spoil first," she said, explaining her choices.

Neither wanted to say their thoughts out loud. They ate in silence, sipping a little lemonade. Addie picked up the empty container, leaned over the side of the boat, and swished it through the water. Bits of potato, celery, and onion floated on top of the swells. The mayonnaise made a small slick of oil. A few skuas circling far overhead came screeching and squabbled over the debris. They scavenged the edible bits and veered off.

"What fierce birds they are!" exclaimed Addie.

"Seabirds have to be. Imagine flying over the sea every day looking for food. And when you find it, there's a crowd ready to snatch it away. I would be fierce, too. I wouldn't care how pretty I was, so long as I could fly hard against the wind and have a quick eye to spot a fish wiggling below."

Maud gazed at the never-ending ocean stretching in every direction. "Addie, will you read some of your book to me?"

"It's *David Copperfield*."

"Start from the beginning."

Addie pulled the book from the hamper where she had stowed it and propped her parasol for shade. Maud stretched the blanket over the rear thwart like a tent and scrunched under it. Addie read and both girls were transported to England.

After an hour or so of reading, they were drowsy with the heat.

"I'm thirsty," said Maud.

Addie licked her lips. "Me too. We haven't touched the water."

"Let's each have one cup."

They shared out the cups and drank thoughtfully, both aware that the water filled only one jar.

"There's still tea and a little lemonade," Addie said.

Maud thought about how long that would last. "That's not very much."

Addie swallowed, realizing how much more water she wanted. "What should we do?"

"We should be careful." Maud's eyes stayed on the jar. "I'm sure we'll be rescued soon."

It was the first time either one of them had mentioned being rescued. The book was forgotten, and they scanned the horizon for a ship or a shoreline. Each girl had searched from time to time but hadn't wanted the other to notice. They stared about them, trying not to feel hopeless.

The boat floated on the ceaseless sea, and the girls broiled beneath their canopies. The water intensified the glare as the sun baked them and sweat trickled down their necks and pricked their arms and legs. Maud's freckles stood out like a galaxy of brown stars, and Addie's complexion lit with sunburn.

"Shall I row some more?" Maud offered.

"Which direction makes sense? Besides, you can't handle the oars with those blisters."

"If we follow the sun west, we would bump into land. And if I wrap my hands, they won't hurt too badly."

Addie didn't want to see Maud struggle against the ocean. She didn't want to know it was hopeless. With her big-sister face she said, "I'll keep reading."

Maud gave in. After a long time, Addie dropped the book into her lap and rested her head against the gunwale.

"I'm hot and thirsty," said Maud. "Wouldn't it be grand if it rained? I'd like a good soaking."

"Mmmm, yes. Isn't it odd," Addie twisted around to look at

her sister, "that we're wishing for water as we sit in the middle
of this?"

"Perhaps we've gone mad. Do you feel mad?"

"No. Well, yes, a little. I mean, I'm so thirsty. Let's have a
little more water. Don't you think it will be all right?"

"I don't know. I want to drink it all, but I'm afraid to."

Addie doled out two small cups of water and they drank it
slowly. It wasn't enough, but it was something. Maud slumped
down off the thwart and rested her head against the gunwale.

"I read something awful in a book once," Addie offered.
"Something we could do if we're desperate." Maud perked up
at the idea of doing something Addie thought was awful. "A
person can live on raw fish. The blood and juice in a fish are
nearly as good as fresh water."

"Could you do that, Addie?"

"No, I don't think so. Could you?"

"I don't know. Besides, we'd have to catch a fish and that
would take some cleverness." Maud squinted up. "At least the
sun is going down."

The sun slid toward the horizon, shooting flaming path-
ways across the water's surface. As dusk crossed the waves,
the breeze slowed, and a muggy pall settled on the sea like a
weighted net. The girls drowsed

The first drops of rain fell in a slow rhythm on the parched
boards of the thwarts and against the hot faces of the girls.
Larger, determined drops plunked, waking first Addie, then
Maud. They lay breathing the cool moist air, soothing against
sunburnt cheeks and arms.

"Ooooh, this feels good," murmured Addie.

Maud sat up. "Quick! Find something to catch the rain."

Addie scrambled and brought up the child's tin bucket. She
set it on the forward thwart. As single drops increased to a
downpour, the girls' spirits rose. Maud tilted her head to the

sky and opened her mouth to let the rain wash in. Addie giggled and did the same. The rain intensified, soaking them until heat turned to drenched shivers.

"Get under the blanket," suggested Addie. "The wool will hold off the rain."

They huddled under the rug and listened to the monotonous drumming as rain made a curtain around their boat. The hypnotic beat put Maud and Addie into a drowse, and they slept through the earliest morning hours. As night gave way to day, utter blackness changed to dense, sodden gray. The wind lifted from the west and chopped waves into whitecaps. The sea underneath the dinghy tilted and the sky churned. Maud knew they were at the edge of something fierce. She watched stronger winds bring rising swells and harder rains.

"Hold tight," Maud said, clutching both gunwales.

The dinghy rose and dropped rapidly on bumping swirls as the wind pitched higher. The sea heaved until rain and waves were indistinguishable. The boat crawled up steep slopes, perched precariously, then plunged into troughs only to climb again.

Addie recoiled in the bottom of the boat, rigid in terror. Maud grabbed the oars and flailed at the thrashing ocean as if beating back a monster. The left oar was nearly wrenched from her hand, and Maud screamed. A wave crashed over the side, drenching them both. Maud pulled in the oars and secured them along the bottom of the dinghy. As the boat spun and plummeted on the seething sea, swirling foam snaked their ankles and rose.

"Bail, Addie! Bail with anything you can find!" Maud grabbed the bucket and threw the ocean back into itself as fast as she could.

"I can't," Addie whispered with stiff lips.

Maud grabbed the potato salad tin and flung it at Addie. "Bail," she demanded.

Addie filled the tin with the salty wash filling around her ankles. The rhythm of filling and emptying the container, moving in unison with Maud, brought Addie out of her paralysis. As the sky roared and waves soared and crashed, Maud sang "The Women of Ipswich," ending with the refrain:

We're the women of Ipswich
No help do we need.
Our spirits run high
While commanding the sea.

"Sing, Addie! You know the words!" Maud shouted over the wind, booming as she pitched pail after pail over the side. Addie's voice trembled, then she too bellowed.

They bent, filled their pails, and tossed water into the ocean. The storm crashed wave after wave over the bow while the sky streamed and the wind whipped their song away. The girls, drenched, cold, and aching, bailed. Still they sang: "Our spirits run high/while commanding the sea!" Maud led every verse until her throat was sandpaper. Addie kept up, bending and pitching, singing wherever Maud led, watching the water in the bottom of the boat rather than the broiling sea.

As the shrieking wind rose, a gust caught the bow of the boat and spun it sideways. Addie and Maud clung with straining hands to the thwarts as a mountainous wave tipped them on end. Addie, crazed with desperation, threw herself against the bow, bringing the boat down with a crash.

The boat rode through the wave nearly sideways. Addie threw up, and Maud grabbed her as the boat shuddered and heaved. The wind boomed like a berserk train, and the girls lay across the bow, Addie's arms flung forward, her head hanging with hair tangled and lank. They cried out as lightning cracked.

Pushing herself up, Addie looked at Maud. "Keep on," she said. Her face was tinged green as she found the tin and bailed. She sobbed but continued to lift and spill water overboard. "Keep on," she repeated.

"Addie, that was ever so brave!" Maud cried. "We can make it."

Addie gave a weak grin. "We can try, Maud." Cold water reached up her legs.

They bailed through terrible hours, frantic to keep from being beaten and swallowed. They sang into the face of the storm. Waves towered and exploded and icy water poured down. In the deepest eye of the storm, the wind keened and sliced the tops of the waves, sending the dinghy spinning from one crest to another. The boat blew north and east, passing Big Tancook Island, Flat Island, and West Ironbound Island, leagues beyond where the fishing fleet dropped their nets. The girls sang and bailed, their arms burning, their legs bruised and cut from scrambling. The hamper floated, the petticoats and carriage rug a sodden heap.

They bailed and bailed, and the storm finally blew itself out. The clouds shredded, letting a pale moon peer at the ravaged sea. Waves no longer attacked, but the boat leaked. Maud plugged the cracks with napkins, but the sea crept in and they bailed. By early morning neither Maud nor Addie could sit upright, much less hold a container of seawater. While the clouds cleared and a soft sky eased the sun on its path, both girls slid into a wretched and exhausted sleep.

5

We're Not Back Where We Started

Hours after the girls had slumped into weary sleep, the little boat bumped along and pushed its nose against a craggy pile of rocks like a dog sniffing for a place to curl up and rest. It was June 13. Maud felt the bump, sat up, and saw tumbled boulders and hissing ocean foam on sand curving between shoulders of grey rock.

"Addie," she whispered, reaching behind her to touch her sleeping sister. She would have shouted, but her throat was parched, and she was afraid noise might make the scene disappear. "Addie," she croaked, bending to shake her sister.

Addie put her hand to her eyes and groaned. "It's no use. Leave me alone." Addie turned away from the glaring sun.

"We've hit land. We really have." Maud pushed against the rocks, trying to free the boat so it could drift to shore. "Addie, help me push," Maud insisted.

Addie squinted through her fingers. The sight of rocks brought her upright. "We're going to crash!"

"Help me push. If we point the boat toward shore, we can land."

"Shore?" Addie tilted her head to see the shore that lay past the rocks. She leaned forward, placed both hands against the rocks, and held the little boat at arm's length.

The ocean caught the boat again and propelled it toward the beach. Maud took up one oar to steer, turning the boat sideways toward the island. Within minutes, they felt the bump and scrape of sand under them.

"Jump!" exclaimed Addie.

"Don't let go of the boat," cautioned Maud.

They jumped into the swirling, waist-deep water, clinging to the boat to keep it from drifting away.

"Pull!" shouted Maud "Pull as hard as you can!"

Their long skirts, weighted with water, fought them as they tried to keep their footing. The boat, which had seemed so small when they were in it, was now an unwieldy bulk as it rode the breaking waves. They hung on each side and made cautious steps, putting their strength into the business of bringing the boat with them.

Addie, exhausted and weak, pushed a mat of hair out of her eyes. A wave surged forward, catching her off guard. She lost her footing and slid half under the boat. Maud felt the forward tug of the boat and ran with it, using her shoulder to urge it as far up onto the beach as she could. The boat slid halfway onto dry beach. Addie sputtered up alongside, threw herself down, looking like a strand of tossed-up seaweed. Maud trudged across the sand and sprawled in a disordered heap. They lay motionless, breathing deeply, feeling the ground beneath them, uncaring and heedless of the sky, the screech of birds, or the persistent wash of tide. They looked like dolls abandoned after a day's rough play, their clothes twisted and rumpled, their hair tangled. They lay an arm's length from each other, more spent than asleep, for several hours. Neither girl dreamed, and the ground beneath them tugged at their still-rocking bodies.

When early evening chill settled across the water, the girls stirred. They found themselves dusted with salt and sand, thirsty and aching, but out of the ocean's reach. Maud sat up and stared at the boat with her elbows on her bent knees. Her lips were cracked, and her throat stung from the salt. She looked at Addie, still prone, but with her blue eyes open and staring up at the softening twilight. "Do you think we can pull the boat further onto the beach?"

Addie rolled onto her side. "We'll have to. High tide will wash it away."

Maud was impressed with this practical suggestion and said so. It earned her a small smile. They stood and plodded toward the dinghy. Without discussion they waded into the shallows and put their shoulders to the transom, pushing with each incoming wave and continuing step by step up the grinding beach until the twelve-foot craft rested beyond the high-water mark under the crest of a dune. They angled the boat away from the shore and then Maud clambered over the side and passed their belongings to Addie, who placed them beside the boat, stacking tins and folding yards of petticoat into bundles. Maud surveyed Addie's work.

"Do you think there's any dry food?"

Addie answered by stooping to open one tin after another.

"A few slices of chicken. Two date squares. Carrot and bean salad. Six slices of cheese and three slices of gingerbread. The date squares and gingerbread are soggy. We have a little lemonade, a little tea, and three quarters of a thermos of water."

Maud dropped to her knees beside Addie. "I'll have a piece of chicken, seasoned with fierce wind and a touch of kelp, please."

"We can feast now that we've landed. Let's finish the chicken and have gingerbread too." Addie joined her on the sand, still warm from the sun. They sat and chewed the rubbery chicken, trying to ignore the salt in each bite.

"Let's have tea. As Mama says, 'We've earned it.'" Addie didn't wait for Maud's answer. She poured the last of the lukewarm tea into cups, and they drank it, washing down half the gingerbread.

"That feels better! We can go home now." Addie gathered the cups and tins and packed them into the hamper. "Everything will be all right here, don't you think? I mean, we don't

have to carry it all with us. Min will send someone for it."
Addie was ready to walk home.

Maud looked at her. "We don't know where we are, Addie,
and it's getting dark."

"But it can't be far."

"Addie, what are you talking about?" Maud stood up.

"Going home. It's over these dunes. We might have to walk
a fair way, but it's straight across the dunes and around the
harbor."

"We didn't sit still out there."

"What do you mean?"

"We were shoved sideways, turned around. The tide, the
current, the wind. We're not back where we started."

"How do you know?" Addie's voice sounded strangled.

"Let's go onto the dunes and look. But we should wait until
morning to walk. We can see our way then, and we won't be so
tired. Aren't you tired, Addie?"

Addie heard the word *tired* and her body sagged. "It's getting cold too." She hugged herself and shivered. Chill night air
rolled on shore.

"We can camp on the beach," Maud promised. "Like at
Clam Harbor when we pitched a tent and built a fire. It will be
the end of our adventure."

Addie sat back down. "Yes, let's finish our adventure here.
One more night won't worry anyone." She spread the carriage
blanket on the sand and lay on half. "It's beautiful to lie here.
It really is…" she said, her voice trailing off.

Maud dropped beside her and let the sand's warmth come
into her body. After a bit, she wrapped her end of the rug
around herself and rolled toward Addie. Addie did the same.
To her surprise, Addie found the cocoon with gentle waves
lapping beyond quite comforting. They turned, with backs
touching, giving each other warmth and belonging. They used
to sleep this way when they were very small. Pushing the boat

on shore had sapped the last of their energy. Wrenched and
sore, they found refuge in sleep, curling into it as stars pricked
overhead.

With the first morning light, Maud was up. June 14 promised to be mild with high trailing clouds. She reached to shake
Addie, then thought better of it. Addie was never good in the
morning. Finding herself sprawled on this beach with sand-
thick hair would not improve her mood.

Maud slid off the rug, stretched her arms, and twisted
from side to side. Her stomach was a deflated balloon, but
she would wait and share breakfast with Addie. She walked to
the water and then faced the beach. The small crescent beach
of hard-packed sand gave way to loose shale and boulders the
size of buckets. These formed an arm that hugged the beach.
Beyond these rocks the land curved away. To her right, she
saw the steep boulders they had encountered yesterday. These
rocks resembled heavy furniture dumped and tumbled about.
Rounded or sharp with flat surfaces, they made a wall at the
other end of the beach. Maud couldn't see the land on the
other side of the rocks.

She turned to the dunes behind the dinghy and blanket
where Addie slept. Maud strode toward them but cut toward a
small gap in the dune and walked up. This path brought her to
solid land sloping gently up and away from shore and leveling
off in a windswept expanse of seaside goldenrod, beach pea,
and marram grass. Past this, the deep leathery green of bay-
berry showed amid mottled colors of rock and sand.

After being swayed and buffeted by one swell after another,
with no idea of direction or place, the sand felt solid beneath
her feet. She was still unsteady from the ocean's sway, so she
picked her way toward one of the sandy hollows and crouched
down. The smell of bracken fern filled her nostrils. "Oh," she
sighed. "I could sleep here for days." But exploring was too
exciting. She popped up and ran back to the beach.

Addie, sitting up now, looked alarmed, as if she was about to shout.

"I'm here!" Maud said and slid down the dune. "Let's eat and then go."

They ate a date square each and washed it down with water. When they were done, Maud folded the rug and walked up the dune.

"We should stay here," said Addie. Maud's words from last night had changed Addie's mind. She sat near the boat as if it might run off like an untrained dog.

"We won't go far," answered Maud. "Just on the dunes a little way and see if there's a path or road or fishing shanty." She looked up and down the small beach, then looked at Addie. "The boat will be fine. No one will touch it. Let's bring cheese and the last of the lemonade."

Addie stared at the high-tide foam hissing along the sand. "What if someone comes while we're gone and doesn't know that we need help?"

"They'll see a stranded boat and the picnic hamper and come back. We can write HELP in the sand."

"Only a short walk. If anyone takes our hamper, Cook will be furious."

Addie drew large, deep letters in the sand with the toe of her boot. It made her feel better. Maud led the way as they climbed the rise onto the dunes. The wind was stronger, blowing their hair to the east and pressing their skirts against their legs. They walked a few paces, then stopped. Scanning from east to west, they saw soft rolling dunes.

Kittiwakes, cormorants, and herring gulls flew overhead. They were small dots and vees moving and changing direction. The girls crossed the first dune, dipped into its hollow, and came up on the second.

Maud said, "Look for a path."

"What kind of path?"

"A small animal track could take us to a house or farm."

"A small animal track will take forever to find. Can't we just walk?"

"We have all day, Addie. We have lunch and a sunny sky. If you lived here, which way would your house be?"

Addie looked as if she'd just been asked why grasshoppers jump. "I wouldn't live here," she said.

"If someone did, I mean. Where would their house be?"

"How am I supposed to know that?" Addie's parasol twirled.

"What I mean," said Maud, her voice dry, "is which way do you want to walk?" Addie shrugged and turned half away. Maud stared at the side of Addie's face, stuck out her chin, and said, "Fine. We'll walk straight across."

And they did, plunging down and sliding up the soft sides of each dune until they reached rockier ground with scrub grass and wintergreen. Off the beach the smell of salt grass and juniper filled their lungs. They walked faster and the sun moved from its low spot on their right to just over their shoulders. The ground was firmer but had pock holes where underlying rocks settled unevenly against one another.

They walked in single file with Addie falling farther and farther behind. Maud arced slightly to the left. It was a slow and instinctive turn, her feet following the rising ground with the animal knowledge that higher ground meant farther away from the ocean. She was also heading more and more directly for a group of trees that blocked the view. To Maud's exploring mind the trees meant possibility, a universe of cold lemonade and hoop games. At the very least, the trees meant a shady place to eat lunch.

Addie didn't notice the change in direction. She followed the way a pull toy bumps behind a child. Addie was content to let Maud lead and was happy left to her own thoughts. She realized that her reappearance in Mahone Bay might cause a stir. Cook would make a fuss and allow the girls strawberry ices or cake. A party was even possible. Addie was sure of hot baths with mounds of bubbles. It would be easy to persuade Mama that a new dress and a carriage ride along the shore would make up for the fright and hunger.

Thoughts of the carriage ride brought Philip Tierney's blue eyes to mind She would be the half-drowned damsel, blown about and made wretched by storm and waves. But she had survived because her heart was true. That's why women in novels survived, she knew. She was a heroine! Her straggled hair no longer made her cross, nor the grimy edges of her dress. Addie slowed and imagined walking across the lawn, her parasol and hat abandoned in the home-coming carriage, her hair blowing about and Philip Tierney waiting on the porch, his worried face turned toward her. She saw fear and concern as he scanned her face for illness or suffering. He left the porch to cut the distance in half and lifted his hands to grasp hers. Addie raised her hands and let herself stumble a little. Philip opened his mouth to say, "Dearest, Addie!" but instead he said, "Watch where you're going!" Addie blinked.

"I don't want you to trip," Maud explained, shading her eyes, her mouth crooked on one side. Addie blushed and set her chin. "Let's sit under the trees," said Maud. "I'm not sure we're going the right way."

The jack pines were stunted, gnarled and misshapen from the wind, leaning to the east as if they couldn't wait for the rising sun or as if listening to news from across the ocean. They covered nearly an acre, their feathery boughs offering shade. Maud walked to the center of the grove and sank down.

As Addie did the same, Maud put out a hand. "Watch where you lean. These are pitchy trees." Addie stepped away from the tree that she had been planning to use as a backrest.

Maud opened the tin and took out a pickle. She held another up and Addie reached for it. Munching in silence, Maud divided the last pickle between them, opened the jar of water, took a drink, and passed it to Addie. Addie drank, let out a long sigh and drank again, passing the jar back. Maud looked at the jar thoughtfully, took another swallow, and capped it.

"We should save the rest for later."

They gazed about, enjoying the shade. Addie stretched and lay on her back, watching deep green needles lace a china blue sky. The pattern wavered as sunlight flickered, and before long she dozed in the soothing air. Maud heard the deep drum of ocean hitting land and birds crying high. Breezes ruffled branches, making a soft hum, but Maud did not hear what she most wanted to hear. There were no sounds of people moving or working. No dogs barked, and no horses clomped. No children laughed or yelled. She heard nothing but the pound of sea, the call of ocean birds, and the whisper of the wind playing with tree branches. Maud walked farther into the pines and out the other side. Cedar shrubs obscured the view.

Maud let Addie sleep. She had learned it was best, especially when things weren't going well. Her mind wandered over the story she would tell Rufus, Hugh, Nathaniel, and especially Tavis, when they arrived home. Would pirates be more thrilling than fog, a whale, and a storm? The wind ruffled Addie's dress, waking her.

"Come on," said Maud. "We should keep going."

They left the shade and continued up the slope of scrub heather and winterberry. The sun had moved from their right shoulders as they passed bunches of struggling juniper, and at no point did a path appear. Maud was still listening.

As if reading her mind, Addie said, "It's awfully quiet. Do you think we're far from anyone? Is there much farther to go?"

Maud halted and listened hard. Nothing.

"We may be on a spit."

They walked on, rising as the land rose through the leathery leaves and brittle branches of heath plants. As they climbed the far side of a particularly large hollow, Maud heard the ocean's familiar thud grow louder. She hesitated. A few more paces would tell her what she suspected. "Addie," she said, "I think we might be quite far from anyone."

Addie heard the dull pounding also and raced up the last bit of ridge. At the crest, the sapphire blue of the ocean glinted like silk.

"Oh!" she said at first. But then her words tumbled. "It can't be an island!"

She looked left to right, searching for the land to continue, trying to make a continent appear. "We landed!" she said. "We landed after all that time in the boat. Wouldn't we have known it was an island right away? Wouldn't you have known? It felt large and solid." Her voice dropped.

Addie dropped onto a rock and put her face in her hands. The tears came quick and hard. Maud stared at the ocean, trying not to think of when she'd first pulled on the oars and set the dinghy toward the mouth of Mahone Bay. To distract herself, she put a hand on her sister's shoulder. It was the wrong thing to do.

Addie's fear and anger released. "We're nowhere, Maud! Do you understand? We are nowhere at all, just here on this empty place without anyone. No one! What are we supposed to do?" Her voice rose and rose until it was a ribbon of wailing. "We're lost!" She shrieked and her voice choked. "The Social was stupid and awful, and I wish I'd never gotten into your horrible little boat!" The sobs came glutted and thick as Addie's face mottled red and her hair stuck to her cheeks.

The words went into Maud and made a dark ball under her heart. She was stiff, facing the limitless sea. Nothing inside her could answer Addie. She wanted to see Cook waving at them to return to the house, or Papa striding over to show them a rock or a beach flower, or even Tavis mocking her for thinking she could find pirates. Her chest was tight and the place behind her eyes burned. She turned her back on the ocean. They were on an island.

The breeze smelled less like sand and more like salt. They had walked a few miles, and looking east, she saw higher ground and rocks that continued twice the distance they had crossed. What could they do? They were stranded, surrounded by depths of water neither had the courage to face again.

"It's a good island," she said. "It's safe enough and big enough for lots of things."

"Big enough to fool us," answered Addie.

"But big enough to maybe show on a map." Addie scrunched her forehead in confusion. "If it's big enough," Maud explained, "then someone knows about it. Maybe they would think to look here."

Addie tried to absorb what Maud had said. "How far do you think we are?"

Maud surveyed the sea. The truth settled on her. There were no other islands in sight. She knew and Addie knew that the harbors and small coves along the shores of Nova Scotia were filled with thousands of islands, islands that ships and boats maneuvered past to get into the open Atlantic. Currents ran fast and hard past the islands. Past the islands meant they were in deep.

6

I Might Have Found Something

"Someone will find us. It's a good island and someone has to know about it," Maud said.

Addie put her parasol up. "Let's go back."

Going back to the boat was the safest thing to do. Because they had landed there, it seemed the likely place to be rescued. They sat on the north rocks, letting the fact of the island sink in. Addie brushed grit from her dress and half-walked, half-skidded down the slope. They retraced their steps through the grove and across the dunes.

When they arrived at the boat, Maud said, "If no one comes today, we can explore the island tomorrow. Maybe we'll find something."

"Like what?"

"I don't know. Something that will tell us when someone was here." Addie sat on the rug and picked up her book. Maud had seen her do this hundreds of times. It meant Addie wanted to disappear. It made Maud angry. "Addie!" Maud said. Addie ignored her. "You can't just sit and read." Addie didn't respond. "This isn't the Social, Addie!"

Addie closed her eyes. When she looked up, her face was tight, and her mouth was a knot. "Someone will come for us. We have to wait right here. There's nothing else we can do." She went back to her book.

Maud stomped her foot, but the sand absorbed the force of her blow. It was late afternoon and the air was cooling off the water. Maud folded her arms across her chest, staring at

Addie, but Addie wouldn't look up. Maud turned away and stacked the tins and the hamper under the overhanging dune. She placed the empty jars next to them, then climbed into the boat and dropped the oars over the side, placing them under the shelter of the dune. Addie's curiosity was caught. She watched Maud out of the corner of her eye.

Maud disappeared around the far side of the boat, huffing and grunting. The boat rocked side to side but remained where it was. It was too much for Addie. She got up and walked around the boat.

"What are you doing?" She had her hands on her hips, her finger still between the pages of her book. Maud shoved at the side of the boat, rocking it harder and harder. "Maud! What are you trying to do?"

Maud puffed her cheeks and pushed hard. The boat wobbled violently but stayed. She stepped back and let out an exasperated breath. She shoved her hair off her forehead and glared at the boat. "I want the boat on its side to keep water out and to make a shelter. Fishermen turn their boats on rainy days."

Addie's hands dropped and hung at her sides. She took her finger out of the book and placed it on the rug. "I'll help," she said.

Together, they pushed against the boat, rolling it up and, as one held it, the other crouched and pushed it further over until the boat lay on its side. "Let it down easy."

"What?"

"We're going to turn it over. Don't let go!"

The boat flopped over and smacked upside down in the sand. It shuddered as it hit. Both girls jumped back. "Sorry." Addie moved away, afraid of the damage.

"It's all right. Now prop it up with rocks. Find big flat ones."

They picked among the rocks for ones of the right size and

shape. These they pushed and rolled back to the boat, placing them under one edge at either side. Soon the boat was a lean-to, offering shade and a roof.

"There," said Addie, as if she had engineered the whole enterprise. "With the rug underneath, we'll have a snuggery."

Maud gave her a baleful glance. "Well, if it rains, we won't get as wet or as cold, anyway."

They crawled inside to test it. To her surprise, Addie found the dim lean-to comforting. "This is quite perfect," she declared, arranging herself on the blanket. "I'm sure someone will come by supper time." She opened her book.

Maud pulled off her shoes and stockings, then ambled to the edge of the water. She hiked her skirt and skipped along the hard-packed sand, her heels hitting puddles and sending up small explosions of spray. It was a day made for the beach, and this little beach was as good as any beach anywhere.

Three kittiwakes, with ringed necks and black-lined wings, more graceful and smaller than their cousins the herring gulls, rode the wind and called to each other. Maud wondered what the island looked like to them. She wondered if they were watching her and if the island looked to them like Tavis's pirate map.

If they could, the birds would have told her that she was an odd, moving figure on a crescent beach that formed part of the southern edge of the island, protected by a rock jetty that jutted from the southeast corner like an arm. It was this arm that the boat had bumped into. The western end of the little bay was more rounded and stood like a claw ready to snap shut on the beach, acting as a buffer from westerly winds. The island had an irregular and jagged outline with the highest point to the northeast. On the northwest corner, a bluff ran down to the sea in large, loose boulders that became smaller as they trailed south. The center of the island formed a bowl, with the lower rim to the south. Below that rim was the beach where Addie read and Maud ran.

As Addie read, Maud inspected the shoreline. The tide was out, her favorite time at the beach. The sun had warmed small leftover pools dotting the flat sand. Maud ignored the first few but stopped at a larger one nestled between embedded rocks. She leaned over a rock, resting her chin to gaze into the pool. She saw tangled green threads of seaweed. Looking closer she saw limpets and snails—pale hard-crusted animals that stuck to seaweed—rocks and some fish. She especially liked the chitons, whose flat, oval shells divided into eight plates. They reminded her of mountain laurel flowers. *They would remind Addie of buttons*, she thought.

The wind shimmered across the water. The submerged seaweed waved, revealing a sea anemone, its circle of feathery pink tentacles waving too. The anemone meant that something else lived in this pool. Maud waited. A small school of fairy shrimp floated from the shadows. Smaller than her little fingernail and just as clear, they drifted rather than swam, and when the sun caught them, they made almost no shadow. Maud put her face close and saw ghostly blobs to one side, almost hidden under the rock. They were crumb-of-bread sponges. She pushed her finger at the sponges that looked like pieces of yellowish broken bread, soggy and floating. A crab sidled out, darted, and froze. Darted and froze. The fairy shrimp floated up. The crab waited, and Maud saw the fish. It was a speck, and it was in danger. The crab waited. The fish fluttered, rose, fluttered, and sank. The crab darted. The fish was gone.

Maud didn't like seeing the fish disappear. She didn't want the crab to lose, but she didn't want it to be so fierce. Not against that small daydreaming fish. The fish made her think of Addie and that made her feel even worse. She pushed herself up and looked around. She dashed down the beach, feeling the stretch of her legs and the pound of her feet in the sand. The beach ended with tumbled flat rocks, leading to rounder and bigger rocks above. She climbed and balanced from rock to rock, moving upward but mostly across to see what was beyond. She found the western edge of the island as it curved to the north, becoming steeper and rockier. She crawled over and between these rocks and found strands of rockweed, with grape-like bunches of dark brown-gold bubbles. Thousands of brown-banded periwinkles dotted the higher rocks, along with chalky barnacles. Dog whelks clung, larger and lighter than periwinkles, with a similar spiral shell.

Maud climbed to the biggest rocks low to the water and submerged when the tide came in. A startled Jonah crab, with its pale orange speckled shell, snapped its claw at her. It made her think Addie might be missing her, and she decided to go back. It wasn't Addie's fault they were here.

Maud climbed back, striding past the tide pools. She noticed her shadow stretching out behind her, and her stomach growled. Addie was on the dune above the boat with her hand over her eyes, looking east. "What do you see?" Maud asked.

"Oh!" Addie jumped. "Nothing. That's the problem. Dark blue water stretches out to nothing, pale blue sky climbing to nothing, and sand blowing into everything."

"Let's eat." Maud knew Addie had been looking for a ship. "What's left in the hamper?"

"Nothing worth eating." Addie sat next to the hamper but didn't open it. "I want a breaded pork chop with mashed potatoes and a slice of lemon meringue pie. Isn't it Cook's night to make pie?"

"If you're going to be like that, I want lobster with butter and chocolate cake. I want lemonade too."

"I want a bath and clean clothes."

"I want to swing on the rope swing."

"I want to lie on the rug in the library and read."

"I want to walk with Papa and go to Isaacson's for ice cream."

"I want to shop for dresses with Mama. I want to go home."

They stopped. Silence fell as their differences, hurts, and the inescapable fact of being lost rose and sank in them. Maud opened her mouth to say something terrible and balled her fists, ready to strike.

Addie shrank, knowing that if she had not lifted Min's laudanum to her mouth, Maud would not have had to maneuver the boat alone against the current and tide. She dug into the basket. "We have carrot and bean salad and cheese. A bit of gingerbread and the last of the lemonade."

Addie divided it onto plates and they ate. "There's no more food." She speared the last carrot.

Maud picked up the water jar. There was barely enough to fill one medium glass. She poured half the lemonade into her cup and passed the jar to Addie, who did the same.

"I read that you can collect water by setting out dishes overnight," said Addie, as if they had been in the middle of a discussion. "Dew or condensation happens, and you have water in the morning." Maud turned this idea over. "You don't believe it?" Addie asked into Maud's silence.

"I don't know. I've seen Overly lick his dish in the morning before Cook puts food into it. Maybe he's licking condensation."

"Yes," said Addie, excited. "We could put the tins under big rocks and collect the water."

"Do you think it will be enough?"

"Enough for what?"

"To drink."

"Someone will come tomorrow, first thing."

Maud nodded, but the idea of licking tins for water didn't match the joy of finding whelks and mussels. She didn't say this, however. After eating, they took tins and placed them in the cool overhang of a rock and went back to the boat.

Evening shadows bunched into each other until shapes up and down the beach blurred. The ocean hissed and thudded and the evening star glowed. The girls played cards until they couldn't tell hearts from clubs, and Addie accused Maud of cheating. As the world darkened, they discovered their exhaustion again. The air grew damp, sending shivers through Addie. She clasped her arms around her chest and thought the ocean was much too large and the island much too small. Maud was nearly asleep when Addie asked, "Do you think they'll be cross?"

Maud knew she meant Mama, Papa, and Min, but especially Cook. "No, they'll be happy first." She closed her eyes and let the night surround her.

In the morning, June 15, they ate the last of the gingerbread. They didn't touch the water jar. Instead, they went to the two tins in deep shadow and found a thin skin of damp. Maud licked the entire inside of a tin and Addie did the same, with small sideways glances as if someone was watching. Their mouths got wet.

Addie's idea had failed. She was embarrassed and thirsty and knew Maud was too. It was impossible to be so thirsty. Cool, fresh water had always been ready, pumped into the kitchen from the well and stored in a thick crock with a spigot. Addie was frightened.

"We should stay still," she announced with an intensity that made Maud look at her sharply.

"What are you talking about?"

"We shouldn't move too much. It will make us more thirsty."

"We have to move." Maud had no patience for Addie's logic.

"Then wear your hat."

"It makes me hot."

"We need to stay in the shade, or the sun will dry us out!"

Addie's urgency rose and with it grew Maud's irritation. The more irritated she got, the hotter she got, and the more she wanted the spring behind the church where water bubbled over mossy stones.

"Put on your hat!" Addie repeated.

"Stop it! Just because you're fried to a red crisp doesn't mean you can boss me. A hat won't make me less thirsty." Maud scrunched her mouth in annoyance. "Someone will come."

She was furious at saying the same thing Addie had said. She didn't want to be afraid like Addie and ran to the boat. Addie followed and they packed the tins, busying themselves so they wouldn't notice they were still alone.

Addie slumped onto the sand and picked up her book. Maud walked the beach, as if pacing at a train station. Agitated and annoyed, she kicked sand, then stomped the water until it splashed and flew, wetting the bottom of her skirt. She didn't care. Waiting was like getting quizzed on grammar. No one liked it. She spun and made herself dizzy, but that made her angrier because it was something small children did. She flopped on the sand, arms and legs spread, and stared at the clouds. She thought about herself as a speck on a marble, spinning and spinning. It gave her a floaty-headed feeling, but it didn't last. She sat up, sand stuck to the back of her head, and stared at Addie.

With a giving-up sigh, she trudged up the beach. "Will you read more of the story to me?" she asked.

"I've already gone past the part we read together."

"Come on. You've read the book over and over. What's the difference if you reread a bit now?"

Addie knew Maud was desperate. "Sit down."

"It's where David is sent off to school. His mother is a right mess, crying, and Barkus is making eyes at Peggoty."

Addie laughed. "You remember a lot for someone who doesn't like stories."

"I do like stories. I just can't sit still and read long ones. Read."

Addie settled and read until Maud could sit no longer. "I think we should walk," she said.

"Walk where? For what?"

"To see what there is. To see what we can find." She didn't want to say food or water. "Walk across the island in a different direction. Maybe we'll see a ship."

Addie considered and agreed. She put the book down, picked up her parasol, and followed Maud. They walked through sharp-bladed marram grass interspersed with softer purple sand grass. As they moved inland, the ground became firmer, growing evergreen juniper with small gray-blue berries and straggling shrubs of beach plum. They passed a few bushes before Maud stooped and straightened up, a few nearly red berries in her hand. She popped one in her mouth.

Addie ate one too. Her face screwed up. "Ew! That's not very good!"

Maud laughed. "No, but they won't kill you." She held out her hand for Addie to take another.

Addie shook her head and they walked on. Instead of walking toward the trees, Maud headed northeast. They walked uphill, and the dune grasses gave way to grass-covered rocks with hollows and pockets. They had to be careful not to step in a hole. This end of the island was the highest and most jagged where it met the sea. Enormous boulders jumbled atop a steep cliff. Rocks piled upon rocks in huge tumbled masses of granite and quartz. Some boulders were as large as carriages, some as pointed as the corner of a house, some so water beaten they were polished smooth. A steep inlet at the northeast corner had sheer sides. Below, the sea crashed and boomed as it slammed forward and gave a sucking howl as it drew back. Addie grabbed Maud's elbow to keep her from creeping too close.

They found rocks with puddles the size of Overly's dish or dinner plates or even one or two the size of the kitchen sink. But all were salty and filled with tiny scudding creatures.

They headed back to camp, tramping over high rocks,

through the dunes, to the beach and the patch of sand with the boat on its side. Neither wanted to say what was obvious. But Maud's stomach rumbled, and Addie groaned. "I'm hungry, Maud."

"I know. Me too."

"It's no good thinking about what used to be in the hamper either."

"I might have found something," Maud said.

"Not bearberries. Our stomachs would be in a twist."

"Better. Come on!" Maud grabbed an empty tin and ran down the beach. She found the dark blue mussels hanging in a bristling cluster. Addie wouldn't argue about mussels! Maud pulled a few loose.

Addie ran after and found Maud tucked between rocks exposed by low tide.

"Mussels, Addie!" Maud smiled up and tugged a dark blue shell free. Their hold was strong, but before long she had two dozen loose. "How many do you think you can eat?"

"All of them," answered Addie.

They trotted back along the water's edge, where Addie stopped short. "How are we going to eat them?" she asked.

"We can smash them open and eat them the way the gulls do."

"That's revolting."

Maud broke one open with a rock and dug out the rubbery meat with a piece of shell. She slid it into her mouth, chewed and swallowed hard. "Maybe they should be swallowed like oysters without chewing." She looked at the bucket of intense blue-black shells.

"I'm not eating them raw. I'm not. Steamed is the only way." Addie had her chin up.

"You didn't even try one." Addie refused to look at Maud. "Steam them how?" Maud asked. She smashed another open and swallowed it.

Addie eyed her, her stomach rumbling. "You do the smash-ing."

Maud complied, crushing and prying the raw meat out of the shells. "Don't think. Just swallow," she told Addie.

They crouched on the beach, filling their stomachs with mussels. One dozen each. Every once in a while one of them shuddered. When the mussels were gone, Maud said, "Not so bad."

"At least I don't feel empty," Addie added.

They lay on the blanket and watched birds looping across the sky. Maud was pointing to two gulls arguing when Addie said, "I don't feel so good."

Maud had been trying to ignore the greenish feeling that had come over her, but as soon as Addie spoke, Maud got up and ran for the dunes. All the mussels poured out of her, and she heard Addie throwing up too. It was the kind of throwing up that didn't stop, even after everything was out. Their stomachs twisted, and they heaved in the sand until they were wrung dry.

Maud crawled back to the blanket and flopped face down. Addie staggered back and curled into a ball. Neither moved until hours later and the day was more than half gone.

7

Make Yourself Useful

Maud leaned up on her elbow, yawned, and stretched. She sat up, hugged her knees, and gazed at the gently swelling sea with its wisps of afternoon mist. The sun was two hand spans over the western horizon and a flock of kittiwakes swooped and dipped in pursuit of food.

Her stomach felt squeezed thin. She hugged her knees tighter and tried not to think about food. Her gaze followed the sun's sheen on the low tide sand. Soft browns streaked through purple and light pink, with thin outlines of glistening silver. The sun sank another degree over the smooth expanse of beach.

Sheeny pools looked like pieces of blue and silver glass shattered from a perfect sky. *Clams*, Maud thought. But the idea made her throat close.

Beside her, Addie rustled and groaned. "Are we alive?" she muttered.

"We have to make a fire," Maud said.

"What?"

"We can't eat raw food again. Let's look for wood."

"What will we cook if we do start a fire? I can't eat mussels ever again, not even steamed ones."

"Clams?" asked Maud.

Addie threw herself back onto the blanket. "I can't."

"Let's look for wood. You go one way, and I'll go the other."

"We'll go the same way." Addie didn't want to admit she was nervous without Maud, so she delivered this statement with authority.

Maud wasn't fooled. "Come on then."

They searched among the rocks for driftwood. The storm that had brought them to the island had also delivered debris. After an hour, each had a small armful.

"Some of this is soggy," Maud said, dropping her bundle. "Let's sort it."

The dry kindling amounted to a few sticks and three arm-long branches. "We can't start a fire until we have something to cook. Which is it, Addie? Mussels or clams?"

"Clams. But I don't know if I can eat them."

Maud glanced around for something to use as a shovel or rake. The dinghy's oar was too long, and Addie's parasol offered nothing but a point. The forks were too small. Maud made a slow semi-circle away from the boat. She found a thin stone with tapered edge, something like a curved spade. She walked to the exposed beach with the stone clasped to her chest and dropped to her knees in the sand. Small bubbling holes showed where clams lay hidden. She scooped the sand with a thrust of her stone spade, and, one by one, revealed a dozen clams. She pulled them from their beds and piled them next to her.

Bending over the pile of clams, Addie thought about breakfast at home: griddlecakes or muffins, a soft-boiled egg in her favorite eggcup, and a slice or two of bacon. Tea and berries, if they were in season. Her stomach ached. "Isn't there something else?"

Maud was used to Addie's morning grumpiness. But this was beyond tolerance. She didn't answer. Addie walked back to camp. Maud trudged to the boat and picked up the bucket and a tin. "Make yourself useful," she said.

It was one of Cook's sayings and she liked using it now. She put half the clams into the tin. Addie grudgingly got up and carried the pail to the ocean to fill it with saltwater. Maud poured half the water over the clams in the tin, then submerged the rest of the clams in the pail. She covered both pail and tin with wet seaweed.

"Those should keep for a bit," said Maud. "Now let's build a fire."

They set flattish stones into a ring. Maud squatted over the driftwood, setting wetter pieces aside. She sorted the rest, splintering smaller pieces for kindling. These she placed inside the stones. She wiped her hands on her skirt.

"It's not going to work," Addie said. She sat with her knees tucked up under her chin, her skirt spread. "We don't have any matches."

Ignoring her, Maud took two sticks and rubbed them together with an intensity that should have set the whole island ablaze. The sticks clicked and whirred as Maud found a rhythm.

"Faster!" said Addie.

Maud gritted her teeth and pressed her lips together. She hunched tighter and made the sticks twirl as her arms pumped. A thread of gray spun from between the sticks and a scorched wood smell met her nostrils. Maud's pressure increased and Addie stood up. A thicker slip of smoke curled around Maud's hands. She kept her pace, trying not to let her breathing slow her down. A flicker of flame darted out.

"Oh!" Maud exhaled. She lowered the glowing sticks to the wood and kept rubbing. The flame caught a strand of seaweed, flared up, then died out with a brief red glow. Maud blew gently on the sticks as she rubbed, and again a lash of flame sparked. "Addie, come blow on it!"

Addie knelt beside Maud, giving short puffs when she saw a spark, but each time it fizzled and went cold. "It's no use." She flung herself on her back beside Maud's kindling and lay staring at the sky.

Maud got up and paced. A few steps one way, a few the other, looking all the time at the pile of sticks. She stopped and focused on Addie. She looked up at the sun. "Give me your glasses," she said. Addie didn't move. "Addie, give me your glasses." Maud stood over her sister, one hand outstretched.

"I need them to read. You can't break them."

"I won't. Let me have them." They eyed each other. "I promise nothing will happen to them," Maud added.

With a doubtful frown, Addie pulled her reading glasses from her pouch. She couldn't read her novels without them. If Maud damaged them, Addie's world would shrink. She fiddled with them, then handed them to her sister.

Maud opened the frames so nothing blocked the lenses. "It's all right, Addie. I won't hurt them." She crouched over the piled wood, glanced at the sun, and angled the glasses so they caught a stream of light. The wood grain magnified under the glasses, small pinpricks became insect homes, and salt crystals shimmered as a beam refracted through the lens. Maud adjusted the distance between the wood and the glasses until a ring of orange-yellow light appeared. Holding still, Maud focused the light, keeping the angle. Light struck the convex glass and gathered itself, bursting through the other side in a tight orange halo. Maud steadied her hand on her knee and slowed her breath. She counted so she would know how long it would take the next time.

"Ten,   eleven…twenty-four…twenty-eight…thirty-one!" A tongue of smoke and an adder of fire licked around the twigs. Another flame and another started up. Maud put the glasses behind her and bowed over the small fire, letting out a slow breath. A crackle, and a dancing yellow-red flame spread through the pile. A real blaze warmed her face.

"That's it!" shouted Addie.

"Not yet," answered Maud. She made sure each twig caught fire before adding another.

"A fire, Maud! A real fire!" Addie grabbed her sister round the waist, and they galloped around the fire, laughing until they were out of breath. The fire gave them energy. Addie especially believed in its power to make everything right. They added two larger pieces of driftwood and the fire flared.

They steamed the clams and ate so the taste was on their hands and in the smoke. "Better?" asked Maud

"Yes," Addie answered. They both knew it had to be enough for now, so they sat and watched the flames crackle. Addie said, "We should make a signal."

"What kind of signal?"

"For being rescued!"

"Yes, I know, but how?"

"I'm not sure."

They were quiet as Maud worked on the fire. "We could spell out HELP in seashells on the beach," she suggested.

"No one would see it." Addie lay on her back.

"A bonfire would signal passing ships," announced Maud with authority. "We'd be rescued in no time."

"No ships have gone by," replied Addie. "This island isn't in the shipping lanes."

"Shipping lanes?" exclaimed Maud. "What do you mean by that? You sound as if ships move across the ocean like carriages on roads."

"That's exactly what they do," Addie responded. "They follow established routes to take advantage of winds and tides and avoid perils."

"You're reciting from a book," scoffed Maud. "If I were a ship's captain, half the fun would be going where I pleased and exploring where no one else had been."

"Yes, well, that would be very good if you owned your own ship and didn't have cargo or passengers that were expected in port," Addie replied. "I did read about them in a novel."

"Oh, it's fiction then," said Maud.

Addie remained silent. For several minutes they stared in

opposite directions. Finally, Addie said, "We only have a little wood and we need it for cooking. We shouldn't burn it in one big fire."

"We have to do something!" blurted Maud. "I can't sit and long for a handsome pirate to rescue me."

"That's not fair," retorted Addie. "I'm not saying we do nothing."

"Then what are we going to do? I say we try a big fire."

Addie saw Maud's eyes and relented. "All right, we'll make a signal."

They sat again, considering. "What about smoke signals?" Maud offered.

"Smoke signals?"

"Mr. Crandle showed me when he was burning leaves. Damp leaves smolder and let off lots of smoke. Indians send messages by covering and uncovering the fire to let off puffs of smoke. The puffs are like Morse Code. We don't have leaves, though."

"We have seaweed," said Addie. "We can dry it out a bit and it should smolder and send up lots of smoke."

The girls worked their way along the shore, gathering up strands of rubbery kelp or feather-like seaweed and hauling it beyond the high tide mark. The sun beat down, making them thirsty. Maud combed the upper rocks for lengths of half-dried seaweed. She returned trailing lengths of dull brown kelp like a bedraggled mermaid bride.

"Ugh! You smell like clam flats at low tide," Addie said as Maud neared. Maud curtseyed and dumped the seaweed next to the fire stones.

"Don't put the seaweed on too thick," Addie directed. "The fire could get smothered even if the seaweed is dry."

Maud placed more wood into a cone, forming airshafts and overlapping pieces to catch fire from one another. She surveyed her work. "We want white billowing smoke," Maud said, as if they were choosing ten-penny or smooth-headed nails at the hardware store. "If the smoke is thin or dark no one will see it."

Addie stepped back and watched as Maud laid a strand of kelp across the flames. The smell of singed seaweed darted up and burned the insides of their noses. Addie stepped away, but Maud grunted and placed another length on the fire. The edges curled and crisped, the center hissed and writhed as the heat came through. A sickly finger of gray streamed up, then another. Maud studied it, bent, and laid two strips across the first. A lighter cloud puffed from between layers. Addie clapped her hands.

Maud ran to the overturned dinghy, grabbed her discarded petticoat, and returned to swing it over the spitting fire.

"Put more on!" urged Addie.

"Not yet." Maud waved the petticoat and watched smoke fan away but not up. She put more seaweed on. "The Indians use a blanket," she said. She looked at Addie, waving the petticoat a few more times.

"Not the carriage rug," said Addie.

Maud looked at the smoldering seaweed and nodded. She waved the petticoat back and forth and managed another cloud of gray-green smoke, but it fell apart as quickly as it appeared above their heads. The day was muggy and full of damp salt. The air turned rank and acidic from the smell. Maud tried once more, laying on more seaweed and waving her petticoat until her arms felt as if they would come loose at the shoulders.

Addie trudged to the dinghy and threw herself onto the blanket.

"Someone's sure to see it, don't you think?" asked Maud, assessing her work.

"It's still daylight," answered Addie.

Maud fanned the smoke until her eyes and nose streamed and she smelled like burning clam flats. The fire hissed and the smoke rolled out low to the ground, enveloping Maud. She choked and threw the petticoat onto the sand. Coughing, she sat down. "It's no use," she sputtered. "A bit of smoke isn't going to make anyone come." She lay on her back and put her arm over her eyes.

Addie curled into a ball. It took a few minutes before Maud realized that her sister was crying. Not just crying but sobbing so that her body shook with ragged breaths. Maud didn't move. Addie stayed within herself, dark thoughts coming down on her and closing in. She had no ideas, no way out, no way off the island. This wasn't a game and it wasn't an adventure, not even for Maud, no matter how much she pretended it was. Addie felt helpless and stupid. Her ideas never amounted to anything. She wanted to call out for Mama. She just wanted to call out. She wanted someone to hear her. She wanted someone to answer. She pulled herself tighter to muffle the aching sobs that rattled her. A black terror nearly stopped her breath. As she struggled to let in air, a high shriek erupted, then hiccupping, gulping sobs. Maud knelt over her and hugged her. Addie turned.

"We're lost!" she shrieked again and again. "We're lost."

Maud kept her arms around Addie. There was nothing to say. When Addie had quieted, Maud went back to the fire, poking it to keep it going. The smoke stayed low and parallel to the water, then lifted toward the dunes. Maud hunched down and put her chin on her knees.

Addie stared at nothing for a long while, then opened her book and began to read. She fell asleep, dreaming of nothing. When she woke it was nearly dusk and Maud was off exploring. Addie climbed to the dunes. Bunches of bearberry appeared as the sand changed to rock outcroppings where silt collected and persistent beach pea tendrils, low-growing spurge, and pitch pines took hold. Orange-red berries, hard and wax coated, clustered under thick bearberry leaves. Addie inspected them and broke one from its stem, rolling it between her fingers. Hungry as she was, she didn't want to put in her mouth. She split the berry with her fingernail, squinted at the white flesh inside, sniffed at it, then gave the cut surface a little lick. A tang sprang into her mouth. She frowned at the split berry on the ends of her finger.

For the first time Addie took note of the plants around her. There were bushes of glossy bearberry green, beach grass of pale gray-green, trees of deep-forest pitch-pine green, and heather in shades of blue and green. Then, she spotted the tell-tale blue-green of small leaves and compact branches. "Blueberries!" she shouted. Seagulls cried back at her.

She stooped for a closer look. Tough seaside plants scraped against her shins and let off a spiced scent as she moved through them. These were not the lush shrubs of Cook's garden—those produced blueberries the size of her thumb that floated in plump circles in her oatmeal.

Addie turned over the branches. These wild plants withstood constant wind and battering salt spray. Beneath the leathery leaves, small white bell-shaped blossoms winked at her. It would be weeks before blossoms turned to berries. Addie sat back. A sob started to rise, but she stopped herself, stood, and turned toward the beach.

Maud was coming up the beach with a handful of driftwood. She dropped the wood and met her sister near the boat.

"I thought I found wild blueberries for us to eat," said Addie. She led Maud to the low bushes and pointed. Maud saw the tiny buds. "They'll be here for the birds, anyway. There's no good wishing about them."

The tide was out, just as it had gone out twice a day, leaving the beach exposed and glistening with small pools swaying as if remembering the pull of the ocean. Maud climbed absently over exposed rocks at the far end of the beach. Addie watched her with irritation and hope.

Maud wasn't bothered that they had to eat whatever they could find. She believed the island would offer something. Addie was annoyed at Maud's refusal to be worried and at the fact that they would have to keep eating clams and mussels. Her hope came from Maud being clever, so Addie sat like Patience and watched Maud clamber over rocks, pausing to stare in a tidal pool before disappearing behind a boulder.

Addie didn't know that Maud was worried too. Maud didn't know whether they would eat or what they would eat. She was mostly worried about Addie's fear. She didn't want Addie to be afraid. She didn't like to see her sister sad. She also didn't want to think that maybe Addie knew better than she did, that there was no hope. Maud stopped at a tide pool and lay with her face nearly touching the surface, letting her eyes adjust to the nearly microscopic view. Miniature pieces of seaweed, small as filaments, swayed against the stones over pink, amber, clear, and slate-blue grains of sand. Out of the corner of her eye, Maud caught the darting, sideways motion of several small shrimp. They were no thicker than her bootlace and only as long as the first section of her little finger. They made her think of grubs. Grubs, Maud knew from fishing, were bait for catching mackerel.

When she went back to the boat, Addie was near the fire. Maud put two more twigs into the flames. "Just tonight we can have a fire for company," she said.

They fed the fire and stayed close to it into the night. It was the friendliest thing they had found, and they didn't want to let it go out. The fire warned off mosquitoes that came at dusk and took away the night chill and the feeling of being so very small at the edge of an enormous sea.

"A line and hook," Maud said aloud the next morning, June 16. She looked to the waves breaking off the island's point. Maud continued climbing over the rocks away from Addie. She needed something right away, something that wouldn't take patience, skill, and time. She would figure out the hook and line. Fishing would come later; that, and building a better fire pit for cooking. She wondered if she could teach Addie to fish and giggled at the image of her sister unhooking a wriggling mackerel. She would need the right fishing spot, and she turned her mind to that as she explored.

In a gap between two rocks, Maud found a bird carcass with flies buzzing around it. Most of the flesh was gone, but the feathers and bones kept the flies interested. Maud poked it to see what kind of bird it was. Probably a gull, judging by the size and color of the feathers. She pulled at the bones, turning them to see how they had been put together. A few small bones detached from the frame and a few feathers fell away. She knelt over the carcass. She separated the bones and laid them in organized piles. She sorted the feathers, discarding the fractured and crushed ones, saving those with hollow shafts and sharp ends. She shooed the flies and lifted a handful of bones. Carrying them to the nearest tide pool, she soaked and rinsed them, repeating this until each bone and feather was clean.

Maud gathered the edges of her skirt to form a pouch for the white bits and walked back to camp. "Look, Addie!" Addie peered into the hollow of Maud's gathered skirt and frowned. "Eggs." Maud gave her skirt a little shake.

"Eggs?"

"Don't you see?"

"I see bones, Maud. A pile of small bones."

"Bird bones." Maud shook her skirt. She waited, but Addie only stared, puzzled. Maud gave up. "If there are birds, then there are eggs."

Addie stepped back and relaxed the frown lines from her forehead. These, however, were replaced by a pucker around her mouth. "Eat them how?" she asked.

"Any way you like! Come on, we'll search. Gulls must nest on the island, maybe kittiwakes or terns, too."

Maud placed the bones on the sand near the boat. "Put on your hat and bring your parasol. I'll get the water jar. Would you like them poached or scrambled? We could make clam omelets!" Maud continued talking as she strode up the dune. Addie heard Maud's voice but not the words as her body disappeared in the grass.

Addie shrugged and followed. As she did, she had to face the fact that eating meant work. She ran to catch up. Her fear of being alone was greater than her dislike of clambering over rocks in the hope of finding an egg. She caught up to Maud as she tramped along. "Do you know where you're going?" Maud nodded and began to whistle. "How do you know?"

Maud stopped and faced her sister. "I've been up here while you've been reading. I think I know where the birds nest." Maud resumed her march.

For a while Addie's mind stayed on the puzzle of eggs, rocks, and the tins swinging from Maud's hands, but a grasshopper jumped and landed on her skirt, clinging with sticky barbed legs to the fabric. The blue of her skirt set off the grasshopper's pea-green body and its eyes and folded wings glittered like malachite. The grasshopper looked as if it belonged in Mama's jewelry box with the onyx brooch and mother-of-pearl pinpoints. She had tried on Mama's jewelry many times and knew which earrings flattered her eyes and how a pendant made her neck look slender. Under a chandelier, jeweled earlobes flashed. A waltz at three-quarter time forced her knees to dip and her skirt to swirl. A turn of the head, sliding just a breath backwards, a touch of smile as she glanced—

"Addie! Watch where you're going!"

Maud put out an arm to keep her sister from stepping off the edge of a large rock. "I told you there would be birds."

They skirted the rock edge and looked across the shelf of land near the cliffs. The steady wind was a relief from the muggy beach. Sand coated their forearms, foreheads, and necks. Maud inched toward the edge and looked down. Just as she had hoped, birds clustered and roosted on small shelves in the layered and tumbled stones. "Puffins!" she exclaimed.

"What?" Addie came forward slowly.

"Puffins!" Maud repeated.

Nests wedged into rock crevices, and behind the cliff many more puffins had dug burrows into the sandy ground. They were like little clowns with orange webbed feet and triangular, tri-colored beaks. Yellow outlined the beak where it touched the face, then a thick dark spot, almost slate gray, followed by another yellow line. The outer beak edge was bright orange, matching the feet. The puffins' faces were white, as were their chests. Their backs and tail feathers were black, giving them a formal air. Maud loved their eyes most. Bright black pupils, rimmed with orange, then a black line half an inch straight up from the top of their eye and another line from the back edge of their eye to the black feathers on the back of their heads. The longer line made a little crease, making it look as though the puffins had cheeks. The puffins were comical with a hint of something sad. They were the most wonderful birds Maud had ever seen.

Those guarding nests gave chuffing barks to ward off herring gulls screeching overhead. Maud watched one female, smaller than her ten-inch mate, dig the burrow entrance partially collapsed from last night's rain. The puffin used her thick beak to shovel and her webbed feet to kick sand. After about ten minutes, the burrow opening looked perfect to Maud, but the puffin was not satisfied. She kept on until the mouth of the burrow sloped down and away on both sides of the opening.

Maud had said eggs, and here were the birds—birds in burrows, birds on cliffs, birds everywhere. Addie looked at Maud to see if she was serious.

8

You're Full of Nonsense

"It's not going to be easy," Maud said. "They're not seagulls—their nests are in little hollows in the rocks. Sort of underground."

Maud had Addie's attention now. "Underground?"

"They burrow and make little hollows. And they only lay one egg. We won't get as many as I'd hoped."

Addie knew some of this, but not nearly as much as Maud. On walks with Papa, while Maud listened and asked questions, Addie thought about the size of her shadow. Often, when Maud and Papa went off together, Addie stayed home to read or listen to Cook's gossip.

Maud moved again to the edge of the rock and peered over. "There's a great colony of them here. Maybe the puffins aren't a good idea." She screwed her mouth to one side and twisted her fingers. Kittiwakes and terns spiraled overhead, the kittiwakes landing on the cliff edges. Nests spilled from crevices all along the cliff face. A tern wheeled and dove, landing several yards from them in a tumbled stretch of grass-covered rocks and then disappeared. Maud remembered the fierce shriek of the tern that had landed on the boat. This was a much larger bird with a wingspan of nearly thirty inches.

"Perhaps we should try the isolated ones on the cliff."

Addie flicked her eyes from where the bird had landed next to Maud. "How are you going to carry the eggs?" she asked.

That stopped Maud. She put her hands in her pockets as a way to test their suitability, looked at Addie, opened her mouth to say something, then closed it, eyeing Addie's hat.

"No, Maud. You're not putting eggs in my hat."

"Nothing will happen to it. I promise. We haven't anything else. We'll have eggs any way you like by teatime."

Maud didn't wait. She started down the steep rock face. After a moment, she climbed back, removed her shoes and stockings, and put out her hand for the hat. Addie undid the bow and handed her hat to Maud.

Maud tied it over her arm and worked her way down toward the sea. Several gray and black kittiwakes nested on a grassed-over shelf. Maud inched toward them as they watched her suspiciously. One stood, adjusting its feathers; another gave a warning whine. Maud paused and waited for them to settle down. Not sure of Maud's intent, they quieted, but kept their beady eyes on her. She whistled low, and the birds turned to the sound, distracted. Maud pulled herself closer and put her hand toward them. The closest one called shrilly, but Maud left her arm outstretched, balanced, and found footholds as she went forward. She was close enough to see where the curved beak met feathers and the watching in their eyes.

She thrust her hand under the closest bird and felt the warm round of an egg. She pulled it free. The bird flapped, its yellow beak trying to find her fingers. She dropped the egg into the hat and reached under the next bird. She found another egg, but both birds screamed and flapped. One flew at her face. Maud screamed, dropped the egg and nearly lost the hat. She knew Addie was yelling but couldn't make out words. Turning her face to the rocks, she reached again and closed her hand around another warm egg. She held and gave a shrill whistle. The startled birds sheered off, giving Maud time to put the egg into the hat and scramble up the rocks.

"I've got two!" Maud panted as she came over the edge.

Addie was frozen, not believing what she had seen Maud do. "Don't ever! Not ever again," she scolded Maud.

"But it worked!" Maud held out the eggs.

Addie couldn't speak. She walked away, trying to shake off the vision of Maud tumbling off the cliff into the thrashing sea below. Maud called after her, but she kept on, caught between anger and fear. Would everything be like this? Would every day be full of risk and failure? Balancing from one rock to another, Addie found herself amid the largest rocks on the island. Massive stones were wedged and shouldered into one another. She climbed from one to the other until she came to a level surface atop a house-sized rock. On it sat another giant stone. Addie halted.

"Maud!" she cried. "Maud, come quickly!"

Maud followed her sister's voice and found Addie leaning over an enormous stone bowl.

"It's from the glaciers," said Addie.

She was right. A remnant of the last glacier, this gigantic stone had been tumbled and ground against another enormous stone like a socket and ball until the basin was worn into a fourteen-foot oval, six feet deep. Set just below the highest point of the island, the stone was perfectly positioned to allow the girls to kneel at its upper rim and bend over it. The huge dish caught rain high above the salt spray pounding the cliffs. And the smooth sides prevented lichen or moss from taking hold. The sun struck the water, lighting it with a refracted glow.

"It's a fountain in a fairy tale," Addie said.

"It's a magic pool from *The Arabian Nights*." Maud wet her finger and put it in her mouth. "Not salty," she said.

"Is it safe to drink?"

Maud put her face to the water and drank. "It tastes like rock," said Maud.

Addie drank too. "I've been so thirsty."

"Me too, but I haven't wanted to say."

With face still wet, Addie sank back on her heels and said, "It's a huge bathtub."

Maud's turned quickly. "We can't get in. Not ever. This is for drinking." Addie started to argue, then saw how serious Maud was. "We can take water out, but this pool is magic. We can't spoil it." Addie didn't know why, but Maud's insistence frightened her. At the same time she was glad that her sister had taken charge.

They traversed the island and brought back the jar and thermoses, along with two tins. The tins were to wash their faces. "I wish we had soap," said Addie. "Can we wash our hair?"

"It's not a good idea." Washing her hair hadn't occurred to Maud.

"I can't stand it. Just once?"

"What difference does it make? No one can see you."

"I don't want to be found like this! I'm sticky and awful, and there's gallons here."

"It might not rain again for a long time," said Maud.

Addie stared at the surface, then refocused her eyes. The sun shone along the rim of stone. Only faintly could she see to the bottom. The words "long time" could have been pebbles that Maud had dropped into the water.

"All right," Maud said. "One face washing in the morning."

Back at the boat, they put the water under the rocks to keep it cool, coaxed a small fire from the coals, and put the eggs on the hot stones nearby. Addie counted from one to three hundred.

"I guess that's long enough," she said.

They cracked their eggs and ate them.

"Smoked eggs!" crowed Maud.

"Well done, Maud. Although I feel bad for the birds."

"Don't think about it. Read some more of the book."

The wind backed around to the west and stalled just as the sun marked the middle of the afternoon. The marram grass went still and grasshoppers sang louder in the muggy heat.

"It's too hot to move." Addie lay on her back, trying to get the most shade from the boat.

"Come swim with me." Maud jumped up and pulled her middy blouse over her head, then stepped out of her skirt. Neither she nor Addie had worn stockings or shoes for days.

"Maud! You can't undress right here on the beach!"

"There's no one here, Addie. Aren't you boiling? I feel like a cooked lobster." She kicked her clothes to the side and walked toward the ocean.

Addie looked at Maud's bare arms, neck, and legs, with only her chemise and bloomers as cover. Light white cotton. She watched Maud swing her arms and break into a skip. Lace itched Addie's neck. A snake of sweat slid along her back. Her skirts weighed on her legs. Maud danced along the water's edge.

Addie closed her eyes, lay still for a second, then sprang up. She opened rows of buttons, undid ties and hooks, peeled off petticoats. She gave everything a shake, folded it carefully, and faced the dune as if to keep the ocean from seeing. Maud's shouts came up the beach and Addie stood stiff. She touched the boat as if letting go of something and then raced after Maud, feeling the breeze flutter the legs of her bloomers and reach inside her chemise.

"It's perfect!" yelled Maud, surfacing from a shallow dive several yards offshore. Addie walked in up to her ankles. She gasped as water clasped her legs. "Run in! Don't wait!" Maud dove and came up with her hair plastered and streaming. Addie took another few steps and water sloshed over her bloomers. "You're wet now!" Maud lunged at her.

Addie screamed as the splash sprayed her chest and face. Her body tensed for anger, but she ran forward, straight on until she was waist deep and then dove, arms out, kicking hard. She turned on her back and floated, letting her limbs drift and the water lap into her ears and around her face. Her chemise swayed around her.

Maud's face, freckled and wet, appeared beside her. "Don't you love it?" She was grinning, the dimple on her cheek deep, and her eyes picking up the green from the sea.

Addie laughed back at her, and they set off in a race that both knew Addie would win. Her arms and legs were made for swimming, but neither cared who won. It was enough to be in the ocean and safe. To be swimming. It was heaven to be free of skirts and blouses.

As the tide came in, rolling waves broke just offshore. They rode them in, crashing with the water onto the pebbled sand, then turning right around and swimming back for the next one. Over and over, they laughed as a wave broke too soon and submerged them, or hooted as they stayed afloat, carried like driftwood and nearly thrown onto the beach.

Finally they had had enough and dragged themselves, puckered and weak, from the sea. They threw themselves onto the sand and panted, still laughing, and let the late sun dry them through.

"We should put up a flag," suggested Addie.

Maud was sorting through her pockets. "What for?"

"A signal for passing ships."

"What would we use and where would we put it?"

"We could use your petticoat. You're not using it and we could tie it to one of the trees on the bluff."

Maud paused her sorting. "I'll think about it."

"You don't care about your petticoat, do you?"

"No. But it won't do any good."

She didn't want to say the real reason she didn't want to follow Addie's idea. If she was going to fly a flag, it wasn't going to be her petticoat. She wanted a Jolly Roger or a made-up country flag. A petticoat was awful to wear but hanging it out for rescue would be the worst kind of embarrassment.

To distract Addie, Maud said, "If I had a line, I could catch fish."

"Use your string." Addie liked the idea of eating fish.

"It's too thick. The fish will see it. I have a hook." Maud held up a bit of bird bone. I can use raw clam for bait."

Addie looked at her, shading her eyes. "I don't have any good ideas." She shrugged.

"We have thread."

Addie was puzzled. Maud pointed to the hamper. "Aren't your gloves in there? You could unravel them."

Addie stood between Maud and the hamper. "You're not using my gloves!"

"We don't have anything else. The thread would be perfect. It's thin."

"It's silk!" They glared at each other, neither moving. "It's not fair!" Addie dropped her shoulders.

"It's the only thing," Maud said finally. "Mama will buy you a new pair."

"All right, but I'm doing the unraveling."

Addie sat in the shade of the boat, unraveling a lace glove, pulling at the crocheted loops and winding the thread round her fingers. She tied the ribbons that had braced the cuffs into her hair. *The fish won't get these*, she thought. As she pulled and rolled, she remembered the day she had gotten them. Mama had taken her to Spring Garden Road. They had looked at ready-made dresses and low-cut shoes at The New York Dress Company. Mama had taken her to tea at Highbury's, and they had shopped for hats. Addie saw her mother standing in the shop smiling at her in the mirror. Mama's hair was a rich gold and she had a few freckles across her nose. But Addie saw Mama's eyes, green-gold and laughing.

"Too much?" she had asked.

Addie was thrilled to be consulted. The hat, made of tightly woven white straw with a wide brim, was adorned with an emerald ribbon circling the crown and ended in a voluptuous bow.

"Oh no!" Addie breathed. "It's perfect!"

Satisfied, Mama told the clerk to wrap it up and then asked to see the gloves. As the drawer opened, Addie saw pale blue froth, with seed-pearl buttons and deeper blue ribbons in tight florets at each wrist. Mama saw her gaze and pointed for the clerk to take them out of the drawer.

"Try them on, Addie."

Once on, she could never put them back. She held her hands before her and turned them over. Mama watched, her head slightly tilted. "We'll take those too," she said, and Addie had squealed.

"They're for something special, Mama. They're the best gloves ever!"

Maud's shadow fell before her on the open sand. "Is the string ready?"

"It's silk thread, Maud. Silk."

"Is the silk ready?"

Addie held up the ball and felt the thread's cool slipperiness. She pinched her lips and handed it up to her sister.

Maud trotted toward the big flat rock that was perfect for fishing. When she was on top, she sorted the bird bones in her pocket and selected one the length of her little finger. One end had a knob so she snapped it off, leaving a jagged point. She unwound several feet of thread and tied a piece of clam near the end. The very end, she wound around the bird bone until it was knotted just below the clam. Putting the rest of the ball into her pocket and holding the bone and clam dangling before her, she crouched over the deep, cool waters where codfish hid from the sun.

Lying full length, stretched with arms and head over the edge, she waited for her eyes to adjust to the shadows in the

water after the glint of the sun. She wiggled farther out over
the water and lay still, watching.

Yes. A large-mouth fish nosed into the rock crevices for sea
shrimp and minnows. With slow, smooth movements, Maud
lowered her thread into the water and took the ball from her
pocket. This, she gripped in one hand while she suspended
the length of thread over the surface. With a gliding motion,
she dragged the line through the water, ever so slowly just
within the cod's sight. She reversed direction and made a slow
curve in the water. Two brownish gray bodies turned to it and
followed the clam.

Maud brought the line to a standstill, blinked to clear her
eyes, then jigged the line up and down slightly. One cod darted
forward at the line. Maud scrambled to her feet and pulled her
arm up. The end of the line stayed just below the surface and
she could feel the weight of the fish. She dropped the ball of
thread between two rocks and took hold of the line with both
hands. Hand over hand she pulled the line up, stepping on the
slack line as she pulled it in, the cod just below the surface. She
felt its weight and energy. Snap! The line went limp and the
fish darted away. Her line was empty and bitten. Maud tried
again, but nothing came close.

The sea was flat and sluggish, and the temperature rose.
Sweat covered her forehead and neck and her hair was soaked.
They had been five days on the island with no sign of help.
Maud made a small scratch with a sharp rock on the handle
of her knife. There were eight scratches for every day they had
been gone.

Addie was on the sand between the rocks, peering into shallows. She tried walking fast, striding away her anger at Maud
until she knew it wasn't really Maud she was mad at. She was
mad because things were not looking good. Not so good at all.
She slowed and wandered among the rocks. The silver-blue of
a fish flashed from between the rocks like a signal mirror. She

hunched over and poked at a dead wizened herring. *I feel the same*, she thought. And she felt awful. She wanted to preserve the fish, its arrested action. She committed the fish to memory, then strode back to camp and picked up her book.

Maud walked back to camp, thinking about bait, fishing rods, contests, racing, and marbles. The marbles in her pocket were sure shots, never failing her aim. She took them out and rolled them in her hand. One was a robin's-egg blue that hinted at green; the second was mottled orange and white like a planet only she had discovered.

Her favorite marble didn't look like much, kind of like a mongrel dog. It was mossy green with blotches of white and specks of brown where dirt had stained it. At one end clear glass showed through and sparkled when she rolled it. Three marbles weren't much, but they were enough.

"Come on, Addie, play!" This was the third time Maud had asked. Addie kept reading. Maud kicked a small spray of sand, but it fell short of her sister. She tried to will Addie to put the book down. Her frustration snapped. She stamped her foot twice and grunted. "Book nose!"

Maud stamped her foot and liked the dense feel of the sand beneath her foot. The thick sand gave a little, then packed down. It grabbed her anger and held it. Maud stamped and stamped some more. She lifted her knees and pounded the sand with her feet, bending forward and down, compressing her body to give her stamping more thrust. She stamped everywhere, in every direction, but soon she stamped in a rhythm and made a hard, flat circle six feet across. She looked it over and began again, pounding harder on one side than the other.

"What are you doing?"

"Don't step on it!" Maud waved Addie back. She pounded a spot with her left foot.

Addie's finger marked the page of the closed book. "What are you doing?" she repeated.

"We need a proper, level pitch. Otherwise it wouldn't be fair. I'd win every time."

"You're full of nonsense."

"Try me."

Addie knelt and rolled a marble. Slitting her eyes, she put her nose very close to the edge of the pitch and flicked her fingers so the marble followed the line she wanted. She didn't win, but she gave Maud a good go.

"Where did you learn to do that?" Maud asked, gathering her marbles.

"From watching you."

"You can't learn from watching. You have to practice." Maud couldn't believe her sister was simply good at marbles. That went beyond all rules of how the world should work.

"I don't know. I pretended I was you, and the marbles did what I wanted."

That satisfied Maud. They leaned back on their arms and let the sun warm their faces. Addie drew pictures in the sand. She drew a flight of wings, a horse dashing left, and the outline of the island, as she understood it. Between each sketch she smoothed the sand with her hand. After the last image, she picked up a handful and looked at it closely.

"How many colors do you see in the sand?" She sat cross-legged with her head bowed so she could inspect the particles.

Maud was half reclined on one elbow, facing away from Addie, her legs crossed at the ankles.

"The sand is brown, Addie. Dark brown, light brown, pale brown, dense brown. It's brown."

"That's four colors right there," answered Addie. "But don't you see green and flecks of pink?"

"Pink?" Maud came up off her elbow and turned toward Addie. "Sand isn't ever pink."

"Look carefully. You'll see orange and pieces that are clear like grains of salt. And definitely green, there's lots of green.

On some beaches the sand is almost pure white, and I've heard that in the Pacific some of the islands have sand as black as crow's feathers."

Reluctantly, Maud took a handful of sand and spread it like a paste on her palm. She tilted it toward the sun and squinted. Little flecks of silver and black jet sparkled as she rolled her hand slightly back and forth. A small gleam of gold caught the light and she brought her hand closer.

"All the grains have different shapes," she said aloud without considering that Addie's curiosity had caught her. "They're like snowflakes, I suppose."

"Just think, Maud, this very sand we're sitting on runs along the ocean's bottom and all the way to Crescent Beach. If there weren't all that water, we could walk home."

Maud looked at Addie and laughed. She looked down the beach and out across all that water. "That makes it sound like we're not so very far from home."

Addie didn't answer, and the two girls watched little hissing waves advance, leaving less and less beach between them and the sea.

All at once Maud jumped up with a sly smile. "We can't walk back but we can practice swimming!" Maud removed her skirt and unbuttoned her blouse. Addie laughed at this repeat of their earlier swim. But at the water's edge, Maud looked back at Addie and stepped out of her bloomers, pulled off her chemise and ran naked into the waves, making a great splash.

"Maud! Maud!" yelled Addie. "You can't do that!"

Addie was on her feet, rigid as she watched her sister paddle and roll in the slow breakers.

"It's wonderful! Try it!" Maud called. "It's glorious!" she called again and made circles doing a vigorous crawl, then a leisurely sidestroke.

Stiffly, Addie moved closer to the water, without taking her eyes from Maud. "Aren't you afraid of sharks?" she called.

"Sharks don't care if you have clothes on. Aren't you hot, Addie? Wouldn't you love the freedom?"

Maud did slow spins in the water and kicked the surface. Addie pulled off her chemise and dropped her pantaloons, startled at her nakedness in the bright of day. She glanced at Maud who was watching with a wry grin. Addie, laughing at their boldness, ran headlong into the waves. When she surfaced, she was grinning too.

"Oh, it's lovely! I feel like I'm made of air!"

"Swim with big, long strokes. It feels good to move after being so sticky."

Addie paddled in short spurts, stopping every few minutes to turn on her back and float with eyes closed. "It's wonderful, Maud," she murmured. "Who will ever believe us? Someday, when we're grown and proper ladies, we will remember swimming naked in the ocean like all the world's fishes."

"This won't be the last time, Addie. I plan to do this often."

They swam and raced and floated for much of that hot, sticky afternoon. As the sun began to drop, they clambered back to the beach. Maud shook her hair out of her face and lay on the warm sand to dry. Addie stretched out a little ways away to lie in the sun also.

When they were both dry, they pulled their chemises and bloomers back on. Addie headed to camp to get her dress. Maud followed, but didn't reach for her blouse or skirt.

"I'm not putting them back on," she declared.

Addie stopped mid-motion, her arms inside her dress. She looked at Maud with her mouth open. "No one's here. It's too hot for these clothes."

"But...we're supposed to wear clothes."

"I'm wearing all the clothes I need." Maud pointed to herself. "Why drag around all those skirts?"

Addie could think of no good reason why they should get dressed. Her dress, still draped across her arms, confused her.

She let it drop, and it was like letting go of worry. She picked it up, folded it, and put it under the boat. Then she ran back down the beach, jumping as high as she could and kicking with each jump. To Maud, she looked like a circus act they had once seen.

Late that night, Addie rolled to face Maud. "I've been thinking. Do you realize Mama and Papa don't know what's happened to us?"

Maud leaned up on her elbows, her eyes bright in the dark. "I was thinking the same thing. I bet Cook is frantic."

"What about Min? Do you think she's doing anything to find us?"

They were quiet for a while, each picturing the summer house with Cook in the kitchen and Min on the chaise longue.

"I think they called the police," Maud finally said.

"The police? We didn't commit a crime. What could the police do?"

"Organize a search. That must be in one of your books."

"Do you think Min's helping?" Addie's voice had a catch to it, then she answered herself. "How can you tell what anyone will do? We don't really know her."

"I think she might," Maud said. "I think it's exactly because we don't know her that we can't guess badly of her. There are probably all sorts of unexpected things about her."

"Maybe," said Addie. "But maybe we're just wishing someone is taking charge of finding us."

"Of course we are. And hoping it isn't Mrs. Beal!" Maud hooted, and Addie pushed her off her elbows.

They rolled around giggling until they fell asleep.

9

Here's a Spot of Trouble Coming

"Addie! Addie, wake up!" Maud shook Addie so hard the morning of June 17, she was instantly awake.

"Stop it! What are you doing?" Addie looked like a bird blown off course.

"There's a ship! Look! A ship!" Maud shouted and pointed. She half turned and shook her arm at the sea. She hopped up and down. "A ship!"

Addie scrambled up and looked where Maud's finger pointed, her face intent. She hopped up and down too. "Oh! Oh! Hello! Helllloooooooo!"

"They can't hear us." Maud ran and climbed the nearest boulder.

"What'll we do? Helllooooo! Make a fire! Quick, Maud, make a fire!"

Maud raced around and pushed the leftover driftwood into last night's fire. "Give me your glasses."

Addie put them into Maud's outstretched hand. "Hurry!"

"I need dry kindling. This is soggy and the bigger pieces are charred." She angled the glasses, trying to catch the thin morning light.

"Hurry!"

"I'm trying. Get me some small pieces."

Addie scurried around rocks and sprinted onto the dunes. She came back with a handful of twigs and grass. She dumped them on the smoldering sticks Maud had managed to coax toward a fire. The grasses caught, singed and smoked, smothering the little flame.

"No!" yelled Maud. "Dry twigs, Addie, not grass!"

"There aren't any." Addie danced next to Maud, twisting her fingers and looking out to sea.

Maud crouched, feeding bits of sticks to the warm coals. She moved Addie's glasses up and down, back and forth.

"It's taking too long," Addie said and blew out a choppy breath. "Come on, Maud!"

"It's not working. Not yet."

Addie threw a look out to sea and ran onto the dunes. Her hair flew as her feet pounded across the island, across the grassy hummocks and around the humped boulders, until she came panting to the high rock at the eastern tip.

"HAAALLLOOOO!" she screamed, waving her arms over her head and jumping up and down. "HAAAAALLLLL-LOOOOOO!" She caught her breath and watched the white ship, a scant spot on ever-and-ever blue. Opening her parasol, she swung it high over her head. "HEEEELLLLLP! HEEEELLLLP! HEEEELLLLP!" She screamed the word over and over until her throat was raw.

Maud bent over the listless strands of smoke and then ran onto the rocks, shouting," Help!" too. She waved and waved, then trotted back to the fire, blowing a little, feeding bits of sticks, blowing a little more and nearly dropping Addie's glasses into the ashes. She blew again until she was lightheaded, dashed back to the rock, and jumped up and down. Defeated, she faced the sea.

The ship shrank and was lost in the waves. No ship outline anywhere. Gone as though it had never existed. It was as though Maud had made it up. Now the day was misshapen.

Addie came back and dropped to the rug. Maud couldn't look at her, couldn't look anywhere. She went back to the fire and let the acrid smoke drift into her hair, stinging her eyes, making them water. She spat hard at the fire. It was the vilest thing she knew how to do. She kicked sand at it, bent, and threw fistfuls of sand again and again, kicking and spitting.

"Stupid! Stupid!" she yelled. She flung stones and shells at the fire, flung them everywhere. Slammed one of the larger stones around the fire onto another. Smashed it down with all her strength, brought it up, and smashed it again. Again and again, something coming from her lungs like a growl.

"Stupid! I hate...! I won't...! I can't...! I can't...!" She brought the stone down again and it split into pieces. She panted, "I can't..."

Addie grabbed her arms, saying something, wiping the tears from her face. She didn't know how her own face had gotten wet.

"I can't, Addie. I can't," Maud croaked.

Addie took Maud by the shoulders and pressed down, as if her sister were going to fly away or fly apart if Addie didn't hold her still. Maud crumpled onto the sand, hanging her head. Addie sat beside her and held her hand. The fire steamed and sank.

The day crept over the island like damp wool. The ship had taken all the fine dry air with it and left a film and heat that pulled at the girls. They didn't talk for a long time. They didn't want to name what had happened. Stillness came over everything. The whole island felt different. Nothing moved that torpid, airless day. Not the eel grass on the dunes, not the kittiwakes that usually cartwheeled across the sky, not the scuttle crabs in the flattened tide pools. Even the sea seemed too heavy to do more than slump against the beach. The sun was smudged smoky yellow by the humidity. Under it, Addie and Maud sprawled, their chemises clung like wet tissue paper and their hair frizzed.

"This heat is murderous," groaned Addie.

Neither moved the merest fraction, and they stared in different directions as if a lack of focus might lessen the temperature.

"I feel as stupid as a clod of dirt," Addie continued.

Maud turned her head and stared at her sister.

"What?" asked Addie. "I do."

Maud started to say something, then changed her mind. Instead she said, "This kind of weather brings lightning."

They drifted into their own thoughts—Addie tasting electricity in the air, and Maud considering which rock to hide under. "It would be heat lightning," Maud said thoughtfully. "Nothing to worry about."

"I miss Overly." As soon as Addie said it, she wished she hadn't. It was a superstition between them. If they didn't say the words *miss* or *scared* or *wish* then they'd be all right. They could stay with finding clams or swimming in the shallows.

Maud neither turned her head nor answered, which made it worse. Addie could feel Overly soft-stepping onto her lap, the rumbling engine of his purr increasing as he pushed his forehead into her chest. She could smell the fizzy electricity of his fur, and out of the corner of her eye she saw Maud doing rapid string puzzles.

"We could watch for seals," Addie said. But it was no good.

Lightning flashed in the east. They pretended they weren't watching until a straight line of wind caught them under the dinghy. The temperature dropped like sliding coins, and the hair on their arms lifted.

"Under the blanket!" yelled Maud.

Horizontal rain sliced at them with a fingering wind, so they pulled the wool rug tight. The rain hit like driven nails, and Maud said through skittering teeth, "There's ice in it."

They took turns, one furrowed into the lap of the other, swallowed in the plaid wool and shared breath, thinking of Overly checking on them in bed while lightning stabbed the beach like a spider striking for its web. They shuddered, cried, and lay still, each thinking the other was brave.

As the storm swept off, they still didn't move, each letting their minds wander instead of thinking of food or cold or wet. Addie's mind went from lightning to heat strike, to striking while the iron was hot, to hot coals, to hot kettles, and finally to lapsong souchong tea. She gave a satisfied sigh as the stacked wooden boxes came into her mind's eye, some with dragons stamped on the side at the warehouse on the waterfront.

Maud's thoughts were quite different. "Would you go to a rodeo, Addie?"

Addie turned to look directly at Maud. "There are no rodeos in Halifax."

"I know, but if there were, would you go?"

Addie gave a small shrug. "I don't see why I would. It's only bulls and men riding horses in a circle."

"They fire rifles too. At least that's mostly what she shoots."

"Who are you talking about?"

"Annie Oakley. You'd want to see her, wouldn't you?" Again, Addie shrugged. Maud didn't wait for an answer. "She was the best. And she wasn't trying to be like a man. She had her own way of doing things."

"What do you mean?" Addie's tone let Maud know that she didn't think somebody who fired a rifle in a show could have much style.

"She was dead-eye fast. She could shoot behind her using a mirror or galloping a pony. But she wore a skirt with buttons down the front and a blouse with puffed sleeves and a ruffle at the neck." Addie narrowed her eyes to listen better. "She had long curly hair that hung down her back."

"Not braids or anything?"

"No. She'd brush it until it was shiny smooth, then she'd wear a brand new rolled brim hat to match her shoes."

"It matched her shoes? That's nice."

"She didn't want anyone forgetting she was a lady, but she could beat them all."

"Did she wear fringe, Maud?"

Maud looked at Addie for a long moment. "Yes, sometimes there was fringe, but that didn't make her shooting better."

"If there were fringe, I might go," said Addie.

They lapsed into silence, one thinking about the length of Annie Oakley's rifle and the other about the length of her fringe. A steamy drizzle started, confining them to their make-shift lean-to and reducing them to worrying about food. In the past twenty-four hours, they had only eaten a few steamed clams. They curled under the carriage blanket, letting their thoughts drift until Addie said, "Tell me more. Tell me what a whole rodeo would be like."

Maud did her best to describe what she had seen on a poster. She added buffalo and fire dances. She didn't know if these were possible in a rodeo, but she knew they were part of an authentic Indian experience. But soon, even Maud's rodeo imagination gave out.

The rain, however, was endless and the island was dull. They crimped themselves under the boat and watched rain stream across the beach, run off the rocks, and curtain like spun thread over the ocean. It dripped steadily off the edge of the boat. Once in a while they changed places to give themselves a different view.

By late afternoon, the wind died entirely and took most of the rain with it, leaving the air thick and hot. Gray sheets of clouds turned slowly, blotting the sun for slow moments. Addie sat propped against the overturned boat, reading *David Copperfield*, her curls clinging to her neck and forehead.

Maud trailed a fishing line over the edge of a rock. Nothing had bitten for a long time. She had set a stone on end to watch its shadow shift. Pulling herself upright and rolling her wet fishing line into a compact ball, she lay belly down, her head hanging just over the edge of rock, staring down into the water. Her thoughts were wandering when a large school of small fish poured into the pool below the rock. She stood up and watched the dizzying movement of the fish. Along each fish ran a blue-green streak that deepened to violet at its belly. It was like looking at the sky through wet eyelashes or like tiny sequins on her mother's best gown. She saw sudden tension—a stillness followed by a frantic beating against each other and the rocks—before she saw what caused it.

A larger force than the mass of small fins and scales was bearing down. The dorsal fins appeared first, and then, with long whip-like tails, tensile and strong, eel sharks lashed through the school of herring, swallowing several fish whole. The water boiled below her. Dizzy, Maud sank to her knees to keep from toppling into the midst of the frenzied fish. Within seconds the action was over. The sharks had thrashed, eaten, and left. The remaining herrings drifted from one side of the rocks to the other. Maud didn't know she was holding her breath until it was over.

She moved from the higher rocks to the protected pools near the camp and lay on her back in the shallows between two large rock tumbles. It was an open-ended tidal pool that never got cut off from the sea. She had enough water to float if she spread her arms and legs. Her hair fanned like sea dulse. She closed her eyes and let the sun turn the inside of her eyelids red. Tiny silver fish nibbled at her ankles.

Addie sat on the rocks above Maud, not wanting her hair to get salty and matted. The sun was halfway down the sky and it was time for a fire and supper. Tea would be better. *When I get home*, Addie thought, and then she stopped herself. When she thought about home, her parents, or Cook, a hollow spot opened inside her. She couldn't stop the image of Cook at the kitchen table, slicing lemon cake and saying, "Drink your tea, missus, and I'll read your fortunes."

When the tea was gone, Cook would take a china cup in her strong hands, swirl the dregs, and tip them onto a saucer.

Cook would begin with Maud, because Maud didn't believe in it and only sat still for an extra slice of cake. Cook would tell Maud things that made them all laugh, like predicting when Min would forget what she was talking about, or when Overly would fart. Maud would soon run off to a game of marbles or to watch the fishing boats come in.

Serious fortune telling began with Addie's tea leaves.

"There's something here, darlin', no doubt," Cook began, and Addie leaned forward on her elbows. She never asked how Cook could read the soggy green and brown shreds. She liked the mystery.

"Here's a spot of trouble coming," Cook sometimes said. Or, "Look at that. I see a bit of blue sky round the bend."

At this point, Addie took her eyes from Cook's face and peered at the saucer, then her eyes went back to reading Cook's expression. Sometimes it was a glance from Philip Tierney that Cook foresaw, and sometimes it was a rip in a favorite dress. Once Cook warned her of a prank by Evelyn Brighty. All had come true. It never crossed Addie's mind that Cook learned these fortunes while hanging laundry and chatting with the neighbor's maid.

Addie looked down at Maud, floating like Hamlet's Ophelia, and shook herself. She did not want that fortune.

"Maud!" she said too sharply. "Maud," she said, more gently as her sister's head snapped up, glaring. "Are you hungry? Should we start a fire?" Maud still hadn't caught a fish. They were deep in cool waters. "We'll have to find more clams," said Addie.

"What if it keeps raining?" asked Maud.

"Why, what do clams do when it rains?"

"No, that's not what I mean. Clams don't do anything. They get wet."

"So, why can't we go get them?"

"I mean if it's raining really hard and the rocks are slippery or when it's high tide. We should have something else to eat. Something that doesn't need to be cooked."

"We can eat seaweed." Addie said this as if they were just getting cheese and crackers from the cupboard.

"What kind of seaweed?"

"Come on, I'll show you."

They climbed the rocks between high and low tide marks.

"Here, this is dulse." Addie pulled at a dark purple, fleshy stem about a foot long. It was a flat frond with finger-like lobes at the end. "If we dry it, we can eat it."

Maud was impressed. "What does it taste like?"

"I don't know."

"Is this something else you've read about in a book?"

Addie didn't answer. If she said yes, Maud wouldn't take her seriously. If she said no, Maud would want to know how she knew about it. Instead she said, "I listen to Papa too."

They kept going down to the low tide rocks. Addie pointed to very thin, filmy fronds, satiny purple-brown with ruffled edges. "That's laver. I think you should boil it, but we could dry it too. And over there is sea lettuce." This looked similar to laver but was bright green. "I know we can eat it just like it is or dry it. I've seen Irish moss up on the higher rocks. Cook uses it to make pudding."

They pulled at the seaweed, Addie concentrating on the laver and sea lettuce, while Maud gathered dulse and ribbons of kelp. They hauled these back to camp and stretched them over the nearby rocks. "They should be dry in a day or so," said Addie. "I saw plants past the dunes that we could try as well. Lydia's grandmother walked with us one day and showed us plants she used to eat as a girl."

Addie pointed. "Further up there's sea-rocket." She trotted to the right and knelt beside a patch of plants with thick stems and fleshy leaves. "Taste it," she said, breaking a leaf, smelling it, then handing it to Maud.

Maud bit down on it. "It tastes like pepper!" she exclaimed.

"The seedpods are good too. Let's gather a bit." Addie walked to the edge of the dunes. A low plant with leaves in a flat ring sent up a leafless stem with a greenish white flower. "Cook says these are good in salad. I think she's snuck them in without Mama knowing."

Maud picked leaves and put them into the bowl of her skirt. "We have enough for a salad, Addie!"

Addie nodded and laughed. But when they sat down to eat, the greens didn't look so appetizing. "It's all we've got," apologized Addie.

"No, it's fine," said Maud.

"It's nowhere near as good as clams."

Maud stabbed a bunch of leaves with her fork, shoved them into her mouth, and began chewing. It was bitter and tough. She chewed bravely.

"Maybe if we tear it up more," offered Addie, who shredded the leaves, flowers, and stems until they looked minced. She piled her fork with greenery and put it in her mouth. She chewed and she chewed. "It's not bad."

"No, not bad." Maud took another forkful.

They ate in silence, chewing as long as they could. After a few forkfuls, they quit.

"I'm sure it will be better if it dries a little," said Addie.

"I'm glad for them, Addie, and for the seaweed. It's like you said. We need something for rainy days, and I haven't caught anything. Besides, wouldn't Cook be amazed at us eating our greens!"

Addie laughed. "Now I know how cows feel!"

The air stayed hot, and long rolls of thunder threatened more rain, eliminating hope of a cool, dry wind.

"It's too beastly hot to do anything!" Addie climbed onto the dunes and flopped into a sand hollow. She had never been allowed to wear her hair up, but she longed to try the styles in Mama's fashion magazines. Addie thought she would look particularly fetching with one ringlet trailing behind her right ear.

"Who are you preening for?" Maud's voice came over the edge of the hollow and Addie jumped with embarrassment.

"I'm getting my hair off my neck, that's all."

Maud slid down the edge of the hollow and joined Addie in the shade the dune offered. "There's no one here to see you but me," Maud said. "You're like the queen thrown into the stars for being vain. And you're burned to a crisp, you know, despite your parasol."

Addie lifted her nose. "It hurts," she finally said. After another moment's silence, Addie asked, "Do you mean Cassiopeia?"

"I suppose. I don't remember her name or the rest of the story."

"It's a myth. A long story."

Maud settled herself. "Tell me."

Addie yawned, turned on her side, and said, "I'll tell you tonight when the stars are out so you'll see her. But you have to untangle your own mop of hair." Maud squeezed her eyes at Addie. "You know, Maud, you might be attractive if you brushed your hair and rolled it into a low knot at the back. It would make your face look less round." Addie assessed Maud's face as if it were a shrub that needed trimming.

A jolt of lightning came from high overhead, followed by thunder. The girls left their hollow and crawled back under the boat. The rain made them shiver. Addie was the first to pull her dress back on and soon Maud did the same.

"My dress doesn't fit the same," Addie commented. She frowned and tugged at the fabric. "It's too big."

Maud put her fingers into the waistband of her skirt. "Mine too. I think we've shrunk."

"Oh, Maud, we're disappearing!"

"No, but we are getting spare."

They curled into the carriage rug and played Rock, Paper, Scissors, until they fell asleep.

With the dark and the rain came flashes of lightning to the south that kept up until just before dawn on June 18.

10

Don't Say Once Upon A Time

In the morning the air was washed and hung out to dry. The sea, however, was still soggy, as if the rainwater had thickened it and made it lazy. Maud had heard fishermen call it a hunting sea. A hunting sea meant good fishing. It crossed Maud's mind to talk Addie into going out in the boat with her and set lines for fish, but her common sense talked her out of it. The idea of getting back in the boat terrified Addie.

"Who knows where we'll drift off to," was Addie's answer when Maud suggested they circle the island in the boat. It wasn't Addie's words but the way she refused to look at the ocean while they were talking that showed how afraid she was.

Maud pulled off her middy blouse, left on her skirt, and patted each pocket. Satisfied that her pocketknife and ball of string were safe, she walked across the sand to the low boulders that made the rocky point sticking east into the sea. Maud hopped from rock to rock, paused to regain her footing, and then moved toward the outermost stones.

The tide was high and the sluggish ocean slapped with no spray. Maud balanced on two stones, one foot behind the other, and peered into the water. It was deep at high tide, and water covered limpets and barnacles crusting the rocks. A good-sized haddock might be lurking in the rock folds. It took a few minutes for her eyes to adjust to the murky shapes below the surface. What she saw made her smile.

A school of herring, thick as last night's rain and liquid as mercury, filled the cove. Cormorants and kittiwakes circled.

The sun turned the water's surface from steel blue to a glinty shimmer. Maud watched the herring shift like magnetic filings, pulled by currents running along shore. As she watched, an idea came to her. She pulled out her pocketknife, tested the blade against her thumb, and went to work. When she was done, soft curls lay around her and her neck felt the breeze. *As good as swimming naked*, she thought and put her attention to fishing.

Just as she had before, she unrolled the string, tied a bit of mussel pierced by a sharp bird bone to the end. She dropped her line and lay full length on the rock, holding her breath. When the jerk and tug came, she nearly jumped to her feet. Instead, she held firm, letting the fish swallow the bone. When the pull on the line intensified, she brought it slowly up until the fish dangled just below the surface. She took a deep breath, yanked the string in an arc and landed an eight-inch codfish. It twisted and slapped against the rocks, the bone clearly stuck through its lower jaw.

Not daring to believe this had really worked, she dragged the fish onto the flat stone and watched as it flipped its tail and gulped air, the barbell on its chin wagging. The fins shimmered with purplish markings that faded to silver gray with pink. A pale line ran down its side. Maud watched its eyes go flat. She rolled the thread, pulled the bone from the fish's mouth, and hooked her finger into its gill. Holding the fish high, she ran down the beach.

"Addie!" she called.

"What happened to you?" Addie looked as though someone had poured ice water down her back.

"I caught a haddock!" Maud was elated.

"Your hair!"

"What?" Maud concentrated on the fish. She put her hand to her head and remembered. "Oh. I cut it."

Addie walked around her sister. "I can see that. Why?"

"It was in the way. Watching you fuss with yours made me think of it. It's so light."

"Oh, Maud!" It was all Addie could think to say. "I couldn't ever," she finally said.

Maud laughed. "You don't have to. Don't worry, I won't cut yours while you're sleeping." Addie's eyes got wide. Maud put her face close to Addie's. "I promise."

"It's so...you look..."

"Cooler?" Maud offered.

Addie gave a weak laugh. "I guess. And you're right brown too."

She walked away, pretending to see if the seaweed was still rubbery, but she needed to understand what Maud's haircut meant. They would never think of things the same way, but on the island, Addie needed Maud to be as close to her as possible. Cutting hair was drastic, she decided. More drastic than swimming naked. She was jealous, too, that Maud was brown as coffee. Maud was beautiful.

When she came back, it was as if Maud had read her mind. "Let's make sand sculptures," Maud suggested

"Castles, you mean?" That's what Maud made, sturdy architectural shapes with moats and turrets.

"Anything we want."

The wet sand held together but was dry enough for smooth, sharp lines. They chose their spots and agreed not to peek until both sculptures were complete. For most of the afternoon they dug, piled, and shaped the sand. Once in a while, one got up and wandered the shore or went up into the dunes, then returned and continued. Sand coated them past elbows and knees and a patch of sand stuck to Addie's cheek. Finally, Addie called, "Done!"

"Not yet!" yelled Maud over her shoulder. She blocked Addie's view and kept working.

Addie paced the water's edge, rising on her toes and spinning every other step. She was halfway toward camp when Maud shouted, "Done!" She ran up the beach and joined Maud half facing the water.

"All right," said Maud. "We're going to look straight down at the sand and walk up between our sculptures. We're going to go back to back, with me facing your sculpture and you facing mine. Look up when I say *Go*. Ready?"

They positioned themselves according to Maud's instructions and looked up when she gave the word.

"Well done!" said Maud first. She examined a large sculpture of the tree in their backyard. Its rippled trunk had textures, and its leaves were mounded to give the idea of dense foliage. Individual small mounds made perfect, separate leaves. The rope swing swung from a low-hanging branch. Addie had pressed a length of rope from the boat into two sand ridges for the braided pattern. Maud looked up to praise Addie again, but Addie's back was still to her. She hadn't heard anything Maud had said. "What is it, Addie?" Maud came around and stood next to her sister.

When Addie brought her head up on Maud's *Go*, she had expected to see a castle or even a replica of the queen's residence. But a life-sized mermaid lay at her feet. Not only life-sized, but life-like. The likeness astonished her.

"Do you like it?" Maud looked from Addie's face to the sand.

"It's a mermaid!" Addie brought her gaze up to Maud. Maud nodded, smiling a little. Addie looked at Maud closely. "It's me."

Maud nodded again, her smile fading a little. "Yes."

Addie turned back to the sculpture. "It's the most beautiful thing I've ever seen!" she breathed. She walked around it, stooping and tracing where Maud had pressed shells into the tail to make scales, kneeling near the head to get closer where Maud had formed the same curve that Addie's mouth had when she was getting ready to laugh. Maud had grouped and trailed thin strands of seaweed, then sifted sand to create the effect of real hair. A necklace of small shells hung round the mermaid's neck and two perfect clam shells covered her breasts. A blush spread over Addie's face. "I don't—" she began.

Maud finished for her. "Not yet, but soon." She giggled at Addie's wide eyes and deeper blush.

"I want to keep her," said Addie. "I don't want the tide to wash her away."

"When the tide comes, she'll know what to do," answered Maud.

Addie looked at her sister and saw someone not quite the same as she had been before. Addie didn't know if it was because of Maud's hair or if Maud really was different. Or maybe Addie saw something she couldn't see before. "What will she do?" she asked.

"She will swim." Maud skipped away, thinking about dinner. Addie stayed until the thin edge of the ocean crept up and curled around the roots of her tree and touched the fin on Maud's mermaid. Addie couldn't watch, so she joined Maud.

For the rest of the day, they looked for driftwood and searched the high dunes for dried kindling grass and swam once more. As evening fell, they ate half of Maud's haddock. After they had settled near the boat and wrapped themselves in the rug, Maud said, "Tell me a story."

Addie picked up *David Copperfield* and turned pages to find where they had left off.

"No, I don't want you to read. Tell me one of your stories." Maud leaned up on an elbow and stared at Addie, who was lying on her side.

"What do you mean, one of my stories?"

"You know, the ones you made up when we were little. At night, while I was falling asleep."

Surprised, Addie regarded Maud. She didn't know that Maud remembered or even liked the tales conjured out of shadows and slow nighttime breathing.

"The light's going to fade anyway," Maud cajoled.

"All right. I remember one." Addie was pleased. She opened her mouth to begin.

"Don't say 'Once upon a time,'" Maud interrupted.

Addie's mouth closed. Her lips twisted in a knot, and she sighed. "Quiet now and let me begin. This story is called The Proper Conduct Dragon."

The story spun itself around them like the softly falling dark....

Anne Marie wouldn't mind anyone. She knew she was too clever to follow other people's silly rules. She didn't listen to her nanny, so there was always a new one. None of them could make her brush her hair or lace her own shoes or sit straight at the table. She didn't listen to her mother, because her mother would fall to pieces when Anne Marie threw a tantrum. All she had to do was stamp her foot and let her voice rise to a whine and her mother would twist her hands and say, "Well, then, that's all right, I guess."

Anne Marie didn't even listen to her father, although he was tall with a deep voice. She didn't have to obey, because he brought her dolls and fudge and picture books, then went to his study to smoke cigars and read the papers.

Anne Marie ruled her world, and she looked every bit the tyrant that she was. Her hands were usually grimy, and her pockets were always stuffed with pieces of cake or cheese. Her hair knotted up at the back into a little ball that would have made a dormouse very happy. In front, it hung in her eyes, except when she blew a jet of air up over her forehead in exasperation. Her smocks were covered in stains because she slumped over her plate, and no one came to play because she bullied and badgered and bossed until she won every game, had the most blocks, or got to name the family of dolls.

Then one day, after Anne Marie's eighth birthday, a tutor arrived. Her father had determined that his daughter should learn to add, to know the countries of Europe, and to name the Greek gods. If he thought someone could get her to sit still at a piano, he would have hired a music teacher as well.

The tutor was a small, wiry woman with black eyes like a crow's. Her hands were slender and strong. Anne Marie found out just how strong when she tried to squeeze one during their handshake. The tutor's name was Miss Duncan, and she carried a satchel full of books, paper, pens, and maps. She spread these on the table and began to quiz Anne Marie on what she already knew. Anne Marie played dumb, answering most questions incorrectly. To other questions, she gave a shrug and swung her feet. Finally, Miss Duncan stood, looked hard at Anne Marie for a moment, and left the room.

Quick as a flash, Anne Marie dumped the rest of the satchel's contents on the floor. She knelt and poked the things about—a change purse, an address book, a set of keys. Then she spied a small red leather volume with strange markings on the cover. The leather was worn, and when Anne Marie brought it to her face for a closer look, she could smell ages of must and mildew. She drew her fingers across the cover to feel the design in relief and an odd shiver went down her back. Sitting very still, she opened the book and saw inscribed in dark spidery handwriting:

This volume belongs to
The Proper Conduct Dragon

Anne Marie mouthed the words in a half whisper. As the sounds came out of her mouth, she felt the back of her neck grow warm, as though something was breathing hot right behind her. She did not have the courage to turn. She stood, placed the book on the table, and stooped to gather the spilled contents of the satchel. Her hair fell over her face and as she brushed it aside, she saw the toe of Miss Duncan's sturdy black walking shoe. Anne Marie straightened quickly, the satchel dangling by one strap from her hand.

"I..." she began. "I didn't mean...I—"

"I know, Anne Marie," said Miss Duncan. "We seldom *mean*, when we only set out to do. Let's begin at the beginning, shall we?" Anne Marie thought she meant the alphabet or doing sums. She had already figured those out on her own. "What is your best wish, Anne Marie?" asked Miss Duncan.

Anne Marie stood mute. No one had asked her this question or any question like it. She had not even asked it of herself. She had always thought she had everything a child was supposed to wish for, and she had always done only whatever came into her head at any given moment. She had never shaped a "best wish" to hold like a favorite doll or savor like dark chocolate. She couldn't think of anything. Not one thing.

"Well, that's the problem, isn't it?" asked Miss Duncan, watching Anne Marie carefully. "You have to go beyond things."

Maud sat up. "What does that mean you have to go beyond things?" she asked.

"It just means Anne Marie should..." Addie's voice trailed as she thought. "It means children should try..." Her voice stopped.

"Don't you know what it means?"

"Well, not exactly."

"What do you mean, not exactly? Aren't you the one telling the story?"

"Of course I am. But sometimes words come first and meaning comes later."

"That doesn't make sense!" Maud exclaimed.

"The sense will come later as the story gets told." Addie

rearranged the blanket and settled back into the sand. "Maybe if you weren't like Anne Marie, you'd understand."

Maud got to her feet and stood over Addie. "Addie, you are the most priggish girl in the whole world. You're the one like Anne Marie. You don't know a map from a cooking recipe." She stomped down the moonlit beach.

Addie folded her arms and refused to watch. She screwed her mouth and twitched her left foot until it looked as if it were having a spasm. "She doesn't know anything about stories," Addie spat out to the dunes, the stones, the stretch of shimmering sea. "She has no imagination." She flopped back and stared up. The stars stared back, and Addie lay defeated by their sharp sparkle. She had no idea where the story was going. With a sigh, she rose and trudged down the beach after Maud.

Maud walked slowly, dragging one big toe in the wet sand at the water's edge. She turned the words of the story over in her mind like a coin she wanted to spend. "You have to go beyond things," she whispered. She thought of all the things she wanted: kites, marbles, a horse. She thought of things that weren't train rides or a trip to Boston or seeing Rufus Handy get beaten in a race. Were those the things she needed to go beyond? What about getting off the island? Was that a thing to get beyond? The words puzzled her greatly. Maud's toe found the edge of a clam shell.

"Ow!" she yelped, hopping on one foot, then wading into the water up to her ankles. She stared along the shifting silver ribbon the moon made on the water's surface. It came to her that going beyond things would be like walking along that ribbon until she came to… Maud's thoughts stopped. As she turned to yell back up the beach, she nearly collided with Addie.

"Ahhh!" came out of Maud's mouth.

"Oh! Oh!" came out of Addie's.

"I thought you were coming to yell at me again. You look

so serious." Addie's laughter erupted, seeing Maud's eyebrows so fiercely together.

"I thought you crept up to scare me," replied Maud. "But you look more scared than me!" A wave of giggles came over Maud.

When they reached the dry sand, they gave in to giddiness and flopped down. The fine sand was cool and soft, so they lay enjoying the night as they gulped in air.

"It's a good story," said Maud after a while. "I like the idea of A Perfect Conduct Dragon."

"You do?"

"Yes. And I think I know what Miss Duncan means when she says, 'You have to go beyond things.'"

"It didn't mean anything. You were right, and that's why I got so mad."

"It does mean something. It's just not easy to figure out. And I think Anne Marie is smart enough to figure it out too."

"So what does it mean?"

"Oh, Addie, it's your story, you know the answer."

The two girls burst into fits of laughing that startled several curlews stalking the beach. They walked back to the boat and lay down on the rug. Within minutes, Maud was breathing evenly. Addie put her elbows on her knees and watched Maud as she slept. Addie thought about how Anne Marie's story might end, but before she could get there, she fell asleep too.

First thing the next morning, Maud was up and gone. June 19 brought a quick breeze that caught her as she rounded the rock-piled jetty. She landed on a small stretch of beach. Grains of sand spun and lashed her legs, and strands of hair stood out sideways from her face. The wind slapped up small whitecaps, and dark green seaweed threaded ferny patterns over the sand. Maud squatted, pulled a few strands away, and watched the sand crystals change color as clouds covered and uncovered the sun. A ten-ridged whelk almost four inches across lay at her feet. She felt the ribbed whorls. It was yellowish gray with creamy white streaks, and the raised ridges were dark amber. It was a very good find, one to put in her collection. Two herring gulls sailed overhead, making a repeated *kyoo, kyoo*. They were angry at something, and Maud wondered if it was her. Their winged shadows circled then veered off. She looked down again and saw a small hole just three inches from her big toe breathe out a bubble.

"More clams!" she said aloud, putting her hands on her hips. She surveyed the section of beach, then walked the water's edge, looking at high tide marks, the occasional gutted crab shell, rockweed clumps, and the tissue-thin ribbons of sea lettuce. More boulders lay ahead. She climbed them and found a less sandy cove, full of brown kelp and eel grass. As she climbed, the rocks leveled. Climbing higher, almost to the bluff where she and Addie had first realized they were on an island, she thought about using mussels instead of clams for bait, but her thoughts were stopped by the wreck of a fishing boat.

The smashed boat was wedged on a level shelf, high above the highest tide mark, tucked just under the bluff's overhanging rocks and invisible to anyone standing above it. Below, the sea churned in a deep twist of angry current. The boat had settled and softened under the beat of salt spray and wind. Its prow wedged between two boulders and its keel cut deep in the sand.

Climbing around it, Maud stopped at the stern to read the name, now bleached and peeled. A top curve of an *O* or an *M* showed with a half stroke that could be a tall letter. Maud decided *M* was most likely, followed by vowels. She concentrated on the next letter and gave up. "Better for Addie," she said aloud and crawled onto rocks that had fitted themselves into the shore side of the boat. These made access easy, but Maud hesitated. She was careful as she stepped onto the wreck.

11

You Can't Do Things Like That

It was not the Spanish galleon of her fantasies, but for Maud, the fishing boat held more promise and excitement than a vessel filled with gold doubloons. There was nothing on the deck but shreds of old rope and the broken stump of the mast. The boards of the deck held her, so she inched across, knelt, and looked down into the hold. Light flickered from cracks between the boards, now that wind and salt had eaten the caulking.

Maud saw the boat's bottom and the loose grid of a rotting net. She put a foot on a ladder rung to test its strength. Holding the edge of the square opening, she reached for the next rung. It held. She looked down, then up out of the hole. The distance from top to bottom was about twice her height.

With her mouth set straight, she stepped down one more rung, one more, one…but there wasn't one more. Her foot dangled to find a perch, but the rung was gone. Maud stretched her full length, groping until her right foot found the next rung. She loosened her grip and put her weight on the rung. It snapped and gave way. As her body slid, she grabbed for the ladder, but her balance was gone and she crashed, landing in the belly of the boat. The light from above was like a weak spotlight, showing a net, tangled and frayed. Shapes extended into the dark as her eyes adjusted.

Maud peered around, then groped along the sides of the boat, touching stacked lobster traps, crates, and coiled rope. A rusted metal bin sat to one side where fish were dumped when the net was dragged in. The dark made her more nervous than she wanted to admit. She stumbled. A pole lay across her path. A gaff hook. "Good work!" she said and held onto it. Continuing around the hold, she looked back to the small square of light. It looked very far away. A tern crossed the opening. She jumped for the bottom rung, but it might as well have been the tern she was trying to reach. A coil of fear wound in her stomach.

Maud lifted the empty crates to the hatchway and arranged them in a pyramid. Holding the gaff hook as a staff, she steadied herself. The boxes creaked and cracked as she put her weight on them. At this height, she could just reach the bottom rung of the ladder, but it meant letting go of the hook. The hook was a great tool and the boxes were perfect firewood, but she couldn't manage all of it alone.

Sweat dotted her face and arms. She hung the hook on the highest rung she could reach. It stayed. She stood on tiptoe, balancing as the boxes swayed. She jumped. Her right hand caught the rung, but her left hand scrambled at air. She let her body sway, her left arm reached, and this time she gripped the rung with both hands. She lifted herself, hauling her chest as far above the bottom rung as she could until her upper body rested on it. Keeping her left-hand grip, she let go her right and reached for the next rung. She caught hold and breathed. Pulling herself up so that she was kneeling on the bottom rung, she took a deep breath and climbed the rest of the way out, pulling the gaff hook up with her. Once out, she looked down at the boxes. They looked a long way down, and the coil in her stomach gave another small turn. She said, "I'm going to need Addie for this." She went down the rocks and back the way she had come, heading for camp.

"Is that a harpoon?" Addie yelled as Maud came toward her, trotting over hard-packed stretches of beach and scrambling over boulders smoothed by waves. *She looks like a small warrior,*

Addie thought. She had seen drawings in the big volume called *Far and Wide* that Papa had brought back from England. It was full of drawings—turtles bigger than Mama's hatboxes and women with tattoos. She had stared often at those pages.

"It's a gaff hook," Maud answered, pounding down the last distance between them. She held the pole to hurl like a javelin, but it was thicker, shorter, and had a metal hook on the end. Grime and cobwebs covered Maud's legs.

"Where did you find it?" Addie asked. Any tool could mean the difference between fish or kelp for supper.

"In a wrecked fishing boat," answered Maud. Her breathing slowed as she lowered the hook to lie across both her palms. She bounced the pole, feeling its weight and the smooth, hard wood that had resisted years of damp and salt.

"It's not a spear," Addie commented, tilting her head and trying not to sound doubtful.

"No, but I've watched tautogs off the point. They like sea urchins and crabs that scuttle in the cracks. If I can balance above them while they're eating, I might be able to jab one. Come on, let's try!" Maud didn't wait for an answer but trotted to a jumble of boulders as big as sea chests.

Addie didn't budge. The rocks were dry, but there were periwinkles that made her shudder when they slimed between her toes, and the small colonies of volcano-like barnacles cut her feet if she didn't step carefully. It took too much concentration.

An hour later, Maud returned with one six-inch tautog. She cleaned it while Addie built a fire. They used a flat rock to cook the fish. While they ate, Maud told her about the crates. "If I go back down, I can throw them up to you."

Addie put down her empty plate. "You can't do things like that."

"Like what?"

"Putting yourself in a hole and not being able to get out."

"But I did get out."

"You almost didn't. What would happen if you didn't?"

"I did, so it doesn't matter. You can't tell me what I'm allowed to do."

"There's no one else!" Addie cried. Her face flushed and her eyes filled.

Maud's face reddened, too, and her hands were fists. "I'm not a baby!"

"You don't think! You run wild!" Addie yelled back.

"I think about lots of things. I think about fire and food!"

"I think about being safe." Tears ran down Addie's face. "What if you didn't come back? What if you'd gotten really hurt?"

Addie's fear for her surprised Maud. She pressed her lips together and looked sideways at Addie. "I was thinking about firewood."

"You were exploring." Addie pushed her hair off her face, feeling the heat of the fire and her agitation.

"We can go tomorrow and get the crates."

"If you stood on the crates to get out, how will you get out once you've tossed them up to me?"

Maud opened her mouth and closed it. For once Addie saw the way something worked before she did. This time it was the way things wouldn't work. She slumped next to the boat and stared at the ocean. It was a puzzle. It was like the puzzle story Papa told, only there would be no magic trick.

"We'll poke a hole in the side," she said.

"Okay," Addie said. She doubted it would work, but she had pushed Maud far enough. "Okay," she said again. "Tomorrow we'll do it."

In the morning, however, before they could go back to the boat, Addie said they had to eat. It was June 20, and one small piece of fish or a few clams every day meant they were always hungry.

"Okay. Let's find something to eat," Maud answered.

When Addie stood up in answer, Maud told her to bring her parasol.

They walked together off the beach and onto the high ground of the island.

"Give me your parasol," Maud said.

"What?"

"You're right. It's better if you do it."

"Do what? Maud, what are you talking about?"

"Open the parasol and follow me. Take my hat and keep it out of the way." Addie was bewildered. "Hold it way above our heads. Flap it open and closed. Now run!"

Maud dashed toward the burrows where the terns landed. Birds were coming in and finding their nests. "Come on, Addie!" she cried. "Keep up!"

Addie chased after, trying to do as she was told. She held the open parasol over her head, waving it frantically. Maud stooped, reached into a nest and came out with a dark blotchy egg. The tern swooped and dove at her head.

"The parasol, Addie! Keep the parasol up!"

With a blood-curdling scream the bird dove again, but this time it dove for the parasol as the highest point of the intruder.

Maud found another nest and found another egg. "Take these and put them in the hat. Run!"

Addie didn't need to be told twice. She grabbed the eggs, ran for the hat, and flew off the rocks and across the island to the camp. Maud scrambled behind some rocks and waited until the birds quieted down. When she was sure they wouldn't attack again, she crept out, took the jar, and filled it at the basin. Then she ran for the dunes and their camp.

That afternoon, Maud led Addie to the fishing boat.

"How long do you think it's been here?" asked Addie. She walked the length of the boat, then examined the transom where only a few strokes of its name remained.

"Long enough for beetles and crabs to clean away any food

and for the weather to pull the boards apart. It'll be easy to work them free. We're going to have great fires now!"

Maud scrambled over the lee side of the boat onto the main deck. She stamped her feet in places to test the solidity of the boards under her. They creaked and sagged, but nothing gave way.

"Come down into the hold. There are broken boards toward the back. We can start there." Maud held the gaff hook. When Addie came around to the side, Maud extended the hook like a stair rail. "Take your shoes off so you don't slip on the rocks," Maud cautioned.

"Do I have to go down?" Addie peered into the hole with her nose wrinkled. "Why can't we pry the boards loose from outside?"

Maud pointed to the rocks around the boat. Addie could see there would be no firm footing.

"Besides," Maud said, "poking the boards from the inside out is easier than trying to push them from the outside in. They're already curved out."

This logic satisfied Addie, but her mouth was scrunched at the idea of slime or spiders or crabs. "I'm not going barefoot in this boat. You don't know what could be down there."

"There's nothing. At least not much." Maud didn't count spider webs or small crabs. "The light's perfect. It's pouring down the hole like a little window." Maud turned away from Addie and stopped over the hatch. "I'll go first," she said and lowered herself into the opening. *Crash!*

"Ow!" floated up from below; then, "The bottom is fine." Addie could hear Maud pulling the crates away. "You'll have to jump down after the last rung," came Maud's voice again.

Addie peered into the square hole. Maud's face floated below like a freckled fish. Addie swung her legs over the edge and stepped down the rungs. When she reached the last one, she pushed off and landed on her bottom with a "humph!"

Before getting up, she looked at the streaky light and the shad-
owed curves of the boat's hold. She felt the soft floorboards
and the grit of sand. The nails, rusted and shrunken, allowed
gaps between the planks.

Maud held the gaff hook next to the splintered boards. "We
can use this as a crowbar." She wedged the hook between two
boards, but the handle was too long, and as much as Maud
tried she couldn't control the pole.

"Addie, take the far end and I'll tell you to move it left or
right, up or down. I'll work the hook end and get it to stick."

Addie followed Maud's instructions.

"Up more. To the right. Up again. Push straight forward."

A sharp crack answered their efforts.

"Push down hard," directed Maud. She walked backward
down the pole and joined Addie at the end. They pushed and
struggled to lever the board away from the boat.

"Sit on it, Addie!" snapped Maud.

"What?"

"Sit on the end of the pole. I'll hold it."

Addie sat sideways on the end of the pole. Her weight was
enough to sink the pole a foot deeper. Another crack and another as the pole sank further. A slow creaking release came
as a board swung free. Excited, Maud let go of the pole and
Addie tumbled onto the floor of the boat.

But there was daylight and a gap.

"Push again!" shouted Maud.

And they did. The board snapped away with a crack, leaving
a hole showing rocks and the ocean beyond.

"It's not big enough," said Addie.

"Of course not. We have to do it again."

They worked for the rest of the afternoon, prying boards
loose and piling them on the rocks. By the time the sun shone
directly across the water, they had a hole big enough for the
crates and themselves.

The next morning, June 21, Maud went back to the fishing boat alone. She didn't know why—maybe because Addie had been so bossy. She liked being by herself to wonder inside the boat. The storm must have been tremendous to push the boat so far up. Even on this clear summer day, at high tide the water at this end of the island swirled and thrashed with waves crawling far up the rocks like grasping fingers. Anything approaching the island from that direction would find itself crumpled and battered. Maud hadn't given up on treasure. The hold might be empty, but maybe there was a map in the cabin, which was nose first between boulders.

The cabin door resisted, but with a few sharp tugs, its hinges gave way and hung crookedly in its frame. With the door open, the still air in the cabin collapsed like an escaping sigh. New air hesitated. A boulder as big as a leather chair sat just outside the angled window, blocking most of the light. The boat's cabin flickered as if underwater with only late afternoon light entering. Maud had chosen the right moment to explore.

She stepped over the threshold and let her eyes adjust to the murky light. She half turned her head and froze.

The slender, pale bones and staring skull of a man returned her gaze. Air escaped her lips with a hiss, and she took an involuntary step backward. But she didn't run. The man's posture, the position of the skeleton, sparked sympathy in her. She crouched and scanned.

The skeleton was half sitting, half reclining against the side wall of the cabin. The legs were stretched out full, but the thigh bone of his left leg was cracked in two and shreds of trousers covered him. His fisherman's boots looked oversized and heavy on the bare ankle bones. The face was turned toward the window, making Maud think he had watched the sea come for him as he sat, unable to fight his way out. His arms showed her that he knew he was in a tight spot. His right arm was fully extended and covered, like his chest, with the rags of a plaid flannel shirt. His hand still held fast to the wheel of his craft with the bones bent tight on a wooden spoke. Maud pictured him trying to steer in rough waves, though he couldn't stand. His left arm was folded at the elbow and the finger bones clung to a rusted tin box. The skeleton's hands were long, the bones like fine small flutes as they tapered, and the skull suggested a high forehead. The jaw line was even and strong. She thought this was not an old man who had crashed on these rocks. Pieces of shirt hung from the shoulders.

Maud looked long and carefully and felt very sad. She didn't touch anything. This was too important to do by herself. She went back to camp and told Addie what she had found.

"I don't want to see a skeleton," Addie said.

"It's important." Maud couldn't say why, but something in her voice made Addie change her mind.

They returned together that afternoon.

Addie stood before the doorway of the cabin. Maud, unaware of her sister's hesitation, swung the door open with a series of rasping creaks that made Addie rigid. The early afternoon light hadn't found its way into the cabin.

"You have to step over the frame," cautioned Maud. She moved through the doorway and was swallowed in shadow.

"Maud!" The syllable came like a bird call.

Maud's face reappeared in the doorway like a moon suddenly risen.

"It's all right, Addie. He's dead."

Maud waited until Addie came forward then moved back so Addie could enter the cabin too.

The skeleton looked the same, but to Maud it looked gentler because of the thinking she had done about him. She felt protective of the man.

"He must have cared an awful lot about his boat. See how his leg is broken? The big thigh bone is broken right through. That must have happened during a storm."

Addie barely heard Maud. Her wide eyes never moved from the head, tilted toward the sky, the eye sockets still searching.

Maud pointed to the bones of his hand. A rope lashed over the boat's wheel and looped around the man's wrist. The rope and the man's bones had been together so long they looked worn down to the same elemental substance.

"Do you think someone tied him here?" Addie whispered, as if she could wake the half-reclining skeleton.

Maud touched the rope where it rose away from the wrist and circled the wheel. Wrist, rope, and wheel looked fused together so that particles of one were particles of the others. The rope was stiff and dense, the wooden wheel bleached and pitted, more porous now, but gray and brittle, and the hands and wrist clung to both, showing the fine grain and mottles of exposed and weathered bone. Maud inspected the point where all three met.

"No," she said. "He was trying to save himself. It was the last and only thing he could do."

"What do you mean, the last thing?" Addie inched closer.

Maud heaved a sigh and turned to look at her sister. "Look at his right leg, Addie. See that great bone splintered and smashed in the middle?"

Addie looked, uncomprehending. Her head nodded to show that her mind was following, but fear was getting the best of her.

"His leg is broken," went on Maud. "Maybe the mast fell on his leg when it snapped. He was out here in a storm by himself. His leg was smashed and the only thing he could do was tie himself to the wheel so he could steer."

The girls stood in the dimly lit cabin and stared at the broken thigh bone and the rope holding the wrist to the wheel. What they saw was a man, wet through from a storm, knocked about by an angry sea, pulling himself along the deck of a shattered boat to try this one last thing, to give himself a small chance by tying his faith to the boat.

After very long minutes, Addie said, "But it didn't work!"

Maud's head came up quickly and she smiled. "Oh, but it did. He didn't drown, and he didn't lose his boat."

"Then why did he die?" The words came out in a wail.

Maud looked steadily at the man's skull, the face tipped toward the window. "He just did, Addie."

Neither knew what to say or do next.

"We're the only ones," said Addie.

"What do you mean?"

"We're the only ones to take care of him, to understand what happened. Maybe no one knows but us. And we don't even know who he is."

"He's brave—we know that," said Maud.

"Why do you say that?"

"See how he holds the wheel? I bet he was strong. I bet the storm came up suddenly. Why else would he be out fishing? Did you notice how the mast was gone? The wind probably snapped it. He might have been pinned under it for a while. There must have been blood everywhere. I think he fought hard. There was something or somebody he wanted to get home to. Look at the box he's holding."

Only then did Addie see the metal box in the grip of his skeletal fingers. "We can't leave him here," was her answer.

They pondered the length of bones before them. The cabin smelled of seaweed and rotting wood.

"We should bury him on the bluff just above us." Addie said, nodding her head. "Yes, the bluff would be right."

Maud didn't argue, but part of her didn't want to lose the man. She knew this skeleton had something to tell them and she hadn't figured out what it was yet.

12

Take One End

"Let's take the box and see what's in it. It must be important, or he wouldn't be holding it like that," suggested Maud. She shivered in the murk of the cabin and pulled her attention away from the skeleton. Peering into corners, she saw a latched cabinet. *Neatly stowed* came into her head and she pulled the doors open though they stuck, rusty and warped.

"Tins, Addie!" Maud exclaimed and lifted one out. The paper cover had disintegrated and the metal was rusted, but the contents hadn't leaked. Four food tins and another smaller tin with a removable lid sat on a shelf. Maud stacked these on top of the box, and they made their way back to camp.

"How are we going to open the tins?" Addie asked.

They knew it was pork and beans. The only tinned food available was Van de Camp's Pork & Beans. Sometimes tinned pineapple could be bought, but not very often. A fisherman would bring beans for a quick meal at sea.

Maud pulled the lid off the small tin and laughed. She tilted it so Addie could see what was inside.

"Tea! Oh, tea!"

"It must be terrible stale, though," Maud warned.

"Terribly."

"What?"

"It's terribly stale, not terrible. You sound like Cook."

"Good. I like the way Cook sounds. She has her own voice, not a book voice."

Addie gave this a bit of thought. "Well, anyway, I don't care if it's terrible or terribly stale. It's real tea." She was already at the fire poking bits of splintered wood into a pile and ready to run for water.

"Wait," said Maud. She pulled out her knife and stabbed at the top of a tin. The blade sank into the soft metal. She stabbed again and again around the top until she had a crescent-shaped hole that she could peel back. Addie was tight against her shoulder, their heads nearly touching as the smell of pork and beans rose.

Maud groaned. "Real food."

Addie closed her eyes. "Not ocean food."

"Right quick!" ordered Maud. "You get water. I'll make the fire. And we're only heating one can, hear?"

But Addie was already gone, racing up the dunes for water. She sang, "Tea!" all the way there and back.

"It's so good," Maud said, licking her spoon after all the beans had been eaten.

"And we have three more," answered Addie. "Three more days...." She stopped talking. Saying anything about days was too risky. "What about the box?" she asked.

The paint on the metal box was worn thin by rust, the hinges eaten to corroded lace. Maud knew better than to think it might contain doubloons, but a rattling sound made her think of one gold coin. The shuffling sound confirmed her suspicion of maps.

She pried at the lid, but her small hands couldn't loosen it, so she considered seashells, Addie's fingernails, a stick of driftwood.

"Let me try," said Addie.

Maud didn't want Addie to have a part in the discovery. Wasn't she the one who found the boat and skeleton in the first place?

"I can do it," Maud said and twisted a fork tine into the keyhole.

"You're ruining the fork," Addie said and grabbed the box away. She considered the box, then hurled it at a boulder. It clattered, bounced, dented, but didn't open.

"Hey!" yelled Maud, but Addie threw the box again. The lid sprang open at one corner. Maud grabbed it and bent the lid back further. She shook the box upside down. Two objects tumbled to their feet: a packet of letters tied with pale ribbon and a tarnished brass key. Addie picked up the key and turned it in the light. She had seen one like it on her father's key chain.

Maud took the key from her. The ribbon-bound letters fit Addie's fantasies, not hers. A key was a mystery. A key inside a locked box raised questions. It had an oval loop at the head for hanging on a hook or a chain. She laughed out loud.

"What?" asked Addie.

"It's a skeleton key." Addie looked at her uncomprehending. "Skeleton key?" Maud repeated.

They both grinned. "I wonder what kind of closet this goes to and what a skeleton would keep in there."

"I've heard Cook talk about a neighbor having skeletons in the closet," added Maud.

"Cook knows everyone's skeletons, but she doesn't know ours," said Addie.

They grinned again.

This key went to a difficult lock. This key hid something important. Maud thought about the smashed fishing boat and the man they had found. If he had been a fisherman, why had he been out alone and why did he carry these letters and this key?

They talked late into the night about how they would bury the man and what the contents of the box might mean. Addie was sure they were love letters. Maud agreed. The key was anyone's guess, but they both agreed it went to a fancy box, maybe handmade. They also agreed that the letters and the key should be put back in the box and buried with the man.

In the morning they went about their habits of reading and poking around the rocks. June 22, high up on the eastern cliff facing the north Atlantic, Maud watched the puffins. One female waddled to the edge of the cliff and dove off, and Maud leaned forward to follow its plunge. The puffin barely splashed as it split the water. Maud waited for it to surface. Several seconds went by and the bird did not reappear. More seconds passed and still there was no sign of the bird. Maud realized she was holding her breath. Her eyes darted back and forth and back to the point of entry, watching for the puffin. After nearly thirty seconds, the little bird broke the water's surface, and Maud saw four or five silvery herring crosswise in its beak.

"Good job!" Maud called and two gulls startled off, crying their annoyance. Maud moved herself from rock to rock to get a closer look at the puffins in the water. She didn't know any birds that could stay under water that long. She saw another puffin dive, and this time she was close enough to see several feet into the water. She laughed at what she saw.

"What are you laughing at?" Addie's voice came from behind her.

"Come over and watch!"

Addie crouched next to Maud, who pointed at a puffin two feet below the surface. "They fly underwater!" Maud laughed again. "Look, they use their wings and feet like rudders."

This puffin also broke the surface with a mouthful of herring, scrambled to the top of the water, then flew back to the cliff.

"Their wings were a blur!" said Addie. "What funny birds."

"Oh, look!" shouted Maud. A great, black-backed gull darted after a puffin with its beak full. The gull shrieked and dove, trying to tear the fish from the puffin's bill. The puffin darted like a hummingbird right into the cliff face and disappeared.

"Why don't the gulls catch their own supper?" Addie asked.

Maud pointed. Two large gulls hovered with legs extended

over the waves. They tipped their beaks into the water. Each skimmed off with a mackerel. The girls watched the bright-billed puffins shuffling about the rocks, some puffing themselves up and growling when gulls appeared and others taking turns flinging themselves off the rocks and speeding through the water looking for food.

They waited for the afternoon to give them the best light in the boat's cabin. The black box sat under the curve of their own boat. While Maud tried a little fishing, Addie peeked into the box. The letters were a story no one would ever know. She untied the ribbon and slid one of the letters out of the pack. With a second's hesitation, she put it into her pocket and retied the ribbon. Maud wouldn't notice.

Maud came back with a few clams. Addie went up on the dunes to pee. While she was gone, Maud poked her finger inside the tin box. She pulled out the key and let it lie on the palm of her hand. It wasn't a treasure map, but it was a key to something special. She would never know what that something was, but holding the key was almost enough. Without another thought, she slipped the key into her pocket. She found a thin flat stone and put it in the box and then took a larger stone and hammered the lid flat and shut.

Addie came up behind her.

"I thought it should look the way it was when we found it," Maud improvised.

"Yes, that's thoughtful. Should we go?"

They returned to the fishing boat and made their way into the cabin. Maud held the rolled carriage rug under her arm, and Addie carried Maud's petticoat, folded into a square. They hadn't spoken as they left the sand and climbed from one rock to another to reach the boat. As they stood in the cabin, their silence deepened.

Next to the skeleton, Maud unrolled the rug, its plaid almost lost in the wavery shadows. She adjusted its position and

looked up at Addie. Addie shook out the muslin petticoat.
That morning she had pulled out the seams. It fluttered white,
making Maud think of the curtain in her mother's bedroom.
Her eyes pricked, and she focused on the rug.

"Take one end," Addie said.

Maud saw Addie's eyes above the cloth. They were large
and calm and solemn. Maud leaned and caught the bottom
edge of the muslin, then stopped. "We have to put him on the
rug first," she said. She looked from Addie to the man's skull.
This was the hardest part. "Cover his feet with the cloth and
hold them steady," Maud said softly.

Maud moved to the man's raised arm and placed her hand
over his. She worked her jackknife blade through the old rope.
It gave without much effort. With gentle squeezing, she pulled
each finger bone away from the wheel. As the arm slipped
down, she caught it in both hands and laid it across the man's
lap.

Next she took the skull in her hands the way she had seen
Cook move a steaming bowl to the table. In one motion, Maud
lowered the man's head and torso to the rug. Addie gathered
the legs and feet in the cloth and moved them to the rug also.
Without speaking, the girls nudged the loose bones into place
and arranged the arms along the sides.

Addie lifted the cloth and shook it, and a fine dust sparkled
in the dim light. Maud caught the end and they draped the
muslin over the man, Maud tucking one end around his head
and Addie tucking the other under his feet. They took up their
ends of the rug and moved in slow, soft steps out of the cabin
and across the deck of the boat.

"I'll go first," said Maud as they came to the side. She held
the bunched end of the rug in one hand, steadied herself with
the other, and swung her legs one at a time over the side and
onto a rock. Inching forward, she pulled her part of the rug
with its shroud across the rock and waited.

Addie copied Maud's movements and soon they were a small procession, creeping and shuffling up and over the uneven rocks that barricaded that end of the island. A tern floated overhead and gave a sharp kip, followed by a trailing *kee-arrr*. Gauzy clouds made lines to the east, and the sun stared at their backs as they clambered from jutting rocks to the sandy bluff at the westernmost point.

Neither girl commented on how light the skeleton felt, but they both thought it and they both wondered how a full-grown man, strong enough and brave enough to sail his own boat, could turn into this delicate cage that hardly withstood the trip from boat to high ground.

"He survived this long," Maud said all at once.

Addie turned to her and nodded. Her words needed no explaining. They set the rug down and scooped sand in a long narrow hollow.

They chose a place as close to the edge as possible without danger of wind or surf washing the bluff from under him.

"He should see the setting sun," Addie said.

"He should feel the winds from home," Maud added.

They dug until they were satisfied. They laid the rug in the hollow and tugged gently on one side until the man's bones lay in the grave. Addie placed the muslin around him, tucking in the corners and edges.

The girls stood, hands folded before them, and gazed down at the man they had rescued. Maud knelt and slid the metal box next to his ribs. As she stood, Addie sang, starting quiet and a little thin, but as the melody took shape, she took courage. "Ave Maria, gratia plena...."

It was the church song she liked best. She had sung it at the May festival just over a month ago at St. Alban's. Maud had hated hearing her sister practice it and said she sounded like a mouse stuck in a jar. But now the music and words filled Maud, so her eyes brimmed and a lump burned in her throat.

Addie finished out the last note. At sight of Maud's tears, she said, "Oh, Maud!" and put her arm around her.

They rocked slightly, holding each other while the sun slid toward the sea.

13

Maybe the Ocean Can Be the Music

"Maud, how many days have we been on this island?"

Addie's tone made Maud suspicious, but she kept unrolling her line. The mackerel liked the deep cold cove in the morning. Maud let the question trail out, like her fishing line, when the first answer and then the second came to her. Eleven days. It was June 23. It was Adelaide Suzanna Campbell's twelfth birthday. Maud said, as if to the little slapping waves against the rocks, "It's been around seven or eight days."

Addie threw a stone, not quite over Maud's shoulder, but very near. Maud didn't stir. Addie threw another. It landed with a plop like the one before it and startled any fish that might have been sneaking up on Maud's lure. When Maud still didn't respond, Addie threw a good-sized pebble and clipped the side of Maud's head.

"Ow! Watch what you're doing!" Maud thought it was funny actually, because she knew Addie was peeved about it being her birthday. But Maud wasn't going to let on. She eyed her sister. "Why don't you go soak your head, Addie? You look all worked up."

A red tinge crept up Addie's neck. She bunched her lips and looked ready to cry. Maud started to feel sorry, but Addie swung off the rock, climbed over a few boulders, and strode up the beach. Maud watched her go. Addie skimmed over the sand, hands in front, pulling at her fingers.

A tremor on the line pulled Maud's attention to the fish below. She jigged it and felt a tug followed by a zinging vibration as a large fish swallowed the bait and swam away. "Well, Addie, your birthday hasn't brought us luck," she said.

Maud picked her way across the boulders, intent on the spaces between low-lying rocks along the eastern shore. After an hour, she had two handfuls of Irish sea moss, its purple fronds like bunches of lace. Letting it dry on a flat stone, she went in search of eggs.

First, she went to the basin for water. As she filled the jar, a feeling came over her that she should offer something back. She and Addie were asking a lot from the island. She peered into the depths. It was magic. She pulled her marbles from her pocket and jostled them on her open hand. The moss green marble with white and brown speckles was the right one. She held her favorite to the light. The clear spot at the end showed a murky sparkle—exactly what should be at the bottom of the pool. She put it to her lips, whispered something to herself, and dropped it in. It sank with a soft plunk and disappeared. She turned to find eggs.

Gulls swooped, screaming, as she crossed back over the top of the island, but Maud was armed with the rest of her bait. She threw it and the gulls winged off, preferring an easy meal to fighting. With the birds distracted, Maud found one kittiwake egg and a handful of almost ripe bearberries.

On the beach, Maud coaxed a small fire and set a tin of water to boil. She put the moss into the water with the berries. In another tin she broke the egg and whipped it till foamy. Maud scooped out the moss and poured the beaten egg into the tin. She stirred until egg and water were a smooth yellow foam. She dropped the bearberries into the tin, watching the mixture turn from thick liquid to soft paste. Satisfied, Maud took a clean tin, poured the mix in and set it in cold water, wedged between rocks.

Next she gathered blades of grass and trails of violet-purple beach peas. The blossoms were folded dragonheads with the deepest color at the throat. She left the flowers in the shade while she fashioned a grass circlet. Then she tucked the pea blossoms around the crown and placed it out of sight.

In the meantime, Addie's long strides had slowed. Her disappointment hadn't left, but the sting had burned off. She thought of last year's birthday with lemon cake and coconut icing. A locket from Papa; a book from Mama. *David Copperfield*—here, lost with her. Addie splashed through a low-tide puddle, startling long-legged sandpipers strutting sideways into the shallows. "Stupid birds," Addie muttered.

A seagull landed next to her, its yellow-rimmed eyes and hard beak challenging her for the rock.

"Shoo!" Addie hissed. "Shoo!" The seagull stepped closer. "It's not your birthday, too, is it?"

As Addie came down the dunes, Maud tensed, looking for signs that her mood had worsened. Addie's mouth moved as she talked to herself, transported in an imagined scene. This was Addie at her happiest.

Maud let Addie arrive inside her dream and stop next to the fire. She crouched, poked at the coals, and rested her chin on her arm.

"It's a nice fire, Maud," she finally said.

"Are you hungry?" It wasn't a needed question, but it set them back on good terms. "Stay there."

Addie sneaked a look at Maud's face and decided Maud wasn't making fun, so she went back to poking the fire.

Maud trotted toward the rocks and returned with hands behind her back. "Close your eyes, Addie," she said. As Addie closed her eyes, Maud put the custard on the rock and placed the flower circlet on Addie's head. "Happy birthday, Addie!" She stepped back to get the full effect.

Addie opened her eyes and reached to her hair. She touched the braided grass and the soft flower petals and looked at Maud with the blue of her eyes deepening.

"Oh, Maud," she said, and two big tears rolled down her cheeks.

"It's only grass and flowers, and this isn't cake, just pretend custard." Maud wanted to keep Addie from crying.

Addie stared at the custard, felt a knot tightening in her throat, and said, "It's as good as Cook ever made."

"You haven't eaten it yet, so hold your words."

They didn't bother putting portions onto plates but took spoonfuls from the tin. After the first taste, they looked at each other.

"It's goop," said Maud.

"It's seaweed pudding."

"Don't eat it. It was just an idea."

"A wonderful idea. Thank you."

"You should have a real party. Not this. We can eat another tin of beans in your honor," pronounced Maud. She opened the can and made a face. "It's gone green!"

Addie wrinkled her nose at the smell.

Maud opened another and exhaled. "Good. This one's good."

"But that leaves only one," said Addie, knowing Maud didn't need her to count.

"We can't save them forever," answered Maud and put the beans near the fire.

"It's a grand party," said Addie quickly. "Are there pony rides or lemon ices? Remember how Papa set eight kites flying for your birthday? And Mama's treasure hunts. She makes such clever riddles."

The girls stretched on either side of the fire as evening came on. Maud put more wood in the fire and watched as little blue flames danced along the edges, then flared up, red and yellow to white, encircling the wood. She listened to Addie and saw their backyard, full of Mama's flowers and streaming kites on a late spring wind. She concentrated on the shapes, because if the memory grew, she would see her father tease her mother as she tried to light candles on a cake. They were laughing the way people do when they have everything. The memory almost swamped her, so she pushed her hair off her face and looked at Addie.

"If you could have anything you wanted for your birthday, what would it be? Getting off the island doesn't count."

Addie chewed at the edge of her thumbnail. "I'd really like a new dress."

Maud burst out laughing. Addie half sat up and glared over the flames. Nearly choking, Maud said, "Of course you want a new dress. I want a new dress at this point!" She burst into new fits of laughing.

Addie saw the nonsense in her choice, and she fell onto the sand, laughing so hard she got hiccups.

"What do you want to do now?" Addie asked after a while.

"It's your birthday, you choose."

It was the time between the end of day and the beginning of night. The light was soft, as if a very fine veil had been tossed over everything. The green-topped dunes took on a bluish tinge, the rocks lost their hardest edges, and the sand picked up flecks of violet. The air relaxed, with little currents wafting from the water.

"Teach me to cartwheel," said Addie.

Maud looked up in surprise. "That's what you want to do?"

Addie laughed. "Actually, I want to dance, but you don't know how and probably don't want to learn." She stood up. "Come on. The tide is out, and the sand is perfect."

"The sand is perfect for dancing too," Maud said as she got up. "How about if you teach me to dance, and I'll teach you how to cartwheel?"

She didn't need an answer. They went to the water's edge where the sand was packed hard.

"You're the girl," said Addie, putting her right arm around

Maud's waist. "That means I lead. Put your left hand on my shoulder and hold your right elbow in a firm, graceful square."

"Firm but graceful," repeated Maud.

Addie flicked a glance at her sister to see if she was teasing. Maud's dark eyes laughed in fun, but not at Addie. "The count is one, two, three," she said. "A steady, regular rhythm. When I step forward, you step back with your right foot, then bring your left foot next to it on two. Then step right with your right foot on three. Then repeat."

"That leaves my left foot stranded by itself."

"What?"

"Doesn't the left foot join up again?"

"Yes, of course it does."

"Wouldn't that be four?"

"No. That would be a march."

"I don't understand."

"Let's just try. You move to the music."

"But we haven't any music."

Addie let go of Maud and stepped back. Her eyes were bright, wanting this so much.

"Maybe the ocean can be the music," said Maud.

Addie stared at her. Small, smooth waves broke one after the other in a long, slow beat. Addie put her arm around Maud's waist again. "Yes, listen to the ocean," she said.

They danced and stumbled and laughed and swung each other along the beach. After many tries, they found a kind of rhythm and Maud put her heart into it, so that Addie led her in graceful arcs. The stars were out and the sea left a pearly shine as it washed back from the shore. The moon came up, lopsided, but large enough to send a path across the sea.

Addie let her arms drop. "You know what I'd like?" Maud shook her head. "I'd like to sleep under the pine trees. Just for tonight."

Maud watched her face. "All right."

They walked back to their camp, grabbed the rug and water jar, and trudged up the dunes and across the island to the stand of jack pines.

The smell of pine strengthened, and a thin breeze moved the needles from side to side. Addie let out a long sigh. "Just wait," she said. She closed her eyes and breathed in. "It smells like solid land."

She had asked to sleep here. She hadn't said why. She didn't have to. Night coolness drifted in, and they smelled the salt of the island. They heard the sway and rustle of pine needles as the wind brushed past. It sounded a little bit like home, just for tonight.

14

We're Two Whole Girls

June 24 and the sun baked the sand and turned the slow ocean into silver-blue tin. Very little stirred, and listless breakers collapsed repeatedly down the beach. Biting sand flies erupted in the heat, causing Addie to take her book up onto the rocks, but after twenty minutes, her chemise sticking, she climbed back down. Maud was nowhere in sight.

Probably poking in a tide pool, Addie thought, then wondered if Maud was finding food. She pulled her heavy curls off her neck and piled them on her head. She didn't want Maud's company, the camp, or the dunes. On the island Addie felt exposed. The wind came at her and flapped her clothes as she reached the eastern edge and looked across the glinting sea. She was tired of openness, sun, and wide spaces. She had walked as far as she could, and a boulder blocked her path. She inched around it and found that it was part of a lopsided triangle that formed a shallow cave twenty feet above a small cove.

She dropped to her hands and knees. There was enough room to turn around, sit with her back against the wall, and let her feet stretch over the ledge. She shoved her parasol to the side and sighed deeply. She rested her head and closed her eyes. She would never hide to scare Maud, but she needed this place the way Maud needed to ramble through tide pools.

Addie drew the faded letter from her waistband. She didn't want to share it with Maud. She put on her glasses and unfolded the petal-soft paper. The first word, very dark, like too much ink had come out, was *Dear,* no, not *Dear, Dearest.* The name was blurred. Maybe a *G* or a *C*. Most of the words were smudged with age, but one phrase ran above the fold, protected. *Waiting for you*. Words before it and after, she couldn't make out. Other words scattered about the page: *fleet, tomorrow, father,* and *sometime.*

She put the letter on her lap, took off her glasses, and stared at the very blurry page. The writing was wavery, an almost thing, soon and easily lost. She closed her eyes, chin resting on her knees. The cave could have fit two. Addie didn't want two. She wanted herself and her daydreams. She had learned the word *solitude* early. She imagined the person who wrote the letter and knew it was a woman. A sad, long-ago letter that had been cherished. She thought of the man who had loved her and would never see her again, and then of the woman who had sent the letters and waited. She thought about the last letter the woman had sent.

The sea lifted and slapped as a seal came out of the water and perched below her. Its belly was covered in constellations of shaded speckles, the animal's sleek fur reflecting molasses, mahogany, and near magenta. Its eyes were black velvet buttons and the whiskers spun gold in the fingering afternoon sun.

Addie lay on her stomach, stretched her legs behind her, and rested her head on her folded arms. The seal lay drying and motionless like an enormous egg. Addie thought of the letter. She knew about Selkies, enchanted creatures changing from seal to human. "You're beautiful!" Addie whispered.

The seal slid into the water, its skin glistening as its body curved. Addie had seen hundreds of seals basking on the rocks off Ketch Harbor, barking softly and gliding better than swans. She imagined listening to their husky breathing and running her hand along the smooth sweep of their heads and backs.

She followed the arcs the seal made and put her cheek

against the boulder. The sky was white with heat, and to the east the horizon blurred. The seal came into the shallows and floated. Addie felt an ancient sorrow. She thought of the man they had buried. Maybe this was enchantment. Maybe this Selkie was the woman who had written the letters, searching for him. Now that he was buried, maybe the enchantment was broken.

Addie dozed. When she woke, the seal was gone. Nowhere in the slow swells could she make out its shape. She traced its outline on the wet rocks, and something splashed just offshore.

She walked along the north cliffs with Selkies on her mind, until she heard the high-pitched squawk of a strange bird. It came twice and wasn't anything she had heard before. She followed the bleats, nearing the grove of pine trees, and found the source.

Maud sat under the pines with a blade of grass between her knuckles and held to her mouth. Her cheeks puffed and the sound came again. Addie stopped in front of Maud and sang with the staccato notes: "Row, row, row your boat, gently down the stream. Merrily, merrily, merrily, merrily, life is but a dream."

Maud's face was red from blowing and she burst out laughing at the end of the song. "Not too bad for a grass flute!"

"Do it again," commanded Addie as she sat beside her.

Maud put the reed back to her lips and puffed out the stilted notes while Addie sang the words. They laughed again.

"I wish I had my flute," said Maud.

"I wish I had my piano," answered Addie.

They sat quiet, then Maud said, "I don't think a piano is possible, but the right-sized bird bone could work. I'm going to find one."

"Not now," pleaded Addie. "Stay and sing with me."

Maud leaned against the trunk and said, "Name a song and I'll see if I can play it."

"The Women of Ipswich," was Addie's immediate request.

"That has more notes." Maud put the grass to her lips and blew out a series of squeaks. It almost sounded like a song. She tried again and blew longer on some notes than others.

"That was a goose call."

"You try it." Maud offered the grass to her sister.

"I'm not putting my mouth on that. Not after you've blown all over it."

"Then don't make fun." Maud tried again to blow a tune, but Addie raised and lowered her eyebrows, first one then the other. It was the one trick Maud could never learn to do. Her breath and her concentration went. She blew a great blast of air, then sang the song and Addie joined her. After, they fell quiet.

It was still hot, but there was shade. The jack pines, with low, knobbed branches, made clumped shadows, some of them quite dense. The ground was stubbed with loose stones and sparse grass. "Tell me what you're thinking about," said Addie.

Maud looked at her, a little surprised. "Not much. Kites, I guess."

"You think about kites a lot. Why?"

"It's a way to get started. It moves me along to think about other things."

"Like what?"

"How the wind changes direction without warning. How some birds swoop together, and others fly alone. How string is just strands that aren't strong enough to hold a button but wound together they can pull you down a road or around the world. Things like that."

Addie looked closely at Maud as she talked. "I always thought you just did things, Maud. I never knew you thought about them."

"You have to think about things. Just like you did with the marbles."

Addie considered. Maud added, "I could have said the same thing about you only in reverse."

"What do you mean?"

"That you just thought about things. I never knew you could do them."

"I don't do much."

"That's not true. Think about the seaweed and the plants. And now marbles too."

The sun gave up most of its glare. They walked back to camp and ate a few mussels and dulse. Maud pulled the ball of string from her pocket, unraveled it, and tied the ends together. She wound it around her fingers, crossed it between her hands, and looped it over her thumbs until she had a suspended spider web.

Addie, beside her, leaned against the boat, her eyes drifting to the deepening blue sky. Maud slipped the twists off her middle fingers, adjusted the tightness, made loops onto her thumb and forefingers, and pulled tight, making a string figure called three trees. She let the string droop and shook it off. She re-looped and crossed the string. This time, she used her teeth to pull the string so she could poke in her fingers. She produced a drawbridge in a string frame. She was proud of this one. Even Tavis struggled with it.

As the sun hit the rim of ocean, Addie asked her a question. "How long do you think the fishing boat has been on the island?"

It was the question Maud didn't want to think about. Maud knew why Addie had asked and considered her answer. She loosened the twine, adjusted the loops, and formed a Jacob's ladder.

"A few years," she said.

A gnat hummed with the rhythmic hiss of breakers. Addie stared at the blackened boards from last night's fire. They had been slow to catch, soggy with damp and decay. But the dry seaweed, along with bits of driftwood, had turned the smoldering into a momentary blaze.

"No one's coming for us, are they?" Addie blurted. "No one sees our fire. No one will come around that point to our rescue." Addie's voice rose.

"We don't know if anyone sees the fire or not," Maud answered. The string was slack in her hands as the tide crept up the beach.

"It's no use, Maud. You don't have to pretend. No one came for the fishing boat either."

Maud untied her string and wadded it up. "He was hurt, and he crashed."

"What's the difference?" Addie asked.

"We're not hurt. We didn't crash. We have our boat. We can get off this island."

Addie eyes flew wide and stared into the dark.

Neither slept well. The next morning they were up and across the island, scouting for eggs. By June 25, most eggs were too old or had hatched. Egg-laying season was past. The sky was low and humid with a skittish wind. The marram grass arched and swayed and jittered as if shaken at its base.

They were on the north edge of the island. Addie picked up from the night before. "No one's coming for us." Maud took her elbows off her knees but didn't answer. Addie paced the rocks, whacking the grass. "If no one came for him... I mean, he died and he had a real sailboat. He was a sailor. And he died!" Her voice was strangled. "No, I don't think anyone's coming. It's been too many days."

Maud paced alongside. "But we didn't crash or drown! We're right here! We have to be found!" Addie looked everywhere but at Maud, who flung her arms out to show how easy they were to find.

"I don't know why," said Maud. "They must have looked, but they didn't find us."

"That man, he died here and maybe they looked for him too." Addie dared a look at Maud.

Her eyes reminded Maud of a horse gone wild with terror.

"Maybe, Addie. But he was broken before he landed."

"That doesn't change his not being found. He's still here!" It was an impossible cry and her face shattered.

"I'm scared too," said Maud and hooked her arm through Addie's. They paced in silence, letting the wind say how small they felt.

"There's one difference," said Maud after a long while. "He was alone." Addie pulled in her elbow, pressing Maud's arm closer. "I know what you're going to say," Maud continued, as if warming to an argument. "He was a grown man with all the proper rigging. But any good sailor knows you don't go out alone. We're two whole girls."

Addie stopped dead. "What are you saying?" She shook her head from side to side. "No, Maud. That's not an idea I can allow."

Neither spoke. Addie pulled away from Maud and paced harder. Maud watched, then sat on a rock where she could look down the cliff. The puffins dove, plunging into the sea and surfacing with a dozen herring in their beaks. The eggs were hatched, the little ones plump and new experts at plummeting from rocks. Puffins dropped into the ocean and bobbed about. Maud waited for them to go under or paddle back to the cliff. The largest one tipped left and right as its feet worked underneath, propelling a determined line away from the island. Others followed, making a string, like a rope buoy. More puffins slipped into the water and joined the undulating line.

"Noooo!" she yelled. "You can't goooo!"

"What's wrong?" Addie gripped Maud's arm.

Maud's body shook with gulping sobs. "They can't go!" she cried.

"Who's going?" Addie turned Maud to face her and gave her a little shake. "Maud! Who can't go?"

Maud's sobs overwhelmed her, her head sank, and tears fell down her front and splashed the ground. She pointed.

Addie saw bright dots of puffins, the ripple of waves, herring gulls diving for food, and the ever-changing blue. "What, Maud?" She rubbed the back of her hand over Maud's cheek.

Maud pulled herself free. She wiped her hands over her face and pushed her hair off her forehead. "The puffins," she said. "They're leaving the island."

Addie laughed. "Why would they do that? This is their home." She pointed out to the ocean. "They're swimming the way they always do."

Maud shook her head. "They're not just swimming, Addie. They're leaving because it's time."

Addie looked from Maud to the birds and back again. "Time for what?"

She knew the answer and watched the birds. More birds were in the water working their way out to sea. The first birds were dots, their orange beaks and white faces barely noticeable on the limitless sea. Addie sat beside Maud and put her head in her hands.

"I like their company," said Maud. Addie nodded. "They don't stay all year," Maud added. She sneaked a look at Addie and said, "They have another home."

Maud watched the puffins, still fishing and teaching young ones to dive, and kept her eyes off the string of birds stretching away.

"All right," Addie said. Maud's eyes were questioning. "Let's go." Addie stood up.

"We have to make a plan," answered Maud. "We have to get ready."

Waiting, preparing to leave the island frightened Addie more than launching out right away. She didn't want to think or notice the water or the wind or her own heartbeat. "Can't we just go?"

"Yes," said Maud. "Let's look at the boat."

This satisfied Addie enough to keep fear from swamping her. They tromped back to camp and the walk settled them, brought them back from the fierce cliffs and wild ocean. Their cove was safety, home. Here, the talk of leaving seemed a little foolish and rash. Addie opened her mouth to say so, then saw the fire pit and the bucket of mussels. It wasn't enough that she was sick of mussels and seaweed. Or how often Maud couldn't catch a fish. Summer wouldn't last. She looked, really looked, at their little camp. They wouldn't last.

Maud was around the back of the dinghy. Her pocketknife was out and she poked at the bottom and sides. Addie watched. Maud walked to the stern and wiggled the transom. "This is firm," she said. She walked around the boat, pulling at the gunwales and peering at the centerboard.

"It's the caulking," she announced when she came back to Addie. "It leaked because it wasn't properly caulked." She was going to add "in the storm," but left that part out. A storm wasn't a good thing to think about. "Help me put it flat."

She crawled under the boat and pulled out the hamper, the tins, and their shoes, tossing them to the side and pulling the stones from under the lip of the boat. Addie pulled at the other pile of stones, lowering the boat by inches until it lay flush on the ground. Maud scrambled onto the bottom and inspected the cracks between the boards, brushing her hands along the wood.

"It's not too bad," she announced, sitting up on her heels

and looking down at Addie. "It'll swell in the water and that will help."

Addie squinted up. "Do you think it will hold?" She hadn't forgotten storm water sloshing around their ankles as they bailed.

Maud shrugged and turned her palms up. "It needs to be caulked," she said.

"What exactly is caulking?" Addie asked.

Maud turned in surprise. "It's paste, like glue. It hardens."

"But what's it made of?"

Maud almost said chalk because it sounded like caulk, but that didn't make sense. "Just paste, I guess."

Addie went back to staring at the boat. "There must be something."

Maud kicked the sand with her toe. "We should eat," she said and turned to the mussels. There was nothing left to burn, not even using Addie's glasses. She picked out a bit of mussel and squeezed it between her fingers. "They're like erasers," she said. After swallowing, she added, "I'm tired of being hungry."

Addie squatted next to her. "I'm sick of dried seaweed."

"I think about bread. Bread and soup."

"Bread!" Addie laughed. "I dream of cake and blueberry pie!"

"Roast chicken! Apple turnovers! Cucumbers!"

"Cucumbers? You hate cucumbers."

"Only in sandwiches. Sliced cucumbers and radishes! Summer food."

"Lemon ice."

"Hot tea."

"Mashed potatoes."

"A bath!" They laughed and got quiet.

"It's all right. We'll figure it out," Addie said. Maud didn't look at Addie, and Addie didn't look at her, but she nodded. "Eat some mussels."

Their thoughts stayed with the dinghy as they ate salty, tough mussels. It wasn't a real meal, but it kept their stomachs from crimping for a while.

Maud said, "Let's take the book up to the pines and read."

It was exactly what Addie needed to push away the caulking problem and the image of puffins leaving.

They walked the small path they had worn across the dunes. Maud carried the rug and Addie had the book and water jar. Addie began where David is at school with Traddles and Uriah Heep is very creepy. She read several chapters until Maud snored quietly. Addie closed her eyes and let the story in the novel mix with the story of the island. She was almost asleep when Maud said, "Sap."

15

It Worked in the Book

"What?" Addie blinked.

"Pine sap. It could work." Maud sat up. She pointed at the trees. "We can smear it into the cracks. It might hold."

They fell asleep, but in the morning, Addie said, "Might hold?"

Maud went to a tree and pushed at the bark where sap oozed to the surface. "It's very sticky. Let's try." Maud ran toward the camp. It was June 26.

"What are you doing?" Addie called.

"Getting tools!" came Maud's diminishing voice.

Addie stepped close to a tree and peered at small beads of amber-colored goo seeping from cracks in the bark. She walked to another and looked and then another. By the time Maud came back, Addie had an idea of what the problem might be.

Maud had the beach pail and a clamshell. She got right to work, scraping pitch from the nearest tree. Getting it off the shell and into the bucket was hard work. The sap was excellent glue, but it didn't move as she wanted it to.

"Will it dry?" Addie asked.

"What do you mean?"

Addie pointed to the tree trunks. "This sap has been here for days, maybe weeks. It's not dry."

"It doesn't have to be dry. It just has to cover the cracks."

"Will it spread?"

Maud scraped another glob from a tree and tried to put it

in the bucket. The clamshell stuck to the side of the bucket. "Let's go try," she said.

At the boat, Maud tried to smear sap between two boards. The shell stuck and the sap remained a ball of goo. She worked at it, pushing and prodding the pitch into the seam, but it didn't sink in. Maud's face tightened as she pushed at the sap. The shell chipped and the shard stuck to the side of the boat.

"Hell!" shouted Maud. She clanged the pail and dented it against the boat. She swung again and again. Her face reddened as her arm kept up its arc. The pail dented again and again.

Addie, back on a rock, opened her book and read out loud. At first Maud didn't hear, but the story made a room that let her escape from her anger. Maud dropped the pail and sat down. The story unwound and things got worse and worse for David Copperfield. Both girls despised Uriah Heep very much.

Addie was turning a page in chapter twenty-four, when she said, "Guano!" Maud thought it was part of the novel and waited to hear what it meant. But Addie didn't continue. Maud twisted to look at her sister. "Guano might work," said Addie.

"Guano?" repeated Maud, her face crinkled in disbelief. "Where did you get a word like that? Guano. What does it mean?"

"We can use it to fix the boat." They stood beside the dinghy. "Puffins make it. We can use their guano. Let's go look."

Maud stared at Addie as if she had sprouted antlers.

"Where did you get this idea?" asked Maud.

"I heard it somewhere," Addie answered.

"Oh," said Maud and turned away. "I was afraid of that. You never saw anyone really using it."

"How would I know someone who uses guano?" scoffed Addie. "People wouldn't talk about it at a social or croquet."

Maud had no other ideas, and they had to fix the boat. Pine

sap wouldn't stop the leaks. She shrugged. "All right, show me."

On the island's northern shore, the wind blew fiercely, lifting their hair. "Where is this guano?" demanded Maud, hands on hips.

"You're standing on it," replied Addie. She pointed to the grayish coating on the rocks.

"It's poo, Addie. Nothing but puffin poo!" blurted Maud.

"What did you think guano was?"

"I thought it held their nests together or coated their eggs. Guano!" Maud said the word in a deep, sing-song voice, testing the sound against its meaning. "G...u...a...noooo. G...u...a...n...ooooo. Addie, calling it guano doesn't make it more useful. What made you think we could save ourselves with poo?" Maud was disgusted and turned to walk away.

"I read it in a book," said Addie quietly.

"You read about poo in a book!" Maud swung back toward her sister. "What kind of book talks about guano?" Maud laughed as she talked, but Addie ignored the mocking.

"It was a book about sailors whose ship sank, and they were washed up on a South American shore. Their lifeboat was saved, but it was battered and not seaworthy. They filled the cracks with bird guano." Maud stared, disbelieving. "It worked in the book," Addie added. Then she, too, turned from the smeared rocks and chucking puffins.

Maud looked about. She squatted and poked a finger into the muck. "It's slimy on top," she offered, and dug deeper. "Gooey down further, then it turns pretty hard. I don't know." She sat back on her heels as Addie started to walk away. "It might stop the leaks if we work it between the boards. We don't have anything else to try." Maud stood and squinted around. "There's enough of it. We'll use the pail and one of the tins. Is that okay?"

Addie retraced her steps. "That's what you're good at, Maud, the practical bits that make ideas work."

The wind made little whirls of sand that gritted their skin.

"Let's start before it gets dark."

They raced over the island's uneven crest to gather tools. Using a clam shell, Maud dug guano from between rocks on the bluff. Addie dug powdered caulking from between the dinghy's boards. "Don't scrape it all away," Maud told her. "We can't redo the whole boat. Look for places where daylight shows through the cracks."

Addie combed the boat bottom for soft spots and loose caulking. The sun beat on the back of her neck and hands, but she didn't see the shadows shrinking, then growing long as they rotated from north to east. She was so intent, she jumped when Maud arrived and said, "I have a full bucket, enough to start."

Maud held the bucket of gray-white guano, her hands caked, her cheeks smeared with sand and dirt. Her dark hair was tangled like scrambled seaweed. Grass stains and guano streaked her chemise. Addie looked at her own hands and chemise. Caulking and wood stain embedded her skin. Her hair looked no better than Maud's.

"We have to keep going before it dries." Maud put the tin next to the boat and surveyed Addie's work. Addie waited for criticism about not doing things right. But Maud bit her lip, gave the boat a once over, and said, "It looks good. I'll start here while you finish scraping."

Maud scooped guano from the tin and pasted it into the cracks between each board. Addie resumed scraping. They worked at either end of the boat until Addie stepped back, cocked her head to one side, and said, "That's it. I've scraped it all."

Maud walked the length of the boat, inspecting crevices. "Good. Now help me with the guano." She picked up her shell and continued cramming goo into cracks.

Addie took up her shell and walked to the bucket of bird poo. Holding her breath, she scooped a tablespoon onto her shell and applied it to the boat.

"You have to work it in with your thumbs," Maud pointed out. "Make sure it gets in and sticks."

Addie scooped a bigger glob from the bucket and tried to push it into a space between boards. Acid bit at the back of her throat and stung her eyes. She blew a big breath to clear her lungs and smeared more paste, but another whiff choked her. She coughed, eyes watering. "I can't stand it, Maud. It's no use."

Maud set her chin and kept on, face shiny with sweat and arms covered with guano. Addie threw down the shell. "This is disgusting and it's not working. Do you hear me?"

Maud straightened and glared at Addie, her mouth bunched.

Addie marched to the water's edge, scrubbed her hands and face in the salty water, then walked away from Maud, the boat, and the stench. She had done her part. Every fingernail was split. Her hands blistered, her neck stiff, she talked to herself as she walked. "Maud's so stubborn. Guano won't fix the boat. It's not a real idea."

Addie walked over the dunes until she came to a hollow. She sat rigidly, expecting relief. Small grasshoppers didn't respond nor did the gulls. She flung her head back and stared at the slow clouds, white scraps on dashing blue. She should have stayed to help, but it was ridiculous and disgusting to smear stinking paste into crevices. Why had she suggested it? And it wasn't hardening the way the book described that it should.

Maud whistled "Down by the River Dee." Addie's eyes welled up and spilled over because Maud was trying so hard. Addie felt helpless and stupid. This time Maud was wrong. Maud couldn't be clever enough to get them home, even if she was so full of noticing it spilled out like sunlight through a crack.

Addie uncurled her legs and sweat trickled down her neck. She wanted to disappear, so she pulled off her petticoat and draped it over the hollow, weighing the edges with stones. She crawled under her tent and closed her eyes. Grasses rustled and gulls cried overhead. She was nearly asleep when the petticoat vanished, replaced by Maud, arms akimbo, at the rim of the hollow.

"You are an absolute frivolity, Adelaide Campbell."

The next morning, June 27, the sun floated over the horizon as a pink-orange bubble. Maud opened her eyes and watched sparks of white flash and disappear as the wind clipped the waves. She arched her back, stretched, and looked at her sleeping sister.

Addie's hair covered most of her face and her breathing was deep and steady. Maud rubbed sleep out of her eyes and brushed grit off her arms and legs. She strolled the beach, scattering curlews. The movement brought back her dream. Tavis had taught her to build a kite with butcher paper and dowels, a painted dragon on the front with a gold silk tail.

"That's a right fine kite, Maud," Tavis had said. "She's a goer."

Maud tried not to show how pleased she was. When the dragon danced in the wind, she felt as if she had a live beast on the string. "It's flying ever so high!" she shouted.

Her kite was nothing compared to the box kites, double-winged kites, and butterfly kites that Tavis made. But she had cut, glued, and tied it. Tavis had said, "Send her up!"

The dream made her happy but made her think she had forgotten to tell Addie something. She couldn't think what it was. She found a perfect sand dollar and her worries about the dream disappeared.

When Addie woke, they discussed how to get the boat ready. "Would a petticoat make a good sail?" Addie asked. "We don't have anything else."

Maud agreed they would have to try the petticoat. The rigging had been coiled in the bottom of the boat when they set out and it lay on the sand along with the oars and the dismantled mast and boom. Maud used her string to measure the mast and boom, and the girls laid out stones in a triangle. Addie stretched her petticoat inside the outline.

"It's not the right shape," she called over her shoulder.

Maud, still caulking the dinghy's gaps, didn't answer. Brushing her hair out of her eyes, Addie sat cross-legged and pulled the petticoat toward her. Holding the fabric taut between the fingers of her left hand, she used a wing bone's sharp point to slice the seam threads.

The edges of fabric parted as Addie sliced and pulled, her head bowed over her lap, her fingers working the tension. She imagined the boat under full sail with Maud pulling the boom to catch the wind. She was surprised at how capable her own hands were, one hand tight with tension, the other attacking with the bird bone. With a last stab, the cloth pieces fell apart. Addie shook out the length of muslin and laid it within the triangle of stones.

"It fits!" she called. Maud came to look. "Isn't it perfect?" Addie asked

"It's about the right size, but I don't know if it will hold the wind."

"What do you mean, 'hold the wind'?"

Maud felt the fabric's weight. "A stiff wind needs a stiff sail. Otherwise, it will be a lace flag." She looked from the spread fabric to the overturned boat. She pictured it with the right kind of sail. Her head hurt.

Addie pursed her lips and draped the muslin across her hand. "How stiff does it have to be?" she asked.

"Like canvas."

"We don't have canvas. How much stiffer than this?"

"As stiff as we can make it," Maud replied and walked back to the boat.

Addie had thread from her other glove, but no needle. She examined a slender bone, put on her glasses, and rolled it between thumb and forefinger. Tiny holes let the sun through at one end. Addie licked a thread end and pointed it at the hole. After more tries than she could count, she gave up.

Thinking to split the bone down the center and make a thinner needle, she placed a flat rock on her lap and aligned the edge of a clam shell with the length of the bone. With the ends steady, she pressed down. Nothing. Gritting her teeth, she jabbed the shell down, heard a crack, and felt the shell hit stone. The bird bone lay in three pieces. Addie lifted the longest one. One end had a hairline split to hold the thread. She sharpened the other end until she had a sharp point, very like a needle. She started to shout her success to Maud, but better, she thought, to show Maud the finished sail. Maud would have figured out a needle sooner.

The makeshift needle stuck and puckered the fabric, but Addie got the thread through enough times to hold the two pieces of fabric together. The silk thread often slipped from the needle, but she kept on. Before the island, she would never have worked so hard. She hummed a made up song about the small clouds overhead being mistaken for a swarm of bees. She never looked up, concentrating on how to stiffen the fabric.

Maud didn't notice the clouds as she scooped and smeared guano, using the shell's edge to force it into cracks. She put her face close and crawled along the overturned boat like a beetle. White goo covered her hands and acid burned her nose and eyes. Now and again, she knelt up, shook the hair out of her eyes, and assessed her progress. She worked fast, trying to complete her task before the sun and air dried and hardened the guano into the wood.

"Sap might work now," she said to the boat. She picked up the guano-crusted tin and walked to the water, letting small waves lick her feet. She sat, filled the tin with saltwater, and pushed her hands into the damp sand. The salt and grit bit into her cuts and scratches. Wincing, she pushed deeper, grabbing it through her fingers to rub the guano off. She pulled her hands free and rubbed them against each other, ignoring the red spots sprouting on her skin as she grated the sand back and forth.

Brushing her hands down her chest, Maud felt the guano there. She rubbed sand on her face, her neck, and along her arms and legs, then pulled off her chemise and ground it into the sand. She walked into the ocean until she was waist deep, submerging the chemise, twisting it and scrubbing the cotton. Again and again, she dunked her head and scrubbed her hair until her face and body were red, her hands raw, and her chemise limp. She waded out, wringing the chemise with a fierce twist before pulling it back over her head. The guano left a gray stain, and Maud's efforts to clean it left the chemise a sorry version of itself. She didn't care. The salt water had scoured the guano, but her eyes, nose, and lungs burned.

Addie had inched up one edge of the makeshift sail and down another. As she broke off a length of thread with her teeth, Maud's shadow fell across her hands. She took off her glasses and peered up. "Maud?"

Maud looked strange, pale, with something odd in her eyes. Addie blinked as Maud crouched next to her, but now Maud seemed fine. A trick of the light.

"The caulking is done," said Maud in a low voice. She pushed at her hair with the back of her hand and slumped next to Addie. "I'll put a layer of pine sap over it tomorrow to make sure." She looked at the stitching but didn't really see it. All of a sudden she roused herself and said, "Let's turn the boat over and see if we have rigging."

Addie was about to protest, but Maud's face stopped her. Maud was already out at sea and didn't want anything in her way. It was a stubbornness Addie knew not to argue with.

They rolled the boat right side up. Maud climbed in, and, with Addie's help, fitted the mast through the deck to the hull, making sure the slot for the sail faced the stern. With Addie supporting the boom, Maud attached it to the mast with the gooseneck. She set up the standing rigging ropes that held the mast in place. The shroud lines kept the mast from tipping sideways and ran through turnbuckles on either side of the deck. To keep the mast from wiggling back to front, she ran a line forward to the bow and secured it. The mast wobbled a little, but she didn't know what she could do about it. Finally, she started on the running rigging, called halyards, to pull the sail up and down. She fastened lines called sheets to the boom to move it left and right to catch the wind. As she worked, Maud showed everything to Addie.

Maud talked as if she were running out of time. Addie knew something about sailing; she knew the names of the rigging, the cleats, and the blocks, but she liked Maud's explanations. When the rigging was in place, Maud sat on the rear thwart and looked at the top of the mast.

"It's going to work," said Addie. "Everything we need is here."

"Do you remember about wind, Addie? Do you remember how to tack and haul in the sheets?" Maud's eyes were shining.

Addie thought Maud was excited. "A little bit. But you're the sailor."

Maud had taken the lines and shifted the boom when Papa and Captain Dresner took them out in his sloop. Addie loved the wind in her hair and the thrill of the bow wave as they coursed through the water, but Maud watched how a boat reacted when a line was pulled.

Maud jumped onto the sand and drew diagrams. She drew

a circle divided into fourths. In each quarter, she drew a small boat. "If the wind comes from this direction, you want to sail this way." She pointed to two of the boats. "That's called reaching because the wind is coming at a slant. If you want to go the other way, and the wind is the same, that's called running, because the wind is behind you. Jibing or tacking is when the wind is coming at you from a slant and you want to go forward. You have to change directions by bringing the sail in on one side, letting the boom cross over the boat, and letting the sail out on the other side." Maud talked faster and faster.

"What if the wind comes from this way?" Addie pointed to one of the boats in the circle.

"You have to listen, Addie!" Maud's voice was sharp and high. "I can't explain it again."

Maud's voice frightened Addie. "I'll be your first mate," she said. "You can order me to swab the decks or anything. I'll watch you." Maud rubbed her eyes and sat back on her heels. All the air had gone out of her. "Are you all right, Maud?" Unease rose in Addie as she watched her sister's face.

"My head hurts, that's all. I stayed in the sun too long." Maud walked toward the carriage rug, her eyes closed as a dizzy spiral engulfed her.

Addie stopped asking questions. She knew Maud hated anyone fussing over her. Addie went back to her task, moving the needle in and out around the perimeter. The sun had dropped over the west end of the beach when Addie finished. Smoothing the cloth over the dune grass, she weighted the three corners with stones and admired her work. She was very proud of her sail.

16

Just Like Dancing, Remember

Maud was still asleep on June 28 when Addie woke. Guessing it was because Maud had worked so hard, Addie climbed the dunes and examined the finished sail. As she ran her hand over the fabric, she understood how to stiffen the fabric. "Maud!" she called. "Maud! The sail will hold the wind!" Maud faced east, away from camp, her head hanging between her shoulders. "Maud?"

Maud put up a hand to stop her sister from coming nearer. With a spasm Maud bent forward and threw up. Addie's mouth turned down in disgust, but she didn't turn away. She waited as Maud doubled over and retched. Sweat covered Maud's face and her chest moved rapidly in and out. She tried to take deep breaths to settle her stomach, but another heave thrust her forward. Addie knelt beside Maud. Before she had her hand on Maud's face, Addie knew something was very wrong. Maud's eyes were glassy, and her cheeks were hot.

"I feel rotten," Maud said. "Maybe I ate something bad."

"I ate the same things you did. Maybe it's the sun."

Addie put the back of her hand to Maud's forehead. "How many times did you throw up, Maud?"

"I don't know, a few." Maud moaned and retched again.

When she sat up, her face was pale and her freckles were dark stones after the rain. Quivers went through her as if a chill breeze swept the island.

"Can you come back to camp?" Addie put her arm around her sister's shoulder.

Maud wobbled to her feet and they limped to the boat and

their camp. "Lie down, Maud. You'll feel better in a bit." Addie
pulled the carriage rug under the shade of nearby boulders.
She smoothed the sand and adjusted the rug so that Maud
could lie with her head raised. Maud dropped to the rug and
curled on her side, worn out by retching.

"My head is stabbing all over," Maud said.

"Does anything else hurt?"

"My legs and arms hurt something awful. Like they're being
stretched or someone threw rocks at them. My chest is on
fire." Maud closed her eyes and groaned, breathing with her
mouth open.

"You worked too hard on the boat. You'll be better soon."
Addie patted Maud's shoulder and watched her eyes close.
"Should I read to you?"

Maud nodded yes, and Addie started where little Emily is
lost and her father searches everywhere for her. Addie wished
she had brought a book that didn't have so many troubles. She
wanted to ask Maud questions, to keep her talking. She wanted
Maud's company.

As Addie started a new chapter, Maud moaned. It wasn't
a hurt moan, it was a getting lost moan. Maud's cheek was a
dry flame and she shivered. Addie pulled the rug around her.
"It's all right. It's all right," she repeated. Maud shivered again
and her body spasmed, her eyes wide, not seeing. She slid into
a sleep that wasn't any kind of rest. Addie was terrified. She
hugged Maud, tears coming fast. Then she was up and running. Grass blades whipped her ankles and rocks jutted into
her path as she made for the basin. She held the jar so tight the
edges bit her side.

Addie pounded across the island, interrupting insect drones,
her breath high and shallow. She flung herself beside the basin
to scoop rainwater but froze with the jar inches from the
surface. The sun's angle and the stillness of the pool made a

mirror. Addie saw her scared eyes with the blue irises dwarfed by circling white. Her cheeks matched the gray stones and her mouth was pinched and crooked. Her own fear stopped her. It was as if the running and the task held off the truth of Maud's hot face and clouded eyes. Addie gulped and made herself move. She sank the jar and filled it. Then she wiped her face.

"Stiffen up, Addie," she told herself and turned toward the beach. She trotted, trying not to spill any water, but going as fast as possible. Her hair straggled into her eyes as she stepped clumsily over rocks to the sand. In long strides, she was beside Maud, who lay as still as the boulders.

"Maud," whispered Addie, her voice catching. "Maud, I'm back." She slid her arm underneath Maud's shoulders and pulled her half upright. Maud was senseless and inert. She whimpered and Addie squeezed her as her worst fear evaporated.

"Come on, Maud, let's get you comfortable." Addie rolled one end of the rug into a bolster and leaned Maud's shoulders and head against it. She took her handkerchief out of her pouch, wet it, and squeezed water into Maud's mouth over and over. "It's all right, Maud," she repeated. "Everything is all right." She washed Maud's face, her neck, her shoulders and arms. Every part of her was burning. She soaked the cloth again and left it on Maud's forehead.

"It's just a fever. Some sleep and you'll feel better."

Addie talked to Maud and to herself. She read out loud, but it was the same page over and over. All that day Addie watched over Maud and gave her small drinks of water. Maud shivered violently or lay limp. Addie lay beside Maud, cradling her. She ate a little sea lettuce and two cold mussels. She gave Maud water and bathed her face and arms. Maud mumbled and a tight cough erupted through her cracked lips.

"You know I can't," Addie told her. She tucked the rug

around Maud and hummed. "What am I supposed to do?" Addie cried suddenly. She watched Maud closely and in answer to her own question, said, "Just get on with it!"

Addie carried the sail to the ocean, plunged it in, soaked it through, then rung it out. She spread it flat, weighted with rocks. The sailors in her book had wet their sails to work better. The salt might stiffen this one. When it was dry, she tied the line through holes to the far end of the mast. She pulled the corner as tight to the wooden mast as she could. Copying Cook's trick when putting up the laundry line, Addie pulled the rope tight, wet it, and pulled tight again. When it dried, the cord was like twisted wood and only a sharp knife would pry the loops apart.

As she pulled the fabric tight, her confidence grew. She repeated her steps at the other three points of the triangle, threading the rope through the reinforced holes she had made.

When all was tied, Addie pulled on the line that unfolded the sail and brought it to its most upright position. She pulled the line tight, then wound it with a half hitch onto the gunwale cleat. The sail hung like a dog's dejected ears.

"Never mind," she said aloud. But she was at a loss. She sat on a low rock and watched shallow waves scallop the sand. She read aloud, chewed on kelp, gave Maud water, and read more. Eventually the light dimmed and the page was hard to make out. The sun rolled below the edge of the world and pale pinks shifted into mauve and iris.

"Tomorrow," Addie said to convince herself. She looked at the water, at the immeasurable length and width of the rolling, moving surface, and let out an "oh" that broke her own heart. Her fists clenched in her lap. She suddenly turned her back on the deep currents and the fitful winds. She looked hard at the wooden dinghy from prow to stern, took in the newly caulked slats, the gunwales, the oarlocks, and the mast. She looked at Maud, crumpled in the boat's shadow.

"Tomorrow," she said.

Addie watched the eastern sky all through that strange night. She knew she should sleep and would need strength come morning. She had tried to feel drowsy, but each time her body slid into forgetting, a curl of dread stirred until her eyes startled open and she heard Maud's ragged breath. She nestled with Maud, watching the sky that would bring tomorrow with it.

At first more than a few stars showed through veils of low clouds. As the night moved on, the clouds thickened and the air grew heavier. Addie hunched, her eyes on the ocean to see how it reacted to the thickening air. She wasn't sure what to hope for. A storm meant a reprieve from setting out in the dinghy.

Addie wanted her feet on firm ground, to keep on as they had been doing. But Maud was the reason they had survived. Addie put her head on her knees and rocked. Without Maud, they didn't stand a chance in the dinghy. Maud was sick and needed help now. Addie's chest was tight, and she heard the boom of thunder. A cloud mass hung a fair distance off.

Lightning bolts jagged down from the clouds and the thud echoed back to her. Small and self-contained, the storm drifted south, carrying the damp, unmoving air with it. Addie followed the storm as it crackled and lit up the surface of the sea, the thunder like cannon fire. A torrent of rain swept offshore with silvery lines spinning from sky to water, shifting like silk fringe. The ocean paid little heed, with small whitecaps roiling up where the storm hit and moved on. It was like watching a stage storm or the antics of giant firecrackers.

Maud loved fireworks. Addie listened to her breathing, ragged and shallow. Occasionally a cough rasped out and Maud's chest constricted. Her lips bled. Addie soaked the hanky and squeezed it on Maud's mouth. She pushed Maud's hair off her forehead. She dressed Maud in her skirt and middy blouse, then pulled on her own dress. She placed their shoes and stockings in the boat.

"It's not possible," she said as if someone had argued against her. "I can't do this."

There was no other way. She had to point the dinghy off the island toward the open sea. She listened to Maud's uneven breath, then packed the tins, utensils, and jars into the picnic hamper. She had counted on Maud to see this through and expected Maud to navigate and direct the shifting sail. Addie blinked back tears.

"I'm no good at this!" She spoke to the ocean's beating wash. She then cried in earnest, huge tears streaming down her cheeks with her gasping sobs.

"I CAN NOT!!" she yelled. She put her head against the gunwale and let fear drown her.

Morning crept up the beach on June 29, and a wind sprang up, fluttering the sail on the boom. Addie looked up and watched it ripple. "It's a real sail!" she breathed.

Addie wiped her eyes and set her chin and placed the basket into the boat. She ran the gaff hook along the bottom and set the oars so they wouldn't swing loose. She went to the rear of the boat and put her back against the transom, dug her heels into the sand, and pushed with her legs. The boat moved a few feet, then jolted to a stop.

A large rock blocked the boat's path.

"Stupid," she told herself. "Maud would have thought of that."

Dropping to her hands and knees, she dug out the rock and rolled it away from the boat. Learning from her mistake, Addie perused the beach for other stones, shells, or driftwood. She trudged back to the boat and stopped directly in front. The centerline of the boat had dug a V in the sand. Addie put her toe to the nose of the boat where it met the sand, dug in her foot, and dragged it back.

"A channel!" She dug and scraped a shallow ditch from the boat to the water. She went to Maud and leaned over her. "Maud," she whispered. "It's time to get in the boat."

Maud didn't move. Addie thought of the man in the fishing boat and cried, "Maud!" She rocked Maud's shoulder and repeated her name. "Maud, we need to get in the boat." She shook harder.

Maud moved her arms, but her eyes didn't open, and her cheeks were on fire. Addie swallowed and sat back on her heels. Herring gulls made high thin shrieks, and something splashed in deep water. Addie drew a great breath and stood up. She made a stairway with stones next to the boat, testing them to make sure they wouldn't topple. She rested for a half hour, staring at the last pale stars strung across the sky, but their magic couldn't reach her. She rolled Maud onto the carriage blanket, making sure she was securely in the center. As she moved Maud's arms and legs, Maud whimpered.

Addie took the corners by Maud's feet and pulled her toward the boat. It wasn't as hard as she had thought it would be. She had never questioned the idea that Maud was stronger, but Maud was so much smaller now, thin and pinched. Looking at Maud folded in the blanket, Addie realized that an older sister was meant to face things first. She reached the stones near the boat. She rolled Maud off the blanket, put the blanket in the boat, and arranged it on the bottom near the rear thwart. She climbed out and said, "We're getting in the boat. I'm going to carry you."

Addie knelt so they were facing the same way and lifted Maud into a sitting position. She slung one of Maud's arms over her shoulder and put her own arm around Maud's waist. "Okay. One, two, three." Addie, with her right knee on the sand and her left foot pressing down, let Maud lean against her, then heaved up to a half crouch. She adjusted her arm around Maud and pulled them both to near standing. A faint wail came from Maud, so Addie tightened her hold, crouched again, and slid Maud onto her shoulders. "Just like dancing, Maud. Remember?" With a grunt, Addie staggered two steps, steadied, and found the stone steps.

Her right foot found balance on the first stone, and her left foot followed. Her right foot went onto the next stone and tested the weight, then her left foot came up to meet it. Both feet reached the top stone and the gunwale of the boat. Maud was still draped across her shoulders. Using her leg muscles to keep steady, Addie lowered herself to a crouch and swung Maud's legs over the side onto the blanket. Addie eased Maud off her shoulders until she was half folded into the boat. Keeping Maud propped against the side, Addie scrambled in and pulled Maud onto the folded blanket. Addie found the water jar and soaked her cloth. She took Maud's chin and squeezed her mouth open so water from the hanky could drip in. Maud's eyes fluttered, and she moved her head back and forth.

Addie scrambled out. With her back to the transom, and using her legs and back, she shoved the dinghy into the shallows. She climbed in. There was no more time. There was nothing else to do. Small breakers pushed the dinghy back toward shore, and the breeze that promised something sputtered and went faint. Addie sat with indigo sky overhead and the first brush of purple at her back. She let the boat rock, thinking the tide would pull it out, but she had forgotten if it was coming in or going out.

Addie's struggle, her focus, had been on getting their belongings and Maud into the boat. Maud was ashen, with a skim of sweat on her forehead and arms as she slumped between the thwarts. Addie rocked the boat from side to side. Grinding sand mixed with water that splashed as the boat rolled.

"Never mind," Addie said. She said again, "Never mind," for reassurance and clambered over the side. She would have to push the boat until it floated free of the island that had caught and held them safe from deep running currents and Atlantic swells.

"Never mind," Addie whispered as she put her shoulder to the transom, dug her heels into the sand, and shoved with every bit of strength. The boat scraped an inch, then another inch. Addie stepped into the work and heaved again. The boat slid, finding smooth ocean floor that slants down to open water. Cold water grabbed her knees. She pushed until it reached her waist. The little boat swung loose from any grasp of land. Addie guided the boat out and out until the water pulled over her chest. Doing what she had seen Maud do, she thrust herself up and used her arms to vault over the side of the boat. She landed with a scrambling roll nearly on top of Maud, but she was inside the boat without tipping it over.

Addie held on to her meager courage and pulled herself onto the rear thwart next to Maud, assessed their position against the rising sun, and pulled on the lines that moved the sail. Puffs of wind fluttered the cloth but weren't strong enough to fill the sail. Addie pulled the lines, straightening and adjusting tension until the cloth was straight in its frame. The small breeze did not deter her from the image of a softly belled curve. Working the fabric, she gathered handfuls until the cloth was aligned. She fully let out the sail and turned the boom to catch the meager wind.

Above her, the sail luffed and fluttered like skittish leaves. Addie pulled the starboard line tighter and shifted the boom so it jutted over the water. The sail gave a flap, then slowly filled. The dinghy felt the urge and glided after. Addie kept her eyes on the sail and the boat's prow, keeping her back straight and her hand tight on the rope. She kept away from collapse or capsize and set everything toward what she thought was west.

The breeze ruffled Maud's hair and she stirred, causing Addie to look at her sister's face resting against her knee. She had tried to make Maud comfortable, cushioning her with the carriage blanket. She wanted Maud close.

The boat swayed with ocean swells and the motion sent its message of departure. Addie looked back. The little beach lay as she had first seen it. But it wasn't at all the same. Sunlight caught the outermost rocks and tinted them deep purple and mauve. Dune grasses stirred in gold filigree, an invitation to lie in the hollows. The groove where the boat had sat was in shadow. Addie saw the incoming tide lick the footprinted sand where she had shoved the dinghy into the water. Soon, no marks would show the girls had ever been there. Three black-backed gulls swooped and screamed over the dunes. The island lay soft cream and pale green with dark gray rocks at the ends of the embracing crescent.

Addie looked to the eastern point where the seal had circled, to the west where clean stones covered the man's bones, and finally to the place that had been their camp. The small ring of stones that had been their fire looked like safety, and her hand tightened to keep the boom steady, as if the boat itself would reverse direction. She remembered her parasol. It was in the cave. Addie faced the island for a long, long while, swallowing hard. Then the island shrank and was beyond her, sliding behind the work ahead.

17

Wherever We're Going, We're Going Sooner

"Here we go," Addie said.

As shore breakers turned into ocean waves, the sail luffed and filled with steady air. Addie did her best to precede the sun's trajectory as it rose. She planted her feet on the wooden boards, put her hand on the tiller, and guided the fluctuations of the sail by holding tight to the stays. The wind wasn't strong, so there was no chance a direct blow from behind would push the boat toward land. Addie assumed land lay to the west.

She thought about Maud's line drawings in the sand. Addie shifted, careful not to disturb Maud. She watched Maud's parched mouth and her ribs, expanding and deflating by little bits. Maud, in fevered sleep, jostled her head so a clump of hair fell over her face. Addie brought the stay to her right hand, clamped it against the tiller, and brushed Maud's hair back.

At Addie's touch, Maud startled and let out a moan, which set off a coughing spasm that shook Maud's frame. Addie kept her hand on Maud's forehead to steady her. "Hush, Maud," Addie murmured. "I'm here."

The sail flapped, calling Addie's attention back to keeping them on course. "I'm tacking, Maud," she said and pulled the stays so that the sail came about with the boom, crossing from one side of the boat to the other. Addie ducked her head, sat upright, and watched the sail fill. She repeated this action over and over as she watched the sail and kept the boat pointed as best she could along the same path as the sun.

During the high noon hours, Addie struggled. The breezes slackened and the sun burned. She dipped her cloth again and again into the water jar, squeezing it on Maud's lips and then squeezing again over her head to cool her. Every six times she completed this task for Maud, she did it once for herself.

By late afternoon, Addie's back ached, and she worried they were heading in no particular direction. The sea spread endlessly on all sides with long, slow rolls across its surface. Addie hadn't seen a bird for hours. Time stood still. She saw their boat as a minute speck in the middle of an infinite nothing. She wanted to turn back to their days on the island and to the pretend idea that they were safe.

Something splashed to the boat's starboard. A sunfish lay on its side, doing exactly what its name implied. The creamy white fish with buttery markings was six feet from snout to fin and was nearly the same across, forming an oval platter. It was enjoying the August sun and its one visible eye stared comically around. It reminded Addie of Mrs. Milledge, who sat on her front porch pretending to tat lace but taking in everything that passed by.

"Hello, Mrs. Milledge!" Addie called out and laughed. "Maud, Mrs. Milledge is eavesdropping. Let's tell her something scandalous."

Addie stroked Maud's hair and asked the fish, "Have you ever swum naked in the sea, Mrs. Milledge? Have you ever stood in chemise and pantaloons in a summer rain? Have you ever peed while puffins watched? Have you ever buried a skeleton without a priest? No, Mrs. Milledge? You haven't? Well, you haven't lived, and I'm sorry for you. Tell me, Mrs. Milledge, what *have* you done?"

The sunfish had nothing to say for itself but bobbed alongside the boat, as if glad of company in this enormous and empty space.

Addie nibbled on a strip of kelp, checking the position of the sun. Maud spasmed with coughing, the wracking barks sounding as if they might shatter her. Sweat ran down the sides of her face, and her head and hands thrashed.

"Maud, please don't. Be still!" Addie begged her. She squeezed water onto Maud's forehead and wiped her dry mouth. "Hold on, please. Just rest."

The coughs subsided and Maud sank against Addie's knee. Addie kept her hand on Maud's cheek, then bent low and kissed the top of her head. "I can't be out here alone, Maud. You know I can't do this by myself. I need you. I need you to show me," Addie whispered so she couldn't quite hear herself say the truth.

Addie's vision was blurry when she sat up. She rubbed her eyes with the back of one hand and looked around. The sunfish had gone. Looking at the spot where the fish had been, Addie said, "Would you like a story, Maud? I won't say 'once upon a time.' In Africa, a long time ago, there was a queen named Cassiopeia.... She turned into stars and now she shines in the sky every summer night as a lesson for those who care too much about being beautiful."

Addie finished her story and sat quietly. She thought about Andromeda, who hadn't boasted about anything but was chained to rocks. She thought about Perseus rescuing her and about the winged horse. She thought that if she had written the story, she might have had Medusa fight Poseidon. She didn't know what she would have done about Andromeda, but she would have given her more things to say.

The wind that had been so fretful from the west, causing Addie to tack and tack all day over a glassy sluggish sea, veered and backed around to the east. The sudden pressure that nearly took the boom out of Addie's hand put the sail into a frenzy. The dinghy wavered wildly. Addie fought the boom, sending the boat skidding sideways. She hauled on the rigging, remembering Maud's wiggly arrows that meant wind and the triangle that was the sail.

"Never put the sail crosswise to the wind," Maud had said.

Addie tugged the sail one way, then another, trying to tame the boat as it galloped, tipped, and caught broadside waves. She pulled the sail nearly parallel with the center beam of the boat and logic took over. The dinghy skimmed along, knifing slightly atilt, and the sail hummed, sounding pleased with itself. Addie knelt forward with the boom locked under her left arm and the sail rigging wound once around her right fist to keep the sail exact, making adjustments as the wind came on or eased.

"Wherever we're going, Maud, we're going sooner," she said aloud. Maud was senseless beside her, and the coughing had stopped. Addie gripped Maud's face and listened hard. When she saw Maud's eyelids twitch, Addie realized she had been holding her breath. "Sooner," she said again and turned back to the sail.

The dinghy ran before the wind as evening blue deepened behind it. Sequin by sequin the stars showed themselves. Addie wanted the wind. She wanted to fly faster and faster, heading for some kind of end. It wasn't possible, this wild push with the two of them racing between depth upon depth and sky over sky. Addie wanted to stand, to be another mast, her arms wide with clothes loose like wings. She wanted the boat to go like a soaring bird until the wind went through her like a hollow thing.

"If I were to tell you that I'm afraid, you wouldn't be surprised." Addie wasn't sure who she was talking to. She adjusted the sail to catch more wind. The sky deepened to match the blue, placid sea. "No one would be surprised." She had been talking for a while, pausing to hear her sister's breathing. With dark thick clouds obscuring the sky, her own breath had a panicky sound.

"Shall I sing for you, Maud?" Addie tilted her head and stared at iris blue filling in to black and the black showing the tingle of stars. Perseus leaned over winged Pegasus. Cassiopeia sat on the northeast horizon. "Do you remember the song Mama sang when we were small?" Addie asked in a husky voice.

Sleep, my child, for the red bee hums
The silent twilight falls
Eva from the gray rock comes
To wrap the world in thralls

Addie hunched herself together to hold off the chill night damp, as if she might dissolve into the seawater that lapped her toes in the bottom of the boat. She peeked at Maud, swaddled in the coach rug. She was terrified Maud wasn't breathing, but Maud rasped and muttered, which gave Addie hope. She clenched the boom to shift the sail and catch the rising wind. The sky was mostly clear, but dark clouds circled from the north around to the east. If the wind increased, she wouldn't be able to control the boat. She refused the horrible question at the back of her mind, so she put her faith into believing they were pointed west toward land. Her back ached and her legs were so stiff she thought she might never be able to stand again. To keep herself awake and believing, she sang "The Women of Ipswich" the way Maud did, loud and high. Over and over she sang the stanzas into the black bumping sea to keep from thinking of the island and whether she had made a terrible mistake in launching the boat.

The wind came steadily from the northeast and the waves sliced into white spumes. The boat skipped over the peaks, rocking as cross waves slapped the side. Addie, with hand tight on the rudder and the line, was numb. The wind picked up speed and the boat ran headlong, determined and reckless. Addie had no strength to curb its momentum. She didn't want to. She tried to fight off sleep but gave in, only to shudder awake moments later. She hadn't given Maud water since the sun had been swallowed by clumping clouds. That must have been late afternoon. The sky opened now toward morning, June 30.

Addie closed her eyes again, let her head droop. The sail flapped and shook. A dark spot bobbed in the water. She jerked upright. Two eyes and a nose.

A seal, Addie thought. *A Selkie!*

The sight cheered her, and then she remembered the buried skeleton. It meant they were too far out. She trailed a hand in the water. The seal swam close. She stretched her hand to touch. The animal came to the boat and under her hand. Addie's fingers touched fur. Her eyes pricked with tears. She ran her hand along the head. There was nothing else but sea.

"Where are you going?" she asked the seal.

The seal surged forward and circled back, coming up again under Addie's hand. Addie wept as the seal swam off, disappearing in the waves. "Don't go!" she called after it. She wanted to let go of the line. She just wanted to let go.

"I'm sorry, Maud. I'm really sorry." She dropped her hand in the water, because there was no help. She let the wind take the sail and tried to hold the dinghy toward where she thought west might be. The sleek head came up again under her fingers. Addie didn't dare pull away or reach for more contact. She wanted company. The animal bobbed alongside, keeping close so Addie could touch. She spread her hand, her thumb ruffling the fur, exploring. She discovered a floppy ear.

"Not a seal!" Addie exclaimed and leaned to look.

The animal floated in place and Addie saw movement below the surface. Not fins. Legs. Massive webbed paws paddled the water like oars.

"But we're nowhere," she said to the dog, for it was a dog.

The bulky head lifted at its name, and Chester gruffed at her. "It *is* you!" she cried. "But how? Maud, it's Chester!"

Nothing but sea was visible. The Newfoundland surged on, curving at times, angling off and circling back. Addie held the sail to the line Chester made. An hour passed, nothing appeared.

"You're not real," she told the dog. "But I don't care. I asked for something and here you are." Chester swam close at the sound of her voice, making sure the girl in the boat didn't stray off course. More hours passed, and Addie was stiff and weary. "I can't," she said.

Chester circled the boat and came up under her dangling hand. Addie rubbed his neck and put her face as close as she could manage. "Maybe you should get in with us," she whispered. "We're very lost." Chester pulled forward, water rippling in his wake. "Wait!" Addie yelled and watched him swim. "Wait!"

Her arm flung forward and she followed its line. She saw a smudge just to starboard, directly beyond Chester's bounding body. "Maud, trees! Trees, Maud!" She couldn't look at her sister. She had to believe they would make it, that Maud would make it. Addie pulled in the boom, the sail tightened, and the dinghy gathered itself in a set course.

A half hour later, and the smudge became a jagged line of trees and a gray wall of boulders—an inlet with a rotting pier.

"Hello!" Addie bellowed.

When they were close, Chester swam forward, clambered onto the shale, shook himself mightily and sounded three sharp barks.

Addie angled the boat as best she could. "Not sideways to the shore," she reminded herself. She held the boom steady, feeling the waves breaking. She pulled up the centerboard almost too late as it scraped bottom. But the dinghy had done this before. It took the choppy shallow water in its stride, rocking, but its wide sides did not tip. The boat bumped along the sand, then Addie dropped over the side and shoved. Chester was back beside her. She got under the transom and dug her feet into the ocean floor, step after step, lurching to get the boat well and truly ashore. She kept pushing until Chester barked again.

"I can't go," Addie said. "I can't leave her." Chester barked and danced from foot to foot. "I can't," she repeated.

Chester barked and dashed off the beach into the trees. She heard him barking as he ran, his deep voice fading. She didn't mean to lie on the stony beach. Didn't mean to close her eyes. Didn't mean to leave Maud in the boat. She didn't mean to stop trying after all the effort of leaving the island. But that was how the man found her.

"Miss?" he said, his hands on his thighs as he bent to inspect this girl washed up out of nowhere. He took her hand and shook her gently. "Miss?"

Her eyes opened and he could tell she was struggling to understand. "You're landed, miss.," he said "You've come in. Your dog brought me round." Chester put his nose into Addie's hair, and she put her arms around his neck. "He's a right smart dog," the man said.

"He's Min's dog," Addie murmured.

"Min? You don't mean Minerva Cosgrove?"

Only then did the man think to look in the boat. "I'll be stove!" he breathed. "You girls are in sore need."

"Please help her," Addie asked.

"I'm not equipped," the man said. He peered at Chester. "There's been worry about you girls up and down the coast. Word went out you're Cosgrove clan." The man eyed Addie, then said, "I'll tow you," and disappeared.

Chester lay next to Addie and she had no strength to contradict him. Minutes later Addie heard the sound of a small motor and a boat breaking the water as a skiff rounded the end of the pier. The man secured his boat to a piling, stepped overboard, and lashed the dinghy to a cleat on his boat.

"Get in," he said, his thumb indicating his skiff. Addie climbed into the dinghy next to Maud, and Chester climbed in after.

"Suit yourself," the man said. He put himself behind the wheel of the skiff and the two boats cut north just beyond the jutting rocks.

Addie was past thinking, and her mind held to the sound of the one-cylinder engine as it said, *potato*, *potato*, *potato*, until she lost track of time. Her arms ached, her head was stone, and she was afraid to check Maud's breathing. Chester lay panting in the bottom, his body snug against Maud's.

It must have been an hour, maybe more, but without explanation, the man cut the engine to idle, climbed over the side, and hauled the boats onto sandy beach. Chester leapt from the boat and charged through trees onto a thin path.

Addie heard him barking and she knew he was wild to make someone understand. He returned, trotting back and forth, filling the air with his deep voice.

18

You Better Do Something Soon

"Chester! Come, boy. Where have you been?" came a voice from the path. A woman appeared. "What on earth!" she exclaimed. "Chester, you mad thing! What have you done?" Then, Min was on Addie, holding her, taking her face in her hands. "You dear girls!"

Addie broke away. "Help Maud! Please somebody help her!" Addie focused on Min's face and tousled hair. Nothing made sense. "Oh, it's not real," she wailed. "She's going to die anyway."

"No! No, it's real! It's just impossible!" Min hugged Addie. "No one's going to die. You're safe. You're here." Then she saw Maud in the bottom of the boat. Her breath left her. "You brave, brave girls!" she cried.

Min moved rapidly, lifting Addie out of the boat, taking her own shawl and wrapping it around her. She half turned and saw black boiling storm clouds coming over the ocean, the wind moving hard, exciting the waves.

"Help her. She's sick." It was all Addie knew to say.

Min asked, "Can she move?"

Addie stumbled toward the boat, losing her footing as waves pulled at her numb legs. Min shoved until the boat scraped all the way out of the water, Maud cradled and unmoving.

Chester circled and Addie touched Maud's hot face, her blistered lips. "We've landed, Maud," Addie whispered. "Min's here, and I don't know why."

Maud wrenched a deep cough and moaned. Climbing back

into the boat, Addie sat Maud up, her head rolling against her shoulder. Addie swallowed rising tears and gave Maud a small shake. "Maud. Maud, can you hear me?" A small noise came, but Maud's eyes stayed closed.

Maud gave a faint whimper. Min didn't pause, bringing Maud forward, legs draping over the gunwale. It was all movement then. The man with Maud in his arms, Addie leaning on Min, Chester huffing and circling.

Layers of pine needles covered the path into the trees. Pines gave way to oaks, elms, and a meadow with goldenrod. The path broke onto a narrow dirt road for a quarter mile, then turned onto a path patched with moss and ferns. Rain spat and wind pushed at upper branches. At the end of the path sat a clapboard house, with a barn behind just large enough for goats or pigs. Two wide stairs led to the door.

Min led Addie and the man into a warm kitchen with a stone floor and a cast-iron stove.

"I'll be getting back," the man said when he'd put Maud onto a day bed. "Storm's coming on."

"You don't know what good you've done," Min told him, squeezing his hands. "You need something for your trouble."

The man reddened. "Glad to help 'em in," he said. "No trouble. I'm George Dalton and I know who you are, ma'am. A bit of that bread would do."

Min sliced him a thick piece, layered it with cheese, and added a jar of hot tea. "You're a good man," she said.

"It's what anyone would do," he said and slipped out the door.

Min turned to Addie. "Is it true? Are you really here?" Chester followed Min's movements. She patted his head, fondled his ears. "How did you know, you clever boy?" She turned to Addie. "You both need care."

Addie choked and said in a rush, "Take care of Maud. She's right sick."

Min fought the clot of emotions that threatened to swamp her. In two strides she was beside Addie. "Dry clothes and soup. Sit here." She left and came back with blankets and a flannel nightgown. "It'll be big, but it will have to do. Help me get her clothes off."

Addie could no more have resisted Min's orders than she could have swum against the tide rising with the storm. She knelt beside Maud and pulled her wet clothes from her. Her sister's pale body had a splotchy red rash across her chest and cheeks. Addie wanted to cover and protect her. Maud's breath rasped and when her chest barely rose, she coughed sharply, her face wincing.

"We'll get the salt off and snuggle her warm." Min stroked Maud's arms, legs, and torso with a soft cloth. She brought a basin of warm water to the bed where Maud lay. "Dry her as I wash her. Her hair is last." Her actions were as efficient as her words. Within minutes Maud was rinsed and rubbed dry.

"She's so small. Please make her well." Addie's tears came as Min pulled a flannel nightgown over Maud's head.

"It's all right. We'll take care of her."

"Can't we get a doctor?"

"The doctor is in Mulgrave, over a day away in good weather." Min tucked a wool blanket around Maud and put the back of her hand on Maud's cheek. "We'll let her rest for now. It's your turn," she said, turning to Addie.

Min filled a galvanized tub and Addie stepped out of her clothes. Min placed a flannel towel over a chair back while Addie sank into the warm water. Min sponged the salt away, letting water run over Addie's hair and shoulders. When Addie was rinsed, Min handed her a towel and a nightgown. She brought a sweater and thick socks. Overhead the wind howled.

"A nor'easter. Could blow for quite a while. You made it within an eyelash. I'll be right back to start supper. Don't move." Min pulled on an oilskin coat and hat, snapped her fingers for Chester, and went out.

Addie hugged the wool sweater to her, her eyes on Maud. She shivered, pulled her knees up, and wrapped her arms around them.

When Min returned she said, "I pulled your boat into the trees and brought the oars, hamper, and blanket onto the porch. No sense letting them wash away."

The image nearly overwhelmed Addie. Losing anything was unbearable, so she pulled herself tighter.

"You need soup," said Min, filling the kettle and putting it on the stove. "And tea." She didn't ask questions or talk aimlessly. She fed the stove and stirred a pot next to the kettle. Soon she put steaming bowls and mugs on the table. "Here," she told Addie. "It's a little glue to put you back together."

While Addie spooned chicken soup into her mouth, she studied Min and was surprised to find that, added to the way she had always liked Min, she trusted her now too. Addie tried to finish her soup, but the stove's warmth made her eyelids heavy. She had no rudder or stays to hold on to, so her head drooped. She tried to bring her bowl and cup to the sink, but Min took the dishes from her.

"You need as much rest as your sister." She pointed to a doorway off the kitchen.

"I won't leave her," said Addie.

Min recognized ferocity when she heard it. "All right," she said. She pulled cushions from the parlor and brought a quilt from the bed.

"Cozy up there," said Min.

"But my sister—" Addie began.

"We'll watch together."

Min carried a rocking chair over to where the girls lay. Chester curled himself next to Addie. Addie did her best to keep vigil as rain whipped the glass and pounded the roof and the wind keened. The stove, the quilt, but above all Chester's deep breathing lulled her into sleep.

When Addie's breath matched that of the dog's, Min pulled the curtains shut. She put her ear to Maud's chest and listened. Her brow creased and the corners of her mouth pulled down.

"She's in trouble," said Min and made up her mind. She took her oilskin from its hook and put it on. "Keep watch," she told the dog and slipped out the door. Not long and she was back, water streaming off her. She shrugged off the coat and took several big onions from the pockets. "These would ripen by next week, but they'll do."

Min got a sheet from a cupboard and cut away a wide strip. From the medicine cabinet in the pantry, she found liniment. The onions she sliced and softened in a pan. After letting them cool, she pulled the covers from Maud. Maud coughed and shuddered. Min loosened the neck of Maud's nightgown, pulled it down, and exposed her chest. Maud's ribs showed and her chest barely moved with breathing.

"All right, little one. I'll do my best." Min put the cloth strip, the liniment, and the onions on a chair and pulled it next to Maud. She smeared liniment and onions near the center of the cloth, rolled it, and wrapped it around Maud's chest. Min replaced the nightgown and covered Maud with a sheet.

Min put two more logs in the stove. She wanted the room warm but didn't want Maud overheated. She poured lukewarm water into a mug and crushed mint into it, letting it steep. Holding Maud's head, she spooned the tea between her lips. Next, she filled a bowl with cool water from the pump and bathed Maud's face, neck, and arms. Maud's breath was jagged, shallow, and dry. The fever stretched Maud's skin hot and tight across her bones, her freckles startling in bluish pale skin.

Min fed Maud tea and broth and washed her face. Through

the night Min repeated her movements, listening to the wispy air from Maud's lips. "Don't let go," Min whispered.

In the morning, Addie woke to Min making oatmeal and tea. Wind wailed around the house and rain drummed on every surface. She knelt beside Maud. "Is she better?" she asked.

"I can't say yet," said Min, bringing oatmeal to the table. "You have more color."

Addie stroked Maud's hair. "She smells awful!" Addie feared the smell meant Maud was worse.

"Onions. A poultice on her chest to draw out lung fever. Have some porridge. You need strength to worry."

Addie didn't take her eyes from Maud. In her exhaustion and fear, Addie had believed everything would be right by morning, fixed by dry clothes and food. Addie had imagined Maud talking about the puffins, the stone basin, and catching fish. Addie wanted a funny story.

Min took Addie's chin in her hand. "We'll share the worry and care. Chester will do his part. Your sister hasn't given up." She saw the question in Addie's eyes. "She'll need time to pull out of this, and she needs you to keep your thoughts on what's possible."

Addie saw kindness in Min. She saw worry, too, and was grateful for it. And she wondered at the change in Min—something firmer with more energy had arrived. Addie's eyes brimmed over, but she nodded. It was her job to stay busy, watch over Maud, and keep dark thoughts away.

"How did Chester know?" Addie asked.

"I was wondering that too," Min answered. "I saw him swim out to sea, and I couldn't call him back. He must have heard something. A whistle?"

"Maud whistles. I don't."

"It's all so strange."

Addie agreed. "I was singing," she said.

"Very loud?"

"Yes, the way Maud says it should be sung."

"That's what he must have heard. And there was no stopping him. I've seen him swim miles out."

Addie put her arms around the dog, her face in his fur, and cried her gratitude, relief, and fear into him.

When she was calm, Min set out mugs of tea. "Tell me."

Addie put her hands around a mug and began. She told how it happened, from being forgotten for the Social, to landing on the island, to eating seaweed, to putting her hand in the water and finding Chester's large head. She told Min almost everything. But one part of the story she couldn't say.

"I failed you," said Min. Addie looked up, startled at Min's directness. "I wasn't thinking of you, and I'm sorry," Min continued.

"But it wasn't your fault."

"Who lets two girls leave the house without a thought?" Min asked, and Addie couldn't answer.

The storm blew itself out by the following morning, leaving the world soaked and tangled. Tree branches lay everywhere, and the sea had tossed debris into the tree line. Addie followed Min on her chores. Six chickens and one goat were hungry, along with Gillhooly, the enormous white goose. Addie helped Min drag limbs straddling the path and the animal pens. She opened windows and swept the kitchen.

"You've earned your keep," Min said. "Chester can take you for a walk. And no argument. Maud needs quiet."

Addie rambled with the Newfoundland. She walked the road and followed paths through meadows and woods. She didn't go to the beach but stayed within sight of the house.

Standing within pine, oak, and elm trees, the blue-gray clapboard house had weathered to match sky and sea. The porch, with its simple railing, made Addie think of a lap to climb into.

The house was clean but not perfectly tidy. The parlor had mismatched cushions and the spinet piano shouldered reams of music with curled edges. Novels slumped in a corner. The cast-iron stove was a squat warrior against cold and hunger. At home, Addie hadn't bothered watching Cook core apples or stir batter. Cook's methods were loud and impatient, answering questions with, "That's not anything you'll likely need to know."

For Min, the stove was an animate being, a fire-hearted companion roaring to braise chicken or whispering simmers to cook fudge. She conversed with it as she worked. Feeding it two split logs each morning, she coaxed a cheerful blaze to boil water and bubble oatmeal. After breakfast she stoked the flames until a huge kettle of washing water steamed the windows. The inside air grew moist and the chores held hope.

Addie surprised herself that afternoon and asked Min how to roll out pie dough. Min handed her the rolling pin. "Roll up your sleeves," she said.

Addie's crust was uneven and ragged, so Min balled it up, and said, "Imagine the best pie crust." She pointed to start again.

Addie made a believable crust that Min filled with raspberries. "Hands that play the piano can also make pastry," she said.

"Can I try cinnamon buns next?" Addie asked.

"That's for company. For now, it's brown bread and clam chowder." The invitation pleased Addie, and the pleasing surprised her. "I've written a letter to Cook to let her and everyone know you're safe," said Min after a pause. "I think a note from you should be included."

"Has she been worried?"

Min laughed. "Everyone's been frantic. All of the eastern shore has been searching. And your parents will need a telegram."

"Oh," said Addie. "Were they told?"

Min brushed back a strand of hair and said, "Cook sent a telegram straight away after you were lost. They're on their way home, but it could be another two weeks before they arrive. They have been heartsick. I came home to watch the northern shoreline. It wasn't right for me to be in their home after you disappeared. I was never supposed to be there."

Addie absorbed this information, thinking about silences and the idea that so many people had tried to find them while she and Maud had been so alone.

Addie wrote out a letter to say that they were safe. She began: *Dear Mother and Father,*

She scratched that out. Addie remembered her mother drifting from the parlor in the afternoon to evening cocktails at the Murcheys', the Barstows', or the Beals'. She thought about counting on people. Addie bent her head over a clean page.

Dear Cook,

I hope this letter finds you in good health and enjoying the mild airs of late Summer.

Addie was pleased with this beginning. It showed good manners and poetic strength. It didn't occur to her that Cook would cry at a letter from girls she thought had washed out to sea.

We are in good health, Addie continued, *and look forward to returning home in a few days, as travel arrangements can be made. Please send money. We have spent the summer unexpectedly and are now lodging with…*

Addie hesitated here. If she wrote Min, would it get their aunt in trouble? She decided on *a new friend.* Addie didn't want to upset anyone.

We are approximately two kilometers south of Canso. It's a lovely, out-of-the-way sort of place, perfect for recuperation.

Addie thought the hint of urgency without alarm sounded good.

We can hire a carriage to Guysborough and from there home. We have missed you.

With affection,
Adelaide Campbell

She reread the letter, smiled, folded it, and slid it into its envelope.

Between and around everything, Min and Addie tended Maud. Min changed the liniment strips and sliced onions. Addie spooned tea and washed Maud's fevered face. Maud wheezed in a sleep that wasn't real. Before she went to bed Addie read *David Copperfield* to Maud, skipping the saddest parts.

Addie helped Min with chores, but Maud was still clammy and spindly. When Addie had fed the chickens, she walked to the road. She looked ahead but was so full of worry she didn't see the tall grasses bending or swifts scissoring and swooping. Under an elm in the meadow's corner, she sat on a stone and put her face in her hands.

Suddenly she straightened, looking toward Min's house.

"Okay, God, you need to listen." Addie balled her fists and cleared her throat. "If getting here alive was your doing, I thank you. But Maud used all her strength and everything she knew to get us through that storm, onto that island, and then fixed the boat. Now she's near to death. She's my little sister, but there's nothing little about her, God, and I won't be going anywhere without her. Tell me what to do to get her well. Chop trees to keep her warm? Walk to Halifax for medicine? Promise I'll never kiss anybody? Tell me, straight out. I'll do it. Are you listening? It's not what Miss Lamont taught in catechism, but I need it this very minute."

Addie shouted, then dropped to a whisper. "You'd better

do something soon. I'll give you half my life to get Maud's back. Take it right now, and I won't miss it as long as I've got my Maud."

Smoke braided from the chimney as Addie gulped sobs and hugged herself. From the porch Min tossed crumbs from her apron to the chickens and Gillhooly honked. Eyes closed, leaf-shadows playing, Addie listened as Min hummed.

A gust of wind shook and startled her. She walked back to the porch and Min studied her. "She's no less determined than you. Do you think she doesn't need you as much as you need her?"

The words caught Addie's breath. She knew Maud's determination; she saw it every day. But she had never thought Maud needed her. An image came of their mother, swirling a paisley shawl around their heads. "See my latest frivolity, girls? Your father sent it from China." Addie remembered herself and Maud jumping to catch the tassels. Later, Maud found Addie primping before the mirror, the shawl draped around her.

"Adelaide, you are the latest frivolity." Maud had said.

Min hooked her arm in Addie's. "The goat needs milking, and you're going to learn."

19

I Don't Want a Fairy Tale

In the kitchen Maud opened her eyes and closed them. She took a breath and opened them again. Nothing about what she saw made sense, but she was too weak to argue with what her eyes told her. She saw the cast-iron stove first, and it comforted her beyond reason by its solid weight and its bowed legs, and by the kettle to one side and the jars and bowls on the upper shelf that held matches, pepper, cinnamon, salt, and dried mustard.

Maud stretched and felt a softness that comes after many washings and the weaving gives in to the cotton. A summer quilt covered her too. She didn't have the patience or the focus to understand its pattern, but her mind filed away the colors and shapes. She trusted that understanding would come. It was enough to lie in this bed in a kitchen bright with sun.

If I have died, Maud thought, *this is the safest heaven I could imagine.*

Her gaze wandered from the stove to the scrubbed table, where two mugs sat, to the open pantry door. Jars filled with fingers of runner beans, new carrots, bristled cucumbers, and peas like thick clusters of fish eggs lined the pantry.

On the countertop rested a loaf of bread so dark it was as if molasses had risen into a shape. Her eyes rested there and closed. She breathed a smile as she slid into sleep.

Maud was deeply asleep when Addie came in with a pitcher of milk and a bowl of eggs. As she put them on the table, she turned to look at Maud. Something had changed.

"Min!" Addie called out the door. "Min!"

When Min hurried in, Addie said, "The worry is gone."

Min touched Maud's face and nodded. "She's fought it through. She's come back."

Addie stayed in the kitchen the rest of the day, reading bits of her book, but mostly watching Maud. Near dusk, Maud opened her eyes. She saw Addie before anything else. Maud's eyes loomed large in her pale face.

Addie bent over her. "We're safe, Maud. We made it back." Confused, Maud looked around the kitchen. "Not home, not Mahone Bay. But Min's here, and she's ever so kind, and Chester found us, and there was another storm." Addie ran out of words. She kissed Maud on the forehead. "You're safe," she whispered.

Min made Maud chicken broth and weak tea, and Addie spooned it to her. Worn out, Maud fell asleep, but it was real sleep, her breathing even. She slept deeply all that night and into the next morning.

When Addie came in from feeding the chickens, Maud was awake. They were alone in the kitchen. "I kept dreaming we were dancing," said Maud.

"Last night?"

"Before last night. In the boat. We had to keep dancing or something would happen." She took a sip of warm tea and lay back on the pillow. "You knew all the steps we had to do, and I tried to follow, but my legs would fade away."

"Fade away? What do you mean?"

"Disappear, so my upper half floated. It felt awful. I was afraid I would float away. A very hot wind drowned out your voice."

"What was I saying? Was I singing?"

"No. You recited multiplication tables, higher and higher. I asked you to stop, because it hurt my head. I wanted to let go, but you said, 'Maud, I'm figuring this out. Stay with me.' We danced again, and you wouldn't let go."

"Were you angry with me?"

"You were so bossy. But when I thought about letting go, I was frightened. You said the multiplications kept the music going, and if we kept dancing we'd figure it out. But I didn't understand what we were trying to figure out."

"It doesn't matter, Maud. It was only a dream. Min says I shouldn't make you talk too much."

"Addie? I almost let go."

"In the dream, Maud?"

"Yes, in the dream." Maud's voice was small.

Addie smoothed the quilt over her sister and walked to the door. Before she stepped out of the room, Maud murmured, "In the dream. And in the boat."

Outside, Addie let tears slide down her face. She cried for a long time, and her heart took up its beat after sticking rigid while in the boat and during Maud's days of searing fever. She wiped her face with the back of her hands and returned to the kitchen. Maud was asleep.

Min eyed Addie and poured her a glass of milk. "She's not the only fighter in the family, you know."

Addie looked at her, puzzled. "She told me about a dream she had."

"I heard her. Did you teach her to dance?"

"Once. She said I was too silly to follow."

"When it mattered, she knew you were the one she could count on. She knew you would fight hard before letting her go."

Addie's eyes spilled over. "It wasn't like that. Maud makes things work. She never gives up."

"That's true. She never gave up believing she could follow you."

Addie's hands jittered and she put down her glass before

the milk spilled. "I didn't think I could do it. I told myself I was the wrong person for the job."

"I know you did. But even you didn't believe that."

The next morning Maud sat up and played a hand of cards with Addie. After arranging her cards, Maud said, "What I said about Min was wrong."

"What did you say?"

"That she doesn't care. And being odd is okay. Maybe better than okay."

"I should think so, being Odd Maud." Addie sneaked a glance at her sister to see how this comment landed.

Maud grinned. "So there!" she exclaimed and put down her cards to show all her points. Then she said, "Remember the sailor and the necessity?"

"Yes, why?"

"Why do you think?" Maud answered.

"Oh! Well, going to Min's outhouse is a challenge. The path is slippery and tall field grasses hide a patrolling gorgon."

"I need to go. I don't want a fairy tale," threatened Maud.

They walked arm in arm, Maud unsteady and Addie offering her experience. "You have to look sharp or Gillhooly the goose will strike. The first time I screamed and ran back to the house. Min says, 'That goose is a better watchdog than Chester.'"

Addie brought old bread, and Gillhooly ate it in seconds, honking and snapping his hard bill at their behinds.

Once in, the problem was how to get out. Gillhooly stood watch like a prison guard. They were trapped until Min noticed and rescued them, saying, "Silly old thing," to Gillhooly. The goose craned his neck and nuzzled Min's hand.

"Next time save something for after," Maud said.

But even with treats for the return, Gillhooly chased them.

That afternoon Min took the laundry to the porch. It was the best place for scrubbing clothes, including the clothes the girls had arrived in. Maud stayed in her nightgown, and Addie wore an old skirt and blouse of Min's, hemmed up and pinned at the waist.

Min's hand fished into Maud's skirt pocket and her hand closed on marbles, the roll of string, and the pocketknife. Her hand dove into the other pocket and felt a key. She pulled it into the light and balanced it on the flat of her hand. Banner clouds streamed overhead and a fur of rain thrashed down, flashing silver. Min let her hand get wet and the key get slippery.

The day turned upside down. She had stood in another day, in another rain, with her hand out flat and this same key stretched along her palm.

"Take it," she had said.

Charlie shook his head no. "The box is no good without the key," he answered.

"Nothing is any good without you," she told him. "You hold the key until you come back."

She grabbed him by the shoulders and felt the wet wool of his peacoat in her hands. "This is my marriage promise to you, Charlie Brice." She spoke up into his face, into the pelting rain. "Until we have rings on our fingers, until you return, I will keep the box safe and you will hold the key. We are together, Charlie. From right now and on and on, we are together."

The wind rose and there was no time. Min slid the key into his pocket as he bent and pulled her into his arms, her face tilted. He held her hard, touched her hair.

"You're the wind and sea, Min. You're the shore I need to find." He tightened his hold once and strode away down the dock.

A few of the fishermen had waited, and as he approached, they brought him into their midst as one of their own. They would go out and follow the rest to answer the transmitted

SOS from the lighthouse. At the end of the dock, the wind had whipped Min's hair.

On the porch, she felt the key press into her hand. The key, like her hand, had changed. The burnish was off them both, but both were strong. She closed her fingers around the shaft, the looped head, and the notched tooth.

"Oh, my Charlie," she said to the afternoon. She finished the girls' clothes, washed and hung to catch tomorrow's dry air. In the kitchen she placed the contents of Maud's pockets in a bowl and put it on the windowsill near the stove. Mixed with marbles and string, the key looked like a child's fantasy. "It's not possible," Min told herself and peeled potatoes.

While they ate, this time with Maud sitting at the table, Addie asked Min how long she had lived in this house.

Min put down her fork. "There's something you need to understand. I'm not your mother's cousin." Addie and Maud put their forks down, too. "I'm her sister."

"But why…?" asked Addie, touching her own nose as she remembered the drawing.

Min nodded. "You might as well hear it. I fell in love with a local fisherman's son. That's how my father saw him, referring to him as 'that Brice fella.' My father wanted to set me up with a Loomis or a Tardif. 'Deep money,' he'd say. But letting me go was more than he could face. Stanford Loomis, with thick red hair and bitten nails, and Gordon Tardif with stiff collars and long fingers, couldn't stand up to father squinting over his pipe.

"'You're the bloom of Halifax, Minerva,' father said when I poured his coffee. 'You give the fire its dance,' he'd say as I drew the curtains. He didn't mean harm, wanting the best for me. I didn't mind being the first 'Cosgrove girl.' I loved my father." Min sat back and closed her eyes.

"Didn't you marry?" Addie blurted. Embarrassed but curious, she asked, "Why are you in this house? Why won't anyone talk to you?"

"No, to your first question," said Min, brushing crumbs off her lap and standing. "Your other questions require a thick rainy day for telling." At Addie's protest, Min continued, "No argument. It's time for bed." She lifted the lid off a burner and poked the stove's flame.

The key was foremost in Min's mind. It was in her hand at breakfast. "I don't pry," she began. "But I found this in one of your pockets. How did you come by it?" She opened her hand to show the key.

Addie looked at Maud, who avoided her eyes. Neither said anything.

Min closed her fist and leaned her elbow on the table. "Seems to me there's a story here."

Maud spoke. "We agreed to bury it, but it's beautiful, so I couldn't. It was all the treasure I was going to find." She stopped and sneaked a look at Addie.

Addie looked at Maud, then across at Min. "I left out bits of the story." She turned to Maud. "You tell her. You found him."

Maud told Min about the fishing boat and the skeleton, the tin box, and what was in it.

When she was done, Min's face was ashen. "You buried him?" she asked.

"Yes," said Addie. "We gave him a proper service and buried him on a bluff facing west so he could look homeward."

Min put her face in her hand and rocked back and forth. Addie and Maud looked at each other, afraid they'd done something horribly wrong. Min shook her head. "It's not possible. When she raised her head, the girls saw sorrow. "Was there a name on the boat?" she asked.

"Addie figured out an *M* and maybe an *R*," said Maud. "The rest was worn away."

"Heaven above!" said Min. She got up and went to a coastal map pinned to the kitchen wall. Along with the shoreline and island clusters, the map showed ocean depths and currents. Min studied it, tracing pale lines with her finger. "The Gulf Stream," she finally said.

Maud and Addie joined her. "What do you mean?" Maud asked.

"It's not likely, none of this is. You left Mahone Bay, south of Halifax, were blown out to sea to an island, then sailed back south of Canso, north of Halifax."

The girls studied the map too, and Addie said, "It doesn't look so very far on the map. Why didn't anyone come?"

"All of Mahone Bay, all of coastal Nova Scotia searched for you two. Cook and I alerted fishing fleets and organized shoreline lookouts with lanterns," Min answered.

Maud finally said what she had wondered. "But no one found us. How hard were you looking?"

Min faced her. "Currents are tricky and it's been a summer of storms. Cook and I decided she would stay in Mahone Bay and I would return here. Patrols went out over and over, and I walked the beach day and night."

All three fell silent, thinking of how each had tried so hard, then Min said, "The Gulf Stream carried you away and back. And storms. A series of happenstance. They took Charlie too. But it was Chester who heard you and went for you."

Addie leaned forward. "Charlie? Do you mean the man on the island?"

Min let out a long breath and nodded. "No finer man in the Nova Scotia counties, with curly hair and brown eyes like the center of a daisy. His hands made me stop and take notice. I was making afternoon tea, and he came to fix the screen door. It was always loose and no one could fix it right. I heard a saw and hammer, and I heard whistling better than most people can sing. I was pouring hot water into the teapot when I glanced up and saw his hands, one grasping a screwdriver, the other bracing the door. Workman's hands. Careful, gentle hands. I watched them put the hinges in place, not forcing anything and understanding what wood and brass want to do. Charlie Brice's hands cajoled life from any material.

"He realized I was staring, because he looked up, right into my eyes. 'Do you need a hand with that?' he asked me.

"I don't know what I answered. I didn't know what he was asking. He put his tools down and took the tea kettle out of my hand.

"'You'll burn yourself if you're not careful.' His mouth had a little smile at the corners, and his voice was deep and soft. He shaped his words like an educated man, not running over the ends the way most folks do. I put out my hand and introduced myself, but I'm sure I sounded like a ninny.

"'What do you do with yourself, Min, when you're not pouring tea?' he asked me."

Addie put her chin in her hands. Min looked beyond Addie, beyond the window with late morning sun turning the chickens' feathers into flicks of flame.

"We talked for quite a while that afternoon. Father was out on business, so Charlie and I talked while he fixed the door and I pretended to drink tea. His father and all his family men were Lunenburg fishermen. But he wanted to be an architect, so his uncles persuaded his father to send him to Boston, to Harvard. No matter how hard the men worked, college was too expensive, and Charlie had to stop before he finished his degree. He described the Louvre in Paris, St. Paul's Cathedral in London, and the Parthenon in Athens. He said those buildings were beautiful because they held the symmetry of a beehive, a sparrow's nest, or a beaver dam. 'Answers are all around. You have to be patient and notice,' he said."

Min watched the wind tease the tall grasses beyond the chicken house.

"Was he right?" Maud asked. "Did you find answers by noticing?"

Min shifted her gaze without moving and looked at Maud. "Yes. Charlie was right. But I stopped believing when I lost him. I heard no answers and noticed nothing."

"What happened?" asked Addie.

"Charlie came by often to visit, but Father wouldn't have it. I never wanted to go against my father, but I loved Charlie from the moment I saw his hands and heard him speak. He loved me too. That was plain. He talked to Father, but it was no good. Charlie saw it. He wrote me letters, and I wrote back for almost a year. Charlie built this house between Whitehead and Canso on a spit of land. In a letter he said the house was for me, for whenever I was ready. Father found the letter, said it wasn't proper. He raged and forbade me to have anything to do with Charlie.

"It was a terrible night. I threw angry words back at him. I told him I was not a child and could do as I liked. I packed a satchel and hired a cart to Lunenburg to meet Charlie. A storm burst by the time I got to Lunenburg, and I found a room at a boarding house where I asked the manager if she knew Charlie Brice." Min stopped and looked at the girls.

"Please don't stop," said Maud. "Did you find him?"

"Earlier he had sent me a box, a surprise for my birthday and I wasn't to open it. The storm was ugly and the fishing fleet was called to help a ship in trouble. I went to the docks with the box, knowing Charlie would volunteer. He said he had to go and he said goodbye." Min opened her hand and there was the key. "This is the key he took with him, and this is the house he built. People talk of deadly currents out past the islands when the sea runs high. I thought the sea had swallowed him. All this time and there he was."

They looked at the key and thought about Charlie Brice. Min remembered a man who filled her world and then disappeared. Maud and Addie remembered a skeleton who became a strong, brave man.

When the supper dishes were put away and Chester had his final walk around the paths, the girls and Min played three-handed cribbage. Addie said, "Your father must have understood in time." Addie didn't want to let Charlie Brice go. She wanted a happy ending even though nothing could change what had happened.

"My father was never going to want his daughter married to a man like Charlie."

"But Charlie was honest and clever and kind," said Maud. "You said so, and that must be true."

"He was all those things. But he wasn't the right kind of man."

"What kind of man should he have been?" Addie's pitched her voice to argue directly with Min's father.

Min pushed hair off her forehead and went to her bedroom. When she returned, she held a framed photograph with the picture pressed against her chest.

"A picture!" Addie was full of excitement. Maud inched forward on her chair. A face for Charlie's name. Posture and expression to clothe buried bones.

"Keep hold of yourselves," said Min and turned the picture around.

Their eyes were eager. Addie's eyebrows darted toward each other, then rose. She pulled them down, glanced at Min, then put her eyes hard on the picture. Maud's eyes steadied on the photograph; then she, too, looked at Min.

"Do you see my Charlie?" Min asked.

Addie stilled. Maud swallowed. Understanding came the way light brings objects out of shadow. "Say it," said Min. She was firm, not angry, not mean. "Say what you see."

"Charlie Brice is a Negro," said Addie. She looked to Min for approval.

Min's face was calm and open.

Addie went to Min, took the photograph in both hands, and studied the man. He wore a suit with a loosely knotted tie. His held a large book, with his right hand resting on top. He acknowledged the camera without a smile, but happiness showed in his eyes. He was the most dignified man Addie had ever seen. Maud took the photograph and held it while Min continued.

"He was in college then, in Boston. He had a scholarship, but it wasn't enough. Every summer he fished to earn money for books and room and board. He couldn't stay in the dormitories like the other men. Charlie was older than most of them anyway."

"Tell us more," said Addie.

Min saw the kitchen, but it was the kitchen on a different day. When she began again, the girls watched her travel back, no longer there with them.

"I will never forget the way that man shucked peas." Min laughed. "He opened the pods by unzipping the seam and letting the green pearls spill like new rain. He never took the rocking chair. Said rolling peas were motion enough. I think he had enough rocking on his boat. I taught him split pea soup for stormy days, and he taught me new peas on toast after a long spring day. He called them easy peasies."

Min looked down at her hands, loose in her lap, and Addie knew she was seeing Charlie's hands.

"They were strong, weren't they, Min?" she asked.

Min looked up, surprised at Addie's understanding. "They were strong enough for tender peas."

20

One Problem Can Take Up the Whole World

Maud and Addie shared a look, and left Min with her thoughts. They walked to the chicken pen and hung over the rail watching the hens scratching in the dirt.

"I shouldn't have kept the key," said Maud by way of apology.

Addie pulled the letter from her pouch and handed it to Maud. Maud's eyebrows went way up.

"Did you read it?"

"There's nothing to read. It's all faded."

"We should give this to her too."

They were uncertain, since Min was already so sad, but they shuffled into the middle of the kitchen.

Min turned from the stove, her eyes red. She exhaled a laugh. "You look as guilty as thieves. What is it?"

Maud elbowed Addie, and Addie stepped forward. "It's this." She held out the letter.

Min cradled it in both hands, not believing the fragile paper and nearly invisible writing.

"We're so sorry," Addie burst out. "We didn't mean to hurt you. We didn't know."

Min face softened. "Of course, you didn't know. It's adventure and mystery. It truly was and is. And you haven't hurt me. You never could. Sometimes tears are about more things than hurt." She took the key from the shelf over the stove and put it and the letter on the table. She went to her bedroom and when she returned, she carried a wooden box. She placed it on the table.

Maud and Addie, afraid they had intruded too much, still leaned toward the box.

"It won't explode! Come closer."

The girls crowded in and peered at the carved box.

"Have you never opened it?" asked Addie.

Maud used her elbow for another poke. "She hasn't had the key."

Min shook her head. "I have only a notion of what's inside."

"What do you think it might be?" Addie wanted to know.

Maud didn't want guessing games; she wanted answers.

"Charlie went to Halifax before I met him in Lunenburg. He was up to something." Min fitted the key into the lock and gave it a half turn. The lid released with a *pock!* Maud imitated the sound. Min pulled back the lid back and the three hovered.

A brass crank wound the barrel of the music box. Next to it curled a red ribbon with two gold rings, one larger than the other. Tucked on the other side of the mechanism was a slim envelope. Min pulled the rings and the envelope from the box. She felt the weight of the rings in her hand and fingered the ribbon. Maud and Addie eyed the envelope. With a finger under the flap, Min opened it. She tilted the envelope and out spilled two pasteboard tickets.

"Railway tickets!" exclaimed Maud.

Min examined them. "This is a surprise and an adventure," she said. She held them so the girls could read the words.

"Round Trip. Canadian Pacific Railway. Quebec City to Vancouver, B.C.," read Addie. She let out a great sigh. "Was it a honeymoon?"

"Charlie was hoping so," she answered.

The girls looked puzzled.

"It wouldn't be easy for a white woman and a Negro man. But Charlie loved the world." Min slid the brass crank onto its stem and wound the mechanism. The barrel turned and the brass pins plinked along the bumps.

Addie waited for a dreamy waltz. The box played a clear and lively version of Scott Joplin's "Maple Leaf Rag." She frowned and Min grinned at her. "He wasn't that sentimental, Addie," Min said and laughed as the music filled the kitchen.

"Will you use the tickets?" asked Maud when the song wound down.

"I don't know if the CP would honor them."

"But they have to!" exclaimed Maud.

Min was taken aback. "You think I should go on this trip?"

Both girls nodded at her. "Charlie wanted you to," said Maud, and Addie nodded again.

"I'm not afraid to travel, but I've got chickens and what would Chester do?" Min put the tickets in the envelope and put it and the rings into the box. She set the box next to the spices near the stove where it was visible from anywhere in the room. "That's enough of yesterdays. Chester would like your company, Maud, for a walk up the path."

So far, Maud had been allowed the front porch or the chicken yard for fresh air. Min directed Addie to go with her. This became the routine, with walks getting longer and Maud talking more. She collected bits of bark, once an osprey wing, and once the skull of a shrew. When she brought her treaures back, Min remarked, "You certainly have a talent for finding what others leave behind."

Maud coughed more than Addie or Min liked, but her freckles weren't so stark even though her clothes hung limply on her frame. While Min chopped wood or made repairs to the house and Addie weeded the garden, Maud took a nap. During the afternoon, when brown grasshoppers worked just as hard as Addie, Min walked between the rows of runner beans to ask Addie to pick some for supper.

"She's nearly well enough to go home," Min said after a

moment. "It's time to end your adventure. You should be in your own beds."

Addie stopped pulling at the beans. Her own bed was a faraway land. But Min had said it, bringing it back. Cook, the house under the big elm, Min on the chaise, and the dressing table full of bottles arrived in a rush. Not knowing what she was saying, Addie's words erupted.

"I shouldn't have done it. I don't know why I did. I mean, I do know, but it was stupid. How could I have been so stupid?" Her words tumbled and huge tears spilled down her face.

Min waited, silently coaxing the rest from Addie.

"It was going to be perfect. My dress, my hat, my parasol. Oh! My parasol!" More tears streaming. "And then you asked me to get it. I wanted my eyes… Oh, it's my fault! It was very wicked. I wanted my eyes…" Addie sobbed, hands to her face. From between fingers she groaned, "I almost killed her. I almost killed Maud because of my own stupidity!"

Min didn't reach for Addie but kept her hands at her sides. "What did I ask for?"

"Medicine." Addie bent forward, her tears wetting her hands.

"And you found laudanum because you knew I had been taking it?"

"I drank some." Her head came up, her eyes wild. "Not a lot! Only a mouthful. I wouldn't have taken more. I wanted my eyes to be beautiful!" Those same eyes flooded and Addie's face crumpled.

"And you thought the laudanum made my eyes look large?" Min asked. Addie nodded. "You wanted your eyes to be large and romantic for the picnic?"

Addie whispered, "She almost died." She rocked back and forth.

Min laid her hands on top of a bean pole. "Maud didn't die. You saved her."

"No!" Again, Addie's head came up. "Maud saved us. I made everything go wrong. From the beginning."

"Does Maud know you drank laudanum?"

Addie shook her head.

"I see," said Min. She put her hand on Addie's head. "You are two brave girls who have a great deal to tell each other. Telling the truth about things we have done takes terrible courage."

"What do you mean?" Addie didn't move under Min's hand.

"Maud deserves to hear this part of the story, and you both need to know how I let you down."

Later, Addie walked with Chester and Maud stayed in the porch rocker. She sat next to Min, who had a bowl of beans in her lap. Min's hands worked independently from her mind. She surveyed past the porch and across the chicken pen.

"Chickens are right peaceful to watch," she said as if Maud had questioned her. "When I'm puzzling something out, I let my mind rest on the feathers. The hens peck about without pattern so ideas can trail after them."

Maud wound her string through her fingers. She made a cat's eye, Jacob's ladder, fish on a dish, and scissors.

"You use that string the same way," Min went on. "You must be solving the problems of the world."

Maud giggled and tucked her head because Min had the truth of it. "Not the whole world," Maud said. She let go the two stars and started on a drawbridge. Min snapped beans into the bowl. She didn't hurry, enjoying the feel of the pods. "Maybe only one problem," Maud said.

"One problem can take up the whole world."

"I know!" Maud's whole frame jolted. "It's like a huge boulder that you can't get around no matter which way you step."

Min worked on, her eyes on the ruffling black bantam feathers.

"I know I have to tell her," Maud continued. "I don't expect her to forgive me, and I won't ever forgive myself, but I have to tell her." The bantams scratched the dirt, finding grain and small insects. "I was looking for pirate caves. That's why we got lost. Addie doesn't know. I rowed us right out into the ocean and we were swept away." Maud's voice tightened, as if her throat were burning. "The whole time I never told her. But it was pirate caves, not wind or tide, or my arms being too weak to row." She swallowed, the string slack in her fingers. She stared over the edge of the porch, but she didn't see the bantams. "I tried every day, right from the beginning, right from that afternoon, to make it right. But I couldn't. Addie was scared, and I was the one who had gotten us lost."

The last bean dropped into the bowl. It lay with the others in a small green mound at the bottom. "You're quite a pair." Min gave her head a little shake and smiled to herself.

"How can I tell her?"

"The same way you told me. But when you tell her, Maud, remember that you didn't start off to take anything away from her."

Maud looked up sharply at Min and studied her profile. Maud realized she had always liked the corners of Min's mouth, how they gave away what she was thinking. And she trusted Min's hands, trusted the work she had seen them do. When she looked back down, she laced the string around her fingers and leaned her head against Min's shoulder.

That evening as they ate dinner, Addie thought, *Min is more complete*. When she looked into Min's eyes, she saw her resolve and her practice of making up her own mind, of letting go, and going on, and of making the best of things. Addie saw sorrow and acceptance, openness and struggle. Addie had thought Min distant and haughty. But here Min was direct with the world. She wore gold earrings and pinned up her thick braids.

Her smile tucked at the corners to conceal secrets. Her light brown eyes were clear and distinct, and small corner creases showed her determination and independence. They were not the eyes Addie had witnessed in Mahone Bay.

The next day, after chores were done, Min called to Chester and told the girls to walk with her along the road. Min took the path down to the water until they reached the boat. Pulled up among the trees, it was like a blown leaf. Its sail drooped and the lines sagged.

Min walked past the boat and down to the water's edge. She pulled off her skirt and blouse and waded into the water in chemise and bloomers. Maud grinned and Addie's face went red. When she was waist deep, Min called, "It's wonderful! Come swim!"

Maud pulled off her clothes and ran to the water. Addie turned half away, folded her clothes, and put them in the boat. She walked slowly into the water. Maud wacked the water next to her, sending up a spray.

"Maud!" Addie screamed.

"Get it over with! Come in!" Maud paddled away.

Addie sank and pushed off with her feet. The water was cool and soft against her skin. The dark pines were huge feathers along the shore, their scent mingling with wet sand and shallow cove water. She closed her eyes, turned on her back, and listened to the gurgles and ripples.

Min swam to Maud. "Stretch your arms all the way when you reach," she instructed. "Give your lungs lots of room."

Maud practiced with Min coaching her how to breathe with each stroke. Then Min struck out toward the ocean, her long arms cutting the water rhythmically, her legs scissoring. Addie thought of kittiwake wings and Maud thought of a locomotive. Just when they began to wonder, Min's body curved, and she pointed back. As she closed in, she submerged and rose, water streaming. She shook her hair and stood laughing. "That's what I needed," she said. She strode from the water, collected her clothes, and said, "See you back at the house."

Addie watched her walk up the path. "Min would never have cared what Evelyn Brighty thinks."

Maud paddled beside her. "Min doesn't know Evelyn."

Addie sank to her shoulders and pulled her legs up to float. "I know. I just mean that Min is her own self and wouldn't have gone to a Social and been foolish."

Maud dipped her face and opened her eyes to see the bottom. The saltwater stung her eyes, but she liked to see the murky, distorted sea bottom. When she pulled her face up, she said, "Min doesn't think like other grown-ups. She puts her eyes to see things at their own level." Maud ducked her head under and swam off.

The girls splashed around in the water for an hour, then went back to the house. By suppertime Min had fish and parsnips ready with a loaf of bread. She put full bowls on the table for the girls, then said she had to bring the wash in.

Maud sat across from Addie and chewed slowly. She couldn't swallow. A parsnip couldn't squeeze its way past the lump in her throat. Every time she looked at her sister, it got tighter and hotter. She put down her spoon and pressed her hand to her forehead.

"Addie." It came out quivery and cracked. Maud's voice made Addie look up, worried. Maud didn't want Addie to be worried about her anymore. She didn't deserve Addie's worry and wet globes formed in Maud's eyes. This was not how she wanted it to go.

"What is it, Maud?"

Tears splashed into Maud's lap.

"I have to tell you something."

Addie opened her mouth and Maud rushed ahead. "I have to. Don't say anything, not anything, until I'm done. You can think anything you want and you have every right to, but let me say it right out to the end. Then you can say what you want when you know what kind of sister you saved."

Addie opened her mouth again, but Maud's eyes were so drowned and fierce, she closed it and leaned forward, forgetting the bread in her hand.

Maud rubbed her eyes and swallowed. "It was about pirates. Tavis Crandle was always going on about pirates. His grandfather has a doubloon and told stories about galleons and walking the plank. He said there were caves in Whynachts Cove." Maud took a deeper breath.

Addie was quite still.

"Tavis had never seen the caves. I wanted to beat him to it, to show him up, to make him think of me as more than 'Odd Maud.' I wanted a doubloon."

Maud saw Addie's eyes widen with understanding. She hurried on. "I had the chance in the rowboat when you fell asleep. I thought I could row around, take a peek at the caves, and get us home before you knew the difference." The words hung in the air. Then she whispered, "It was all my doing. We wouldn't have ended up on that island if I hadn't been stupid and stubborn. I almost killed us both...." The tears came fast and Maud's voice wavered as she gulped out words. "I'm sorry...I didn't mean...you don't have to forgive...I'll make it up...."

Addie was around the table in a flash, her arms around Maud, her own tears falling. "Shhh, shhh. Don't cry. You don't know...it wasn't you...I'm the one...I shouldn't have...I tried the laudanum. I'm so ashamed. You could have died...only to be pretty..." Addie was no more coherent than Maud.

After stumbling starts they got their stories out. Maud heard Addie and Addie heard Maud.

"What I did was far worse," Addie said, pulling away. "I took Min's medicine!"

"Rowing straight into the ocean was worse," countered Maud. "I put us right in danger."

"I was drugged! I wasn't being responsible."

"You don't need to be responsible for me!" Maud's back straightened and she wiped her face.

"If you're looking for pirates, someone should keep an eye out for you!" Addie's mouth formed a line.

"An eye out for me? Who's nipping from Min's bottle? You need a keeper yourself!" Maud glared at her sister.

21

What Exactly did I Win?

Min found them in this state when she came in from hanging the laundry. "I see you've got it straightened out and back to normal," she said, putting on the kettle.

Addie's shoulders inched down. Maud took out two marbles and rolled them in her hand. "Bossy!" she said to Addie. But there was no sting. Addie gave Maud's head a small shove and they were done.

They played cribbage after supper, and as Addie put down a five to make two points, she asked Min, "Why did you take laudanum?"

Min's hand stopped reaching for a peg. "Your asking tells me you don't believe what you've been told." Addie reddened and looked away. Maud looked from Min to her sister. "You're right." Min's hand found the peg and moved it two holes down. "Maybe Rapunzel put herself in the tower."

"What?" asked Maud.

"It was a way to disappear. Yes. I hurt my back and the medicine was for pain. But it healed years ago. I loved Charlie, and I wasn't supposed to. Your mother, your father, my father, my friends decided I was rubbish."

"That couldn't be true!" Addie blurted.

"What did your mother tell you about me? She's my sister, remember."

Addie twisted her fingers. "But you're wonderful."

Min sniffed and folded her cards.

"It hurt. A different kind of pain. Then Charlie, well...I

couldn't exist, so I climbed into a tower room that floated above everything. It proved everyone right. I had no morals, no backbone, no courage."

"Did you like it? The floating room?" It was Addie and Min's conversation now.

Min set her cards down and asked, "Did you?" Addie inhaled, her eyes darting around the room. "Truthfully," Min asked.

"Yes. At first," Addie admitted.

"And then?"

"Then it was awful. Like a sour rag."

"A sour rag," repeated Min. "I like that."

"It couldn't have been like that for you," Addie pressed. "Otherwise you wouldn't have kept doing it."

"It is though, and that's why. More takes the awful away. For a while. It makes the empty room lift and sway, so I don't know where the walls are."

Addie hung her feet on the rungs of the chair. "You haven't done it since we've been here."

"I was trying to stop in Mahone Bay." Min reached across the table and put her hands on Addie's and Maud's arms. "It's my fault. All of it. Neither of you is to blame. Not your mother or anyone. Even when I took it just for the pain in my back, Charlie tried to tell me. Once he took the laudanum and pitched it. He said what we believe about ourselves is what matters most." Min's hands shook. "I'm so, so sorry. I let you go out of self-pity. There's no reason I deserve you back."

Addie and Maud crowded Min and hugged her hard.

"I never thought..." began Min but couldn't finish her sentence.

Addie kissed her cheek and said, "You belong to us."

An hour later a letter from Cook arrived with money to hire a cart and then a carriage to Mahone Bay on July 8. The letter explained that the girls' parents would be home two days after.

Talking about leaving was one thing. Actually leaving felt very different. Not comfortable at all. Going home should be easy, and this last, small piece should be nothing compared to ocean waves like thundering horses and bird-print hieroglyphs on the beach. A buggy ride was a small journey after a voyage with only her hand on the sail and Maud barely breathing.

But now that wishes for new dresses or sponge cake were about to happen, Addie was afraid. In the chicken yard she tossed feed to the pecking birds. The blue-black bantam was her favorite, laying beautiful beige eggs and clucking when Addie came near. The hens minced around the yard, choosing grain carefully.

"She's my favorite too," said Min, putting her arm around Addie's waist. "You've been brave all along, Addie. You'll be brave through this too."

"How did you know I was afraid?"

"Because I would be afraid too."

"It makes no sense! I've longed for home, and Maud has too, though she never says."

"Longing for something you can't get is one thing," Min answered.

Addie watched the bantam. "Now that I am going, I'm afraid nothing will happen. Does that sound odd?" Min put a lock of hair behind Addie's ear but said nothing. "What if it's the same as before? Piano concerts, Cook's pear scones, and Philip being shy?" Her voice rising, Addie added, "What if I forget the island?" Desperate tears appeared.

Min examined Addie's face. The tears fell and the chickens became a blur. "Did you have a favorite chicken before?" Min asked. Addie blinked and swallowed. Her forehead creased and she looked sideways at Min. "Do you think you'll forget about that chicken?" Min put both arms around Addie.

That afternoon, Addie couldn't find Maud or Chester. She walked the dirt road, calling their names until a sharp bark gave her a direction. She found them in the cove. Maud was face down in the water, but her arms reached as she stroked the way Min had taught her. Chester barked, bounded into the water, and paddled alongside Maud. Addie let out her breath. Maud swam back and forth, then waded onto the beach.

"Twenty laps!" she announced. Her eyes danced at her success. She pointed to the width of the cove to show the laps, then walked to the trees and pulled a towel from a low branch.

"We need to fix the dinghy." She nodded toward the boat.

"Fix it for what?" Addie watched her Maud for signs of delirium.

"We can't leave it this way. It got us to the island and here. It deserves recognition for its service."

The dinghy sat, ignored and askew, off the path, sail and lines limp.

"All right," Addie said. "Let's take care of her."

They climbed into the boat and loosened the stays from the cleats, let down the sail, and removed it from mast and boom. The sail would never hold the wind again, but Addie folded it properly. Maud dismantled the boom and mast, laying them along the gunwales. She slid the oars in the bottom of the dinghy. A tiny crab scuttled from behind the centerboard.

"A stowaway!" cried Maud. She scooped it up and brought it to her eyes. The crab waved its larger claw as if to say, *Don't even try to fight!* Maud stepped from the boat, walked to the water's edge, and let the crab onto the sand. "It's not the island, but it's a good place."

When she turned back, Addie was outside the dinghy looking at it as if she had never seen it before. "It's so small," she said.

Maud joined her. "It was big enough and we believed in it."

"We had to," said Addie. "I don't want to leave it."

Maud laughed. "Addie! We can't take it, you know that."

"We never named it."

"Yes, we did."

"What do you mean?"

"What do you think of when you look at it?" Maud got in the boat and sat on the front thwart.

Addie climbed in and sat at the rear. She didn't understand at first, then looked down at the dinghy's curves. "Improbable," she said.

"Only you would think of such a word. The dinghy took us out and it took us back. What's the right word for that?"

They went silent and then Maud hooted a laugh.

"What?" Addie asked.

"Our boat is *The Guano*!"

"We can't name the boat bird poop!"

"Why not?"

Maud's eyes sparkled, and Addie thought of them swimming off the island. "Yes!" She threw her head back and they both laughed.

Min found them there when she came to tell them supper was ready. Chester barked at the girls, dashing up the path and back to the boat until they climbed out.

"He doesn't want to save you again," Min said with a grin.

There was nothing to get ready, but the girls circled the house, yard and paths, putting small things in order. They helped Min tidy the chicken pen and air the blankets. When they cleaned out the picnic hamper, Addie found lots of sand and a purple striped sea urchin with green spines attached. "Part of the island!" she exclaimed. They poured the sand into a glass jar and placed the sea urchin on top. They wanted it as a reminder but, instead, presented it to Min.

Maud said, "So you'll know Charlie is safe."

Min gathered the girls and held them. "When I look at it, I will remember that two brave girls saved me too." She let them go, dried her eyes, and said, "Let's see to the hens."

While Maud and Min gathered eggs for breakfast, Addie

put a handwritten copy of "The Proper Conduct Dragon" on the little desk in Min's bedroom. She tucked it under other papers so that Min wouldn't find it right away. While Min and Addie folded laundry, Maud lifted down the music box, opened the lid, and dropped in her two remaining marbles— one robin's-egg blue and one ringed with orange. "That's Addie and me staying with you and Charlie," she said to the empty kitchen as she replaced the box.

On the day they left, they hugged Chester over and over and cried as they kissed Min. Gillhooly hissed at Addie as she carried the hamper to the cart and nipped at her backside. Addie squealed, which made Maud laugh. "He always did like you best!" she teased.

Min kissed them both and promised she would write. "You're excellent navigators, so it won't be hard to find your way."

Both girls, grinning and crying, climbed onto the cart seat with the hamper and carriage rug tucked behind. The driver tipped his hat to Min and flipped the reins. The dray horse clopped down the road.

"Can I hold the reins?" Maud asked.

Late on July 9, the cart pulled up before the summer house in Mahone Bay with the three church steeples in the background. The yard was full of people. Cook had sounded the news, which meant that dozens had gathered to welcome them back. A cheer went up and someone blasted a tuba.

Cook's face was bright red from trying not to cry. She kept saying, "It hasn't been the same. Not the same at all! Oh, thank heavens!"

A table under the backyard tree held cooked chicken, potato salad, sliced carrots and green beans, molasses cookies, an orange sponge cake, and pitchers of lemonade.

No one knew what to say as Addie and Maud stepped down from the cart until Cook ran forward and squeezed them both.

"You're both right thin, so you are. Let's get you plates."

Suddenly everyone was putting food on plates and asking the girls how much and which they liked best. Mrs. Beal put her hand on Addie's head and said, "Bless you both. You have shown great fortitude."

Evelyn Brighty stepped forward, saw Addie's dress, and said, "You poor thing! Wearing the same dress all summer!"

Addie looked down at her tattered and sun-faded dress with its organdy blue inserts. She leaned close to Evelyn and said, "I wore nothing at all some days." Evelyn's eyebrows disappeared under her bangs and she did a half-step back. "And I peeled," Addie added. "Burnt through."

Lydia Murchey put her arm through Addie's and led her to the edge of the crowd, saying, "Addie, the summer was awful without you. I missed you all the time."

Maud, in her too-big maroon skirt and middy blouse, stayed outside the crowd. Tavis came beside her and said, "You won."

She knew he meant the Social's marble game. She looked at him directly. "What exactly did I win?"

Tavis turned red. "I should have said. I should have stood up to them for you."

Maud was quiet. "Not for me, with me," she said, adding, "Re-match?"

Tavis grinned.

"Bring extra marbles. I gave mine to pirates." Maud laughed as Tavis's mouth made an *O*.

Afternoon turned to dusk and the yard returned to itself as people left. As Cook cleared the table, she looked about for the girls. She had been gossiping with Mr. Crandle and lost track of time. She put down the stack of plates and walked the deepening shadows until she found them curled together on the chaise lounge, deeply asleep. Overly stretched between them, all three breathing in rhythm.

Acknowledgements

Inexpressible gratitude: My fellow workshop writers on Monday and Thursday nights, and Friday mornings who have listened, encouraged, and cheered on Maud and Addie as I followed the girls word by word. They are legion with astounding hearts. Without these writers, I too would surely have been stranded. Pat Schneider and Amherst Writers & Artists for the mission and community. To Michele Rubin, Brianne Johnson and Taylor Templeton at Writers House. For Jaynie Royal and Pam Van Dyk and everyone at Regal House Publishing for saying Yes! and for their attentive respect. Medical examiners Dr. Andrew Sexton and Dr. John Waldman for information on body decomposition rates. Any errors and inaccuracies are mine. Melanie Briand's gift of detailed coastal maps and geographical information of Nova Scotia kept me and the girls within the currents and islands of the North Atlantic. Professor Katherine Conway for incisive editing for plot and character development, giving the girls their day at the Social. Gail Widner, Caroline Raser, and Roberta Wills for listening to plot details and offering practical logistics. Ginny Mayer, Alison Mills, Jan Lamberg, Valerie Haynes-Perry, and especially Nancy Barnes for close reading and astute responses. David Lamb for believing the story should be out in the world. Jared Wills at the very beginning and forever after for an afternoon conversation in the grass that explored the many ways two improbable girls could survive on their wits. Jared truly saved them. My eternal love to Koren, Glynis & Phineas for putting up with me as I talked to Maud and Addie instead of them.